To 1

CW00554609

Truly, Madly, Creepy

Pat Spence

The Master Ghost-Story Teller!

Hope these tales measure up!

Pat Spence x

This book is a work of fiction. The names, characters, incidents and places are products of the writer's imagination or have been used fictitiously and are not to be construed as real. Any resemblance to persons, living or dead, actual events, locales or organisations is entirely coincidental.

ISBN: 9781794474918

Truly, Madly, Creepy

Fair is foul, and foul is fair:
Hover through the fog and filthy air.

Scene 1, Act 1. Macbeth by William Shakespeare.

For everyone who likes a good horror story....

Pat Spence

CONTENTS

INTRODUCTION

Truly, Madly, Creepy…

In the process of creating this collection of short stories and poems, I drew on past experiences and the stories of others. Everyone, it seemed, had a gristly tale to tell, inevitably beginning, "This is a true story…."

That's the 'Truly' part of the title.

What if the horror is not real, but a state of mind? What if the person in the story is deluded, or worse, mad? That's the premise I took when writing some of the stories, which covers the 'Madly' part of the title.

Finally, the common thread running through all the stories, whether telling of hauntings or madness, is a genuine creepiness. And so, the final piece of the title fell into place.

If the mark of good horror is to get under your skin, disturb your thoughts and keep coming back to haunt you, I hope this book gives you some sleepless nights… Happy reading.

Pat Spence.
Hampton-in-Arden January 2019.

*An anti-ageing trial has unbelievable results,
but there's a terrible price to pay…*

Rejuvenate

Maisie MacDonald looked in the mirror and groaned.

"God, I look old." She pulled her face up over her cheekbones, stretching the skin. "D'you think I need a face lift?"

Her husband glanced up from his paper.

"You look fine."

"Maybe to you, but you don't have to run the gauntlet of the school gate every day, with all those gorgeous, mid-twenty, yummy mummies."

"They can't all be mid twenties."

"Well, no. But I am the oldest. By a long way."

Her husband shrugged and returned to his paper. He'd heard it all before. Maisie stared into the mirror, smoothing back the crow's feet and holding up the jowls that had started to hang round her mouth. She didn't regret being an older mum. She was very lucky to have had two children in her mid forties. It was just that she felt so much older than the other mums. She envied their smooth skin, plumped up with youth, highlighting what she was rapidly losing. It was a one-way journey and she was well past the halfway point.

"Get some older friends," suggested her husband. "That'll make you feel younger. It's all relative."

"Comments like that don't help. What I need is surgery. Or a miracle."

"This is what you need."

He read from the paper. "REJUVENATE! Volunteers required to trial a revolutionary new cosmetic product over a six-month period. Designed to turn back the time. No surgery or fees. Details from the Rejuvenation Institute."

He ripped out the advert and gave it to her.

She laughed. "If only it was that easy. One magic cream and all your lines disappear? I don't think so."

She was about to throw it away, but instead, placed it on the dresser, one corner anchored under a vase.

Over the next few days, whenever she walked past, her eyes were drawn to the advert. Then, a chance remark in the playground proved to be the tipping point. An older woman standing next to her, watching the children play, commented, "It's great being a granny, isn't it? You get to hand them back at the end of the day."

Maisie went home in tears.

"I look like a granny," she cried. "I need to do something."

Snatching up the advert, she picked up the phone and dialled.

* * *

The Rejuvenation Institute was located in a smart Georgian building on Rodney Street, just down from Liverpool's Anglican cathedral. It was the city's equivalent of Harley Street, where plastic surgeons nestled alongside orthodontists and private health specialists. A small brass plaque announced the Institute's presence and, nervously, Maisie rang the doorbell. Almost immediately, the door was opened by an impossibly beautiful, blond-haired woman in a crisp white uniform.

"You must be Mrs MacDonald," she said, in a soft, clipped voice. "We've been expecting you. Please, come in."

Maisie stepped over the threshold and the woman closed the door soundlessly behind her.

"Have a seat, please." She indicated a white leather sofa to one side of the reception area and Maisie sat down, feeling nervous. She looked around, dazzled by the smooth white walls and white ceramic floor, unable to see where walls ended and floor began.

The woman sat at a white desk and tapped at the keyboard of a small white computer. She looked up and smiled.

"Everything's in order. You're a perfect candidate for our 'Rejuvenate' trial."

"I am?" asked Maisie, her voice high-pitched. "Don't you need to ask me any medical questions?"

"No, it's all in order. Doctor Jung will see you shortly."

"Doctor Young?" asked Maisie, with a nervous laugh. "He has the right name."

"It's the Swiss spelling. J-U-N-G. As in Carl Jung."

"Right. Sorry."

Maisie swallowed, wondering if she was doing the right thing. She knew the type of women that went to places like this. Rich, pampered play-wives. Not like her. This was way out of her comfort zone.

A drop-down screen appeared on the wall and Maisie watched, intrigued, as a series of 'before' and 'after' images flashed in front of her. She felt the stirrings of hope as she saw middle-aged women turn into fresh-faced twenty-year-olds, as lined brows and crows feet disappeared, wrinkles and marionette-mouth lines were smoothed away, and ageing skin became young and vibrant.

A buzzer sounded.

"Doctor Jung's ready," announced the receptionist. "Follow me, please."

She led the way through a white doorway that seemed to appear from nowhere in one of the walls. It opened onto a white corridor, with white doors leading off. Soft music played and an aroma of orange blossom hung in the air. Maisie followed, admiring the woman's slender figure and graceful movement. At the end of the corridor, she stopped and knocked on a door bearing the words: 'Rejuvenate Trials'.

"Enter." A voice sounded from within.

Maisie was shown into a consulting room, clinical and white, like the reception area. At one side was a white examination bed, partially concealed behind a white curtain, to the other, a large, white desk.

"Hello, Maisie," said the soft voice. "I'm Doctor Jung."

A middle-aged man leant over the desk, hand outstretched.

"Hello," she answered, tentatively, stepping forward and shaking his hand. His grip was firm and cool.

"Don't look so nervous," he said, smiling and sitting back. "Have a seat, please."

He had a faint German accent and was very handsome, with a tanned face, a full head of grey hair and twinkling blue eyes. He was dressed in an immaculate grey suit, with a cream shirt, open at the neck.

She sat down.

"You're here to take part in our 'Rejuvenate' Trial?"

"Yes."

"Let me tell you, we have had some phenomenal results. Over five hundred women have taken part and every one has undergone the most amazing transformation, as perhaps you saw on our slide show?"

"Yes, I did. Very impressive."

"Come, let me take a look at your face."

He moved to Maisie's side of the desk, cupping one hand under her chin and, with the other, patting her skin at various points on her face. She noticed the perfectly manicured nails, the expensive watch and the faint scent of musky aftershave. Everything about him spoke of wealth: his manner, his clothes, his demeanour. This was a world to which she could never aspire and she wondered again if she was doing the right thing.

"You have very good skin for your age," he commented.

"Really? I don't think so."

"But yes. I believe our 'Rejuvenate' product will result in a transformation beyond your wildest dreams. And, of course, because it's a trial, you pay nothing. When it comes to market, the treatment will cost thousands. We expect film stars and celebrities to beat a pathway to our door."

Maisie needed no further persuasion. "Where do I sign?"

He held up his hand. "First, let me tell you about the product. It contains a range of active ingredients: colloidal silver, yeast extracts, black cohosh, along with such staples as hyaluronic acid, omega fatty acids, anthocyanidins and so on. But what really makes this product unique is its anti-ageing ingredient. I'm talking about Purple Algae, found only in an underground lake in Norway. The fish in this lake feed on the algae and live way beyond their allotted lifespan. We harvest it and grow it in our laboratory, turning it into a treatment with unique anti-ageing properties."

"Sounds great," said Maisie, not caring too much about the content, only the result.

"If you wish to take part, you must sign this agreement, acknowledging it is a product under trial and that you will not hold the Rejuvenation Institute liable should you experience adverse side effects."

He held up a form and offered her a pen.

"What kind of side effects?"

He shrugged and smiled. "Just the usual. Minor skin irritation. Nothing more. I can assure you the product is entirely safe. But we cannot get a licence without undertaking trials."

Maisie picked up the pen and signed.

Doctor Jung beamed.

"Our receptionist, Anna, will give you the products and explain how to administer them. By the way, would you believe she's sixty-five? That's the power of 'Rejuvenate'."

Maisie beamed back at him.

* * *

Maisie looked at her face in the mirror. Her skin was taut and firm, not a hint of a wrinkle anywhere. Her eyes were large and sparkling, the baggy lids gone, her eyebrows arching high. Her lips were full and pink, the jowls completely gone. Already she was attracting comments from the other mums at the school gate.

"If you haven't had a facelift, then you've definitely had fillers and collagen," exclaimed one. "Takes one to know one, I've had it all done."

"So have I," said another. "I go for fillers every month. I'd look horrendous if I didn't have Botox on a regular basis. See Joanne over there. She had a full facelift last year."

Maisie was astounded. All the young mums she'd thought were so youthful and natural were all admitting to having had treatment. It was a revelation.

Thanks to 'Rejuvenate', she looked younger than any of them, without any intrusive treatment or surgery.

It wasn't just her face that was reaping the benefits, either. It was her entire body. Her breasts were pert, her stomach flat and her bottom sculpted. She looked like a twenty-year-old. Not a mid-forties mum with two kids.

Sweetest of all, it wasn't costing her a penny. Every month, she went to the Rejuvenation Institute, where Anna supplied her with the products. She applied cream every morning, serum at night and took a vial of liquid supplement after breakfast every day.

After six months, she was transformed. She had the face and body of a teenager. All for free.

"It's almost too good to be true," she whispered, looking in the mirror for the tenth time that day.

* * *

Of course, it was too good to be true. A week later, she received a phone call from Anna.

"I'm sorry. The trial has to stop. There has been an adverse reaction.

"What d'you mean? What kind of reaction?"

"Some clients have developed scaly skin and fish lips. The authorities are refusing to licence the product. They say it requires further development. We must destroy all current stock."

"Destroy?"

Panic seized hold of Maisie.

"It's a set back, nothing more. We'll resume trials in a year or so."

"A year or so?"

Losing her newfound youth was more than Maisie could bear.

"I'll buy the stock from you."

"I'm sorry. That would be unethical. It's not fit for purpose."

"I don't care. Name your price and I'll pay it."

There was a pause.

"Let me speak with Doctor Jung. We'll get back to you."

The offer of hard cash proved too tempting for the 'ethical' doctor and they came to an agreement. Maisie was to make a one-off payment of one hundred and fifty thousand pounds into an anonymous Swiss bank account. In return, she would receive his complete stock, more than a year's worth of the banned 'Rejuvenate' products. Once the transaction was complete, there would be no further contact.

It was way more than she could afford, but she needed 'Rejuvenate' like a junkie needs drugs. And where there's a will, there's a way. Without her husband's knowledge, she remortgaged the house, took out loans, maxed out credit cards and even raided the kids' savings accounts.

For a time, she was able to hide the financial situation from him. She continued to take 'Rejuvenate', pretending she was visiting the Institute every month. In reality, she'd hidden the products in an old cupboard in the garage and was self-administering. To start with, she kept to the recommended amounts, but gradually, as her dependency grew, she upped her usage. After six months, she was applying cream and serum morning, noon and night, and drinking half a dozen vials of the liquid supplement every day.

If their finances were bad, her physical condition was even worse. Thanks to 'Rejuvenate', the ageing process had gone into rapid reverse. She'd passed through adolescence, complete with spots and mood swings, and was now in childhood. Her hips were gone, her bosom flat and she'd lost a foot in height.

"You need to stop taking the trial," her husband told her. "You're no longer a woman, you're a child."

But Maisie couldn't see it. When she looked in the mirror, she saw skin that glistened, a size zero figure and youth beyond her wildest dreams. In her eyes, she'd never looked so good.

Something had to give and it did. Her husband opened a letter advising the house was about to be repossessed. He'd always let Maisie take control of their finances. Now, he began to delve and discovered a nightmare. The accounts were drained, they owed thousands on credit cards and the mortgage hadn't been paid for months. On top of that, he'd lost his job and interest rates were going up. The family was facing financial ruin. But he couldn't admonish her. She was incapable of understanding. The anti-ageing process had gone into freefall. She was now a toddler.

By now, she'd stopped taking 'Rejuvenate'. He'd found her secret stash and destroyed it. But it was too late. The Purple Algae was growing inside her.

In desperation, he went to Rodney Street, searching for the Rejuvenation Institute. He found the premises had been taken over by an orthodontist.

"The Institute closed down," the receptionist told him. "Disappeared overnight. They say Doctor Jung wasn't his real name, that he was a mad scientist who discovered a miraculous anti-ageing cure. He was trying to get it licensed, but it was withdrawn. They say bad things happened to those who used it. I don't know the details."

He went to the bank to see if they could trace the Swiss account, but it was closed. There was no information about the account holder. With bitter regret he remembered the day he'd first shown Maisie the advert.

Eventually, his brother bailed him out. He'd made a fortune selling his software company and had money to spare.

"You'll get it back," Maisie's husband promised. "I'll find a job and we'll get back on our feet."

He told everyone that Maisie had left him, unable to stand the shame of financial ruin. People questioned how she could walk out on such a decent man and two beautiful children.

In truth, she'd never left. In an upstairs room that had once been the nursery, Maisie's husband hid the thing she'd become. She'd passed through childhood into babyhood. Now, she was little more than a partially formed purple foetus. In a short time, she'd become an embryo, then a single fertilised cell, a zygote.

Then, she would, quite simply, cease to exist. The anti-ageing treatment would be 100% successful.

*A man falls in love with his sat nav,
with unforeseen consequences for his wife…*

Miss Hissy

It all started the day they went to the summer fete in the next village. Dan was drinking in the beer tent and Annie was chatting with friends.

As usual, it was a grand affair, well attended in a field behind the pub. The Women's Institute served teas and cakes, the scouts manned the barbecue, and local farmers sold drinks in the beer tent. The usual stalls were positioned around the field: tombola, white elephant, books and toys, plants and home produce, along with the games: Aunt Sally, Coconut Shy, Hoopla, Tin Can Challenge and Soak the Vicar. Children queued for pony rides at the far side of the field, and bales of hay were placed in a circle around a central area, where people sat and watched the sheep dog trial, duck and goose display, ferret racing, girls dancing, a terrifying chainsaw demonstration, and the fete's famous 'Throw the Egg' competition, followed by the inter-village Tug of War. Last but not least, the Prize Draw was announced. This was always an exciting time, as generous prizes had been donated by local businesses.

"I fancy the spa day," said Annie, as they'd purchased their tickets. "Or the 'Meal for Two' at the Malt Shovel. Or the hairdressing session."

"We should win something," retorted Dan. "We've bought enough tickets."

In the event, they weren't aware the Prize Draw was even taking place. Dan had been drinking from the minute he arrived, making a beeline for the beer tent, where old friends and Old Peculiar beckoned. By the time of the Prize Draw, he was three sheets to the wind and involved in a loud argument about Brexit. Or was it football? Or Trump? None of them knew what they were talking about.

Annie was catching up with acquaintances she hadn't seen since last summer's fete, absorbing a year's worth of condensed gossip: who was having an affair, whose marriage had split up, whose daughter was pregnant, whose business had gone bust. She wasn't drinking because she was driving, but she was high on intrigue, and oblivious to the Prize Draw.

"Annie!" called out someone walking by. "They've just announced your name. You've won a prize. Go and collect it."

"Oh my God," she screamed excitedly. "I didn't hear!"

She ran across to the organisers' tent, where she was presented with a box.

"It's a sat nav," explained the organiser. "I think it's a good one."

"Great," she replied, unimpressed, eyeing the unclaimed envelopes marked 'Spa Treatment' and 'Weekend Break'. "Can't I have one of those?"

"Sorry. You've got the sat nav."

She walked back to the beer tent and presented the box to Dan.

"What's this?"

"A sat nav. We've just won it. No good for me. My car's already got one. Might be okay for your old banger."

The old banger to which she referred was Dan's pride and joy. A 1998 C-Class Mercedes estate, built like a tank, without any modern attributes such as sat nav, blue tooth or USB connection.

"I'll fit it tomorrow," announced Dan, taking the box and reading the details through beery eyes. "The Krystyna Sat Nav with preloaded European data, branded points of interest, speed limit display and three route options: Fast, Short and Eco."

"Looks like a cheap Eastern European make to me," laughed one of his friends. "Great for getting round Bosnia. Not so good in the UK."

"We'll see," said Dan, placing the box at his feet.

The next day, he removed the Krystyna Sat Nav from its box and, after some fiddling around with settings and downloading additional information, announced to Annie that the system was in full working order.

"It's perfect," he said. "I'd never have gone for some state-of-the-art, up to the minute gadget. Not in this car. But she is just right. Perfect."

"She?" queried Annie.

"Of course it's a 'she'. I don't want some bloke telling me where to go. Krystyna is the perfect travel companion."

"You do realise you've used the word 'perfect' three times to describe her," pointed out Annie. "Should I be jealous?"

Dan laughed. "Well, she is quite sexy. I don't mind driving round with her in the car."

Annie raised an eyebrow. She wasn't in any hurry to sample the navigational delights of Krystyna. In fact, it wasn't until a couple of weeks later that she encountered Krystyna. Her own car was in the garage having its annual service and she needed to go to Pilates.

"Alright if I take your car?" she asked Dan.

"Sure," he replied, throwing her the keys. "Be nice to Krystyna."

"Oh, I won't be using her. I know my way to the gym."

In the event, she didn't have a choice. Krystyna refused to be turned off. Annie jabbed the 'off' button with the tip of her finger, but the system remained on. She held down the button and counted to ten, but it remained active.

"Where do you wish to go?" asked Krystyna for the third time, in her heavy East European accent. "Please input zip code or location."

"I don't need your help," said Annie with gritted teeth. "But if it keeps you happy, I'll do it." With one fingertip, she jabbed in the postcode of the gym.

"Finding the best route for your journey," announced Krystyna, aggressively.

"I know the best route," said Annie, under her breath. "And I don't like your tone."

"At end of drive, turn right."

Annie tried to quell the sound, but despite pressing the mute button, Krystyna's voice came over loud and clear.

"In two hundred metres, turn left. In one hundred metres, turn left. Turn left, now. Turn left."

She was beginning to irritate Annie and the journey had only just started.

"I don't know how Dan puts up with you. I won't be borrowing the car again if it means listening to you."

She could have sworn Krystyna said, "Suits me", but she was approaching a busy junction and her concentration was elsewhere. Afterwards, she decided she'd imagined it. Krystyna continued her aggressive directions and Annie arrived at the gym in good time but bad spirits.

On the return journey, she took a detour to a friend's house to pick up some tickets and, unsure of the way, input the postcode into the sat nav system. Despite being switched on, the system refused to work. Krystyna was silent.

"Giving me the silent treatment, are you?" laughed Annie. "See if I care. I'll use my Maps app. I don't need you."

Back at home, she handed the keys to Dan.

"Great car. Shame about the sat nav."

Dan looked at her askance. "What d'you mean?"

"She's a right little Miss Hissy. Aggressive on the way there. Silent on the way back, despite being switched on."

Dan laughed. "You probably hadn't set it right."

"Whatever," said Annie, holding up her hands. "As long as I don't have to listen to her again."

A couple of days later, she and Dan sat in his car on the way to the local DIY store to pick up some shelving. Dan turned on the ignition and an accented voice filled the cabin.

"Good morning, Dan. How are you?"

Annie looked at him in disbelief.

"I programmed in my name," admitted Dan, sheepishly. "Makes it more personal, you know."

"Where would you like to go, Dan?"

"Yeah, Dan, press my buttons. You know I like it," mocked Annie.

Dan gave her a venomous look. "I can't believe you're jealous of a sat nav."

"I'm not."

Dan input the postcode of the DIY store and they set off, Krystyna guiding them.

"At the T-junction, turn left, Dan. Go straight over the traffic lights, Dan. Turn right now, Dan. You've reached your destination, Dan."

On the way back home, Annie drove, determined to prove a point. Krystyna knew immediately Dan wasn't driving.

"Turn right in one hundred yards," said her voice, harshly. "Turn right, now."

Annie turned left.

"I said turn right."

"Did you hear that? She is so aggressive!"

"You're imagining it. Anyway, you went the wrong way."

"I can't believe you've been taken in by her."

They drove home in silence, Krystyna's voice the only sound in the car.

For some weeks, Annie forgot about Krystyna. She was busy at work and, along with a full social calendar, had more to think about than a rogue sat nav system. That was, until she borrowed Dan's car again, when her own was in the garage having an MOT test.

As soon as she switched on the ignition, the sat nav system rustled with static and Annie experienced an unpleasant, heavy sensation, as if the cabin was full of white noise. She felt her skin crawl and tried to switch it off. The system remained on.

"Okay, if you won't switch off, you can at least take me where I want to go. I have to visit a new client this morning and I can't be late."

She glanced at her watch. Half an hour. Plenty of time.

Initially, Krystyna behaved, without a hint of the aggressive tone Annie had encountered previously. She began to think Dan was right and she'd imagined it. Until Krystyna led her the wrong way up a one-way street and Annie came face-to-face with a bus. She had no option but to reverse.

"Oh my God, how embarrassing was that? Not to mention dangerous."

Unsure whether she'd turned too soon or it was a deliberate act on Krystyna's part, Annie continued the journey. She was in a part of town she didn't know.

"You have arrived at your destination."

Annie gazed around. Krystyna had led her into a run-down industrial estate, with tumble down fencing, out-of-control weeds and derelict factory units.

"I don't think so," she said angrily, glancing at her watch. "Thanks for nothing, Krystyna. I'm going to be late now."

Something that sounded suspiciously like laughter came from the sat nav.

"You think it's funny? You've done this on purpose, haven't you?"

The system instantly turned itself off and Annie was forced, once again, to use her Maps App, arriving at her client's offices ten minutes late. To make matters worse, she overshot the car parking place, scraping the Mercedes' underside on a low concrete curb.

"Great! Now I've damaged his car. I hope you're happy with your morning's work, Krystyna."

Annie arrived home in a bad mood, having dealt with a sarcastic client and a bill from the local Mercedes dealer for mending a crack to the car's underbody. She hoped Dan wouldn't notice.

"That woman is evil," she said to Dan.

"Who?"

"Your girlfriend, Krystyna. She doesn't like me, Dan, and I'm not imagining it."

"It's a sat nav system. Turn it off if you don't like it." He turned away, calling over his shoulder: "Your car's ready, by the way. They'll drop it off in half an hour."

Next morning, Dan set off early. He was Creative Director at a local advertising agency and had an important pitch that morning. Instead of driving away, he remained on the driveway and appeared to be having an animated conversation.

"Who's he speaking to?" wondered Annie, watching from the bedroom window. "He must be using his mobile hands-free."

On cue, Dan's mobile rang, from the dressing table behind her.

Frowning, she grabbed it and marched downstairs, flinging open the front door and striding across the driveway. She rapped on the car window.

"Who are you talking to?"

He turned, startled, and wound down the window. "Just a call on my mobile."

"I don't think so." She held up his phone and passed it through the window. "It was her, wasn't it? You're talking to Krystyna. Get a life, Dan, for Christ's sake."

Without waiting for an answer, she strode angrily back inside.

From that day, there was a subtle change in their relationship. Nothing was said about the incident, but it marked a change in direction for both of them. They began to drift apart. Dan was withdrawn and secretive. She was irritable, finding fault with everything he did. They didn't row, but there was a bad feeling between them, and what was not said spoke volumes more than angry words.

"He's like a stranger," she confided to a friend over coffee. "I don't know him any more. His sense of humour has gone. It's like there's a black cloud hanging over him. When he's with me, anyway. He clearly doesn't like my company any more."

"Is he having an affair?" asked the friend. "These are classic signs."

"I don't think so," answered Annie, too embarrassed to mention Krystyna. How do you explain that your husband has fallen for his sat nav? That the only voice he wants to hear belongs to a computerised global positioning device? It was just too ridiculous. And yet, the only time she saw him smiling was when he was sitting in the car.

After a couple of months, it became clear the marriage was over. Dan was aloof and unreachable, locked in his own private world. Annie tried talking to him, but he wasn't interested. It all came to a head one Saturday evening. Annie had a works 'do' coming up and needed a 'plus one' to go with.

"Will you come with me, Dan?"

"You know I hate big corporate events. I'll have to wear a suit and make small talk with all those knob-heads."

"I'm getting an award for the highest sales."

"That's great." He couldn't have sounded less bothered if he tried.

"Only it's not, is it Dan? You're not remotely interested in anything I do."

He looked at her with blank eyes. "Sorry, Annie." He shrugged. "I can't do this any more."

"In that case, I can't stay here any more." Her voice was cold and emotionless. "I need to get away, have time to think."

"Where will you go?" His voice sounded brighter already.

"Like you really want to know."

She ran upstairs, fighting back the tears, and threw some clothes in a suitcase. In the hallway, she paused, looking at the two sets of car keys hanging up. She was about to take her own, when she thought better of it and grabbed Dan's car keys.

"I'm taking your car, Dan," she said under her breath, glancing at the closed kitchen door. "And Krystyna. See how you like that."

Zipping up her jacket, she let herself out of the front door.

It was a wild night, large black clouds racing across the sky like grotesque monsters, obscuring any possibility of moonlight. Rain lashed against her skin and she opened the car door quickly, sliding into the driver's seat. She turned on the ignition, wondering where to go.

She remembered a small bed and breakfast establishment she'd noticed on the coast road a few days ago and decided that would make a suitable bolthole. Looking up the address on her phone, she tapped the postcode into the sat nav.

"Okay, Miss Hissy. You win. Dan is all yours. But I'm going to borrow you for a couple of days. Make him sweat a bit, first. Now, take me to the B & B."

Krystyna sprang to life. "Hello, Annie. How are you? Please turn left at the end of the road."

Annie looked at the dashboard incredulously. "How d'you know my name? And what's with polite attitude?"

"Turn left at the end of the road, please Annie," Krystyna replied.

Annie drove for twenty minutes, the storm getting progressively worse. Strong wind whipped the trees so they were nearly bent double and the rain grew so heavy that even the 'fast' setting on her windscreen wipers couldn't clear away the water quickly enough. She slowed down, determined to keep going. Returning home wasn't an option.

"Turn left in one hundred yards," instructed Krystyna, and Annie obeyed.

"Can't see a damn thing," she complained. "I'm in your hands, Krystyna. Be nice."

"Continue for two hundred metres, then turn right."

"Are you sure? Feels like we're going out of our way."

"Turn right now, Annie. Turn right."

Annie obeyed. The headlights bounced off the lashing rain. It was impossible to see anything. She wondered whether to stop, deciding she must be close to her destination and pressing on.

Had she been able to see, she would have realised how dangerously close she was getting to the cliff edge. Krystyna had taken her onto the old coast road that was no longer in use, after a series of rock falls. Too late, Annie realised there was no road ahead, just an empty black space and the churning sea beneath. Before she had time to brake or even think, the car plunged over the cliff, ripping through the wooden safety fencing and bouncing off the rocks beneath, before being swallowed by the swirling black water. Annie knew nothing beyond a split-second of horror as the car left the road. The impact of the car hitting the rock broke her neck and she died instantly.

Next morning, two walkers strolling along the coastal pathway, noticed the broken fence and saw the remains of a vehicle on the rocks two hundred feet below. At low tide, Annie's body and the vehicle were retrieved, and Dan was notified.

The funeral took place three weeks later. There were lots of flowers, the music was upbeat and people wore bright colours. Selected friends and colleagues told stories about Annie in celebration of her life. It was standing room only. Dan never mentioned to anyone the words they'd had on the night Annie left. It was easier to let people think they'd been happily married. Naturally, he'd been shocked by the accident and felt mildly guilty. If he'd been nicer, she wouldn't have taken off. She'd still be there. But if he was honest, he liked having the house to himself. He liked having the space, selecting what he wanted to watch on TV, eating what he chose, not having to make idle chat and constantly do the right thing. So, although he grieved, it was for what they'd had, rather than what they'd become.

His main regret, he admitted only to himself, was the loss of his car. And Krystyna. He missed Krystyna. There'd been no opportunity to say goodbye. Annie had seen to that, and it was something he couldn't forgive. Annie had taken away the two things in his life that had real meaning.

A week after the funeral, there was a knock on the door. A man in a grey overall stood on the doorstep.

"Sorry to trouble you, sir. It's about the recent accident."

"Yes?"

"Condolences for your loss, sir. I'm from the salvage yard. We managed to retrieve something from your car that you might want to keep."

He handed a plastic carrier bag to Dan.

"What is it?"

"It's the sat nav system, sir. Miraculously, it wasn't affected by the crash. Seems to be in full working order. I thought you might have use for it."

Dan's face lit up.

"Thank you. Thank you very much. You don't know what this means to me."

A week later and Dan had tracked down a C-Class Mercedes estate. It was a little older than his previous car and needed some work, but it had the same old-fashioned build quality, the solid feel and exquisite interior craftsmanship. He spent some time lovingly installing the sat nav system. Eventually, he sat back, admiring his handiwork, savouring the anticipation of hearing Krystyna's voice once again. With a click of the button he turned on the system.

"Please input the postcode or destination," the voice instructed him.

Dan frowned and turned up the volume. Something wasn't right. The voice was familiar, but it wasn't Krystyna.

He tapped a postcode into the system.

"At the T-junction, turn right."

"Annie?" he whispered.

"Hello, Dan. How are you? At the T-junction, turn right."

Ripper's Lament

Do not drag me from my rest
To satisfy your game
Do not put me to the test
Finding who's to blame.

There is nothing you can gain
By pulling back the years
You'll only find a life of pain
That embodies your worst fears.

The glass moves on the table
Spelling words you seek
Seeing if I'm able
To find a voice and speak.

Asking if I'm good or bad
How I came to die
Asking of the life I had
In a time gone by.

Sleeping dogs are best left lying
Do not try to raise them
There's no grace in death and in dying
You cannot hope to praise them.

You wake me from the longest sleep
Ask if I'll address you
You seek to delve in matters deep
Not knowing I'll possess you.

So leave me to my gravity
Else you cannot send me back
Or suffer my depravity
The man you know as Jack.

Watch out for the Road Boys if you're driving down the Wixley road. They want you in their gang…

Road Boys

We crouch by the side of the road, watching and waiting. We like bad weather. That can have good results for us. Ice is best, followed by rain. Anything to make the road surface more slippery. We have a favourite place on the road. It's a small section bordered by beech trees. They've been very effective in procuring victims. Impact with a tree at speed invariably causes death. Not that we refer to them as victims. They get to hang out with us, and that's a very exclusive club.

It started with Jezzer and me. That was ten years ago. I'd just got my bike licence and my first bike. I can still remember it. A Suzuki DR 200. Beautiful. I was taking it out for a spin. Jezzer asked if he could come with me. I only had one helmet, but he said he didn't mind. Would go without. Wanted to know how fast my bike would go, its top speed. I said I didn't know, but we'd find out. We went out on the Wixley Road. There's a good stretch of straight road where you can accelerate fast. I could feel Jezzer's arms round my middle, holding tight as I increased speed. I felt the excitement building within him and it was contagious. I began to push the bike, squeezing the throttle. Our speed increased. Trees and fields flashed past in a blur of green. I gave it some more. A light rain started to fall, and that was our downfall. That and the speed.

We got to the section of road where the beech trees stand, five in a row, like sentries, guarding the descent into Wixley. I guess I didn't know the bike too well and didn't anticipate the turn in the road. I thought we could take it at speed. Found out too late we couldn't. The wheels of the bike went from under us, pitching us sideways.

Only one thing could stop us. The beech trees. Well, one in particular. The second one along. Might have been made of steel as far as we were concerned. We slammed into it at 75 mph. I was thrown ten metres, landing at the foot of the fifth beech tree. Jezzer was trapped under the bike and collided with the tree. He hadn't been wearing a helmet and copped it instantly. I took a little longer. Multiple injuries. Didn't take them long to take their toll.

Jezzer and I stood watching as our broken bodies were loaded into the ambulance, blue lights illuminating the dark day. We noticed they'd pulled sheets over our eyes.

"Guess that means we're goners," I said.

"Shit!" was all Jezzer said.

The police cordoned off the area and other drivers were told to turn around and find a different route. I wondered if we knew any of them, whether anyone recognised my bike. Probably not. I hadn't had it long.

Eventually, the ambulance drove away. Some time later, a breakdown truck arrived and took away the bike. They left some of the bike parts lying in the wet grass. That's what got to me most. Why didn't they pick them up?

The police removed the red and white tape and the road opened up again. It was like our accident had never happened. Except that it had and here we were, Jezzer and me, stuck on the roadside, not knowing what to do.

One thing about being dead. You don't feel the cold. Night came and the temperature dropped. But it had no effect on us. I suppose that's a benefit.

Over time, we found we could move around, mainly into the neighbouring fields and woods. We tried going in to a house further down the road but we couldn't get over the threshold. I guess that means we're outside ghosts. But no matter how far we went, an invisible string seemed to pull us back to the scene of the crash. That's where we always ended up.

Jezzer had been my best mate, so I was glad he was there with me. It would have been pretty lonely on my own. But over time, we began to get bored with each other. Some times he really got on my tits. We needed more company.

And just like that, it happened. We didn't plan it. We were standing by the roadside. Jezzer was messing around, playing chicken, running across the road in front of cars as they approached. There wasn't much point, really, because the drivers couldn't see him and if he didn't make it, well, he was already dead.

An old white Fiesta came round the bend. A kid was at the wheel, late teens, wearing a baseball cap. He was driving fast and, at the last second, Jezzer ran across in front of him. The kid saw him. I'm not joking. He actually saw him. I could tell by the look on his face. I practically felt his foot slam on the brake.

He shouldn't have been able to see Jezzer. But he did and that was his downfall. It was raining heavily and, as he touched the brake, the car aquaplaned cross the road, crashing into the first beech tree. The airbag inflated, but it didn't save him. The impact with the tree was too strong. He was still hanging on to life as they put him on the stretcher, then suddenly, he went out like a light and next thing we knew, he was standing next to us.

"Alright, mate?" I said.

"Don't call me mate."

He spoke to Jezzer, "That was your fault. Why d'you run across the road in front of me. I had to brake to avoid hitting you."

"How come you saw me?" asked Jezzer.

"What d'you mean? Of course, I saw you. I couldn't miss seeing you. "

"The thing is, mate," I said, "you shouldn't have been able to. We're dead. No one can see us."

The kid's jaw dropped to the floor. He stared at us like we were winding him up. Then he looked back at his broken body lying on the stretcher and the penny dropped.

He said his name was Ant. He was nineteen, on the way back from his girlfriend's house. He'd just finished with her. Said she was dragging him down, wanting commitment, stuff he couldn't give her. He said he was a free spirit, wanted space, wanted his freedom. Well, ironically, that's just what he got.

It took him a while to adjust. Took him a long time to forgive Jezzer. In the end, he didn't have a choice. He was stuck in the same place as us. He had to get on with it.

So, then there were three of us. Not a great number. It meant one was always left out. We needed someone else. Not long after, Joe joined the gang. This time, you couldn't put the blame on us. The accident was down to his own lack of judgement. It was a dark, rainy night and he was on his pushbike, a lightweight B'Twin Ultra 900 racer in aluminium. He took the bend too fast, lost control and slammed into the first beech tree.

Next thing we knew, he was standing alongside us. We made the introductions, told him what had happened. He wouldn't believe it. But, of course, he didn't have a choice.

With four in the gang, it became more interesting. We were a force, a presence, a number. We were invincible. Unstoppable. We might have missed out on the whole life thing, but who's to say we weren't having more fun than we might otherwise?

The more of us there were, the stronger we felt.

Winter arrived, obliging us with two more members in rapid succession. Black ice, a sharp bend and the presence of the ever-trustworthy beech trees did the trick. We welcomed Jeff and Midge into the group.

Midge was great. A dude, covered in tats, with a 'fuck you' mentality. He was edgy and cool, constantly pushing the boundaries. He questioned, goaded, poked and prodded. He'd been high as a kite when he crashed. Said he'd taken 'spice', although I reckon part of his brain was already missing before impact. He was permanently high, slightly fuzzy round the edges, with a twitchy anxiety and a habit of talking bollocks. He said the world owed him nothing and he was glad he was dead, that death gave him a presence he'd never had in life. He changed the dynamics of the gang, added friction, but he was interesting and, mostly, I was glad he was there.

Jeff was the opposite. Stiff, straight, square. No opinions, no attitude. He'd been a loner, a geek, into his computers, designing programs. He didn't even have an opinion about being dead. Just accepted it with a shrug of his shoulders. I kind of liked his nonchalance. There was an authenticity to it. I mean you knew he wasn't making it up. He was true to himself, unlike Midge, who sometimes tried too hard. Jeff liked me, which was good. It meant I could count on his loyalty and in a group you needed to know who's on your side.

Now there were six of us, hanging out on the roadside. Other groups began to take notice of us, we'd see them on the edge of the fields, transparent, misty figures, watching from a distance, sizing us up. The more the other groups began to appear, the more we realised we needed a bigger gang. Strength in numbers, and all that.

But then the council stepped in, threatening further membership. With so many fatalities in such a short time, road safety experts were sent to investigate. They said the adverse camber was a major factor and closed the road while the surface was levelled. They put up road signs, too, warning of a sharp bend, and a digital sign that lit up, telling drivers to 'Slow Down' if they were going too fast.

We sat on the roadside, watching the workmen. They didn't see us. We were invisible. Until Midge started to make his presence felt. He stood behind one of them, a short, stocky, nervous bloke, and breathed hard down his neck, making him jump and shout out. The other workmen laughed, telling him he was imagining things. Then, one by one, Midge did it to each of them and they began to get spooked. None of them liked being there as it got dark.

"There's something not right here," we heard one of them say.

"It's not exactly a cheerful place, is it?" retorted another. "I mean a load of kids have lost their lives here."

We resented that. For us, this was home. And on the whole, we were a cheerful bunch.

The next day, Midge sat in one of the diggers and managed to raise its mechanical arm. That really freaked them out. A high-vis jacket moving along the verge was the final straw. They refused to go on site. Said it was haunted. A new foreman appeared at that point, a hard-nosed muscle man, who didn't give a shit. Turned out he could see us, and he didn't give a shit about ghosts either.

"I can see you, ya bunch o' wankers," he shouted, as we stood watching on the opposite side of the road. "Bugger off and let us do our job. Don't want any more kids joining ya."

That spooked us, I can tell you. We backed off for a bit. It's unnerving when someone can see you, especially if you don't want to be seen, and especially if it's a wank-brain like that.

For some time after, there were no more fatalities. To make matters worse, a local farmer decided the beech trees were to blame. He came one night, with a tractor and a gang of farmhands armed with chainsaws. By morning, not one of the beech trees was left. Razed to the ground. I thought you had to get permission to cut trees down, but by the time the council found out, the deed was done, carried out by perpetrators unknown. There was nothing they could do.

Without the adverse camber and the beech trees, and with the 'Slow Down' and digital signs, the road was a whole lot safer.

We became resigned to the fact our gang might not grow any more.

Then two things happened. One day, we noticed a group of dark shadows a couple of fields away. There were lots of them and they didn't look friendly. Made Midge very twitchy. And, out of the blue, we gained another member.

Although the road was safer, it wasn't completely safe. It still had a sharp bend. Thomas, on his way to work one morning, late, and trying to take a call on his mobile, approached at speed. Too late, he tried to correct his vehicle and it flipped. It was a survivable accident, but not for him. Lucky for him, we were waiting to greet him.

There were seven of us now.

But there were more than seven in the group of dark shadows. And they were getting closer. We could feel their presence, like a heavy mantle, oppressive and suffocating.

"What are they?" I asked Midge.

"Dunno. Some kind of dark energy. I don't like the look of 'em."

"If they're dark matter, they'll absorb us," said Thomas, our newest recruit.

We all stared at him.

"How do you know?"

"I've read up on stuff like that," he replied. "Dark matter creates a vacuum. Draws everything in. Everything in the same dimension, that is."

"Like us, you mean?"

"I guess. I dunno. Doesn't look too good."

"So, what do we do? How do we scare 'em off?"

He laughed and looked at us pityingly.

"You don't scare off dark matter. It can't be scared. It's all powerful. Like Teflon-coated zombies. The 'living dead' on a mission to kill."

"Teflon-coated zombies?" repeated Midge. "The livin' dead? You 'avin' us on?"

Thomas shrugged. "If you don't believe me, walk up to them. See what happens. Personally, I wouldn't give you two seconds. Before you know it, you'll be on the inside looking out. One of them. Anti-matter."

"Right. So, what do we do, then?"

"It's all about power balance," said Thomas. "If we're more powerful, they'll back off."

"And how do we get more power?" I asked.

"Simple matter of numbers," said Thomas. "There needs to be more of us."

So, out of necessity, our recruitment drive began in earnest.

It started the next night. And this time, it wasn't about getting kids into the gang. It was about getting anybody.

We had to increase our numbers fast and we weren't fussy how we did it.

We found, with practice and concentration, we could make ourselves visible to the human eye. We looked a little fuzzy, like we were glowing with phosphorescence, but that just added to the ghostly impression. The important thing was, we could be seen. People didn't need to be sensitive, they just needed to be looking at the road, at the right time.

Imagine the scenario. You're driving along. Your favourite track is playing or you're listening to a drama on the radio. You're warm, happy, in control. Then, out of the blue, a boy appears on the road in front of you. He's glowing and ghostly. You've no time to think. Instinct takes over. Your immediate reaction is to brake or swerve. You want to avoid hitting him. Self-preservation is secondary. Too late, he's gone and your car is out of control. Next thing, you've crashed and you're dead.

Okay, they didn't always die. With the beech trees gone and the road levelled, the conditions were against us. Sometimes people were injured. Sometimes they walked away. But sometimes, luck was on our side and then, there they were, standing beside us, watching their mangled bodies being carted away.

Over the next month, we welcomed Gina, an old lady in her eighties. She wasn't particularly phased by dying. Just glad it had been short and sweet. And to make things even sweeter, she was surrounded by fit young blokes. No wonder she had a smile on her face. Next came Robert, a local farmhand who'd had one too many in the local pub and attempted to drive home. He never made it. After that, there was a businessman, a woman in her forties, and a mother and baby. We felt bad about the baby, but only because it wouldn't stop crying. As Midge said, "If we'd known it 'ad such a pair of lungs, we'd never have shown ourselves."

The problem was we never knew who was coming. It was just random selection.

Winter arrived, bringing black ice, a slippery road and a whole host of fatalities. It was rich pickings for us and our gang swelled to twenty. Just as well. The dark energy brigade was getting more menacing by the day.

I spoke with Thomas, our resident dark matter expert.

"Have we got enough in our group to overcome an attack?"

He shrugged. "I dunno. The more we have, the safer we are. But I dunno at what point our critical mass tips the odds in our favour."

"How many of them are there?"

"Hard to say. Thirty or so? They're so closely packed, it's impossible to give an accurate assessment. We need someone to take a closer look."

There was only one among us who had the 'cojones' to do that. Midge.

He sauntered over to the far field to estimate the strength of our opponents. And was promptly despatched. Thomas was right about the absorption thing. One minute Midge was approaching them. The next, they were swarming all over him like black flies on meat and he was gone. Just like that. Obliterated in a split second.

Which meant we were one down. And still none the wiser as to their numbers. But we now knew their modus operandi and if we wanted to survive, we had to be smarter and stronger.

We stepped up our crusade. There were now so many of us, we weren't limited to the stretch of road by the former beech trees. We now occupied a good half-mile section. Thanks to a minibus carrying a local netball team and a couple of joggers, we not only swelled our ranks, but also added a female faction. Which made life, or I should say, death, a whole lot more interesting.

It also tipped the power balance in our favour. Just as well, because a week after the netball team joined us, the dark shadows attacked.

One minute, they were watching. The next, they were travelling at speed over the field and then they were on our section of road, a dark mass of swirling matter. We grouped together, standing close, and concentrated on pushing out our energy, creating a force field. We felt them come up against us, seeing contorted faces in the mass. It was like being crushed by cold, molten iron. Like an all-consuming headache was wrapped vice-like around you.

"Hold tight," I shouted, not sure if I could be heard.

The dark matter sucked all air and sound into its midst, closing over us, obliterating sensation, and I felt our gang start to disintegrate, as first one, then another was pulled from us, not strong enough to withstand the pressure. We reformed instantly, filling the gaps left by those departed, desperately pushing our energy into the spaces. And then, just as quickly as it started, it was gone. The dark cloud rescinded with a popping sensation, flowing back at speed over the field and disappearing into the distance.

Cautiously, we disbanded, feeling depleted and empty, surveying the damage. We'd lost four. Not bad, considering the mayhem that could have taken place. We'd lost two netball players, one jogger and our old lady. Amazingly, the baby was still with us, its energy field one of the strongest. On a par with its lungs, I guess.

And that's where you find us now. A ragged bunch of ghosts, torn and frayed, embattled but not overcome. More determined than ever to stand up to our enemy.

And so the recruitment drive begins again. We watch and we wait, crouched at the roadside, looking for opportunities to increase our gang, in readiness for the next attack.

Whoever said death is the end was wrong. It's not. It's a whole new beginning, just as complex as life ever was, with all its nuances, ambiguities, obstacles and dangers. You gotta be vigilant. You've gotta look after yourself. And you've gotta stick together.

Yesterday, the wank-brain weasel from the council came and put up a new sign, announcing thirty-two fatalities over a two-year period. He wasn't happy. Stood there, arms folded, on his side of the road and told us to sod off. We told him to 'do one' from the other side, telling him his sign wouldn't be accurate for long.

So, watch out if you're driving on the Wixley Road, especially if it's a dark, rainy night. Look out for the Road Boys appearing in front of you.

And if you hear a baby crying as you walk over the fields, you'll know we're somewhere near, waiting and watching. We wanna get that sign changed…

Corky the scarecrow keeps birds away from the crop,
but does he have more evil intent?

CORKY

Alice Dempster was excited. She was twelve years old and going to stay with her grandparents, travelling on her own. For the first time, ever.

Her parents were going away for a week to celebrate their wedding anniversary. That's what they said. Dressing it up to sound romantic. Alice knew otherwise. She'd heard the arguments and the accusations. They were going away to patch things up. It was a last ditch attempt to mend their broken relationship. They thought she didn't know. But she heard everything. They were trying to rekindle the spark. Whatever that meant. She hoped they'd succeed. Divorce was messy. She didn't want to have to choose between them.

Her older brother, Tom, was away on a school residential. An adventure week in the Welsh mountains. It sounded fun, but Alice knew where she'd rather be.

She'd be spoilt at Granny and Grampy's. Centre of attention, nothing too much trouble. Better than being told to go to her room, away from the shouting.

Mum took her to the station and Alice boarded the train, feeling grown-up and a little apprehensive. She sat by the window, looking at her reflection. Her blond hair was smooth thanks to the straighteners she'd got for Christmas and her eyes looked big now she'd used eyeliner and mascara. Mum hadn't even noticed.

Granny and Grampy met her off the train and she was soon sitting in their kitchen, warmed by the Aga, enjoying hot chocolate and homemade cherry cake.

"I thought we'd go shopping tomorrow," said Granny. "You can choose some clothes. My treat."

"And I'll buy lunch," said Grampy, crinkly blue eyes twinkling.

Alice beamed. It was going to be a good week.

She stood at her bedroom window, looking over the field behind the house while Granny unpacked her case.

"Who's that?" she asked, peering at the far side of the field. "Looks like a man."

Granny laughed. "It's not a man, silly. It's a scarecrow. The farmer's had a problem with the birds ever since he planted that new crop. There are two more at the end of the field. See? They're doing a good job, keeping the birds away."

"I don't like them," declared Alice, "especially him. He looks real."

"That's the whole idea," said Granny. "He's a bit past it, though. Won't last much longer, unless they give him a new body. The local kids call him Corky."

That afternoon, they went for a walk over the fields and Alice met Corky face to face. She'd been right not to like him. He was even scarier close up. He stood ramrod straight, arms splayed out, held in place by a horizontal pole. The front of his body was sagging and malnourished, straw peeping out from holes in his old black jacket. Twig fingers poked out from the cuffs and dirty grey trousers hung loosely around his straw legs, tucked into muddy brown boots, with the soles flapping loose.

His head was a large turnip, hollowed out like a Hallowe'en lantern, mouldering and discoloured. An old carrot, nobbled and misshapen, formed his nose and someone had gouged out eyeholes, pushing two bits of gleaming black coal into the sockets. A large grin stretched across his face, and used matches, inserted into his blackened turnip gums, created a row of spiky teeth. Clumps of straw stuck out from beneath his hat like matted, unwashed hair.

A dirty red scarf was tied round his neck and his old black hat placed at a rakish angle, giving the impression he'd once been a jaunty kind of fellow. Now he was decrepit, one of life's forgotten creatures.

Alice stared at him. He grinned back, tall and terrifying. The breeze blew gently and the straw rustled with a scritch-scratch noise.

"Can we go, please?" she asked, with a shudder.

That night, Alice couldn't help but look across the field from her bedroom window. There was Corky, silhouetted in the dim light. She frowned and looked a little closer, goose bumps creeping over her arms and neck. When she'd stood in front of him that afternoon, he'd been facing the far hedge. Now he'd turned and was looking right at her. She scrunched her eyes and peeked again. But the light was fading and it was hard to see.

She drew the curtains quickly, cutting him out.

"Stupid," she chided herself. "Scarecrows can't move on their own."

Next morning, she glanced over the field, everything in sharp definition in the bright sunlight. Corky was definitely facing her. She could see his orange nose.

"Probably the farmer," said Grampy, when she told him. "He often moves the scarecrows. Makes them look more real. Keeps the birds on their toes."

Alice nodded, not entirely convinced. There'd been something in Corky's expression when she looked into his face. A familiarity, somehow, an interest, and it hadn't been friendly. Corky was bad news, she was sure of it.

She had a lovely day with Granny and Grampy, wandering around the shops, buying clothes and enjoying a tasty lunch. All the things her mother never had time for. By nightfall, she was exhausted and ready for bed. Once again, she looked out of her bedroom window, allowing her eyes to slide across the field, hoping Corky had turned back to the hedge. Her breath caught sharply as her eyes focused. He'd moved again. Now he was in the middle of the field, black eyes looking straight at her. She drew the curtains sharply, heart thumping in her rib cage. Why did the farmer keep moving him?

In the morning, Corky was still in the middle of the field, grinning up at her, black hat jaunty as ever, arms out wide, as if to say: "Come closer. Let me embrace you." She shuddered and ran downstairs, too embarrassed to say anything to her grandparents.

They had another lovely day, taking a boat out on the river, visiting a butterfly farm, eating ice cream. She should have enjoyed it, but a dark shadow lay at the back of her mind and she couldn't help but think of Corky.

At bedtime, she forced herself to look over the field and breathed a sigh of relief. Corky was nowhere to be seen. The farmer must have moved him down the field and hopefully, that's where he'd remain for the duration of her stay.

Then she flinched, noticing a dark shape behind the trees at the end of her grandparents' garden. Was that a black hat she could see through the branches? Or was it someone walking a dog? It was a cloudy night and darkness was falling, making it impossible to tell.

She drew the curtains and jumped into bed, pulling up the covers, her pulse racing.

"He's not real," she told herself. "He can't hurt you."

But some deep instinct was on high alert.

When she awoke the next day, her fears were realised. As the day dawned, sunny and bright, brilliant blue skies framing the farmland behind the house, she stared aghast. Corky was as close to her grandparents' garden as he could get. He was almost squeezing through the trees at the garden's rear boundary. She could see one of his arms poking through, as if making way for himself. As the breeze parted the foliage, she saw his face, mouth grinning wider than ever, coal-black eyes staring up from beneath the rim of his hat.

Alice ducked out of sight, crouching beneath the window. What did he want? Could a scarecrow really move? Was someone trying to frighten her?

She went downstairs for breakfast, hearing voices in the kitchen.

"Just thought I'd pop in with a dozen eggs," a woman was saying.

"Very kind of you," Granny answered. "How are things? I see Burt's been moving the scarecrows round the back field."

"Not this week, he hasn't," came the reply. "He's at The Three Counties Show. Not due back till Saturday. It's probably the local kids."

Alice felt dizzy. Could it be local children? She hadn't seen anyone playing in the field. It all seemed quiet. She tried to put the matter out of her head, but the thought of the approaching night filled her with dread. Where would Corky appear next? Could he get into the garden?

At bedtime, she didn't look out of the window, just drew the curtains as fast as she could, jumped into bed and waited for sleep to come. Somehow, she drifted off and began to dream.

In her dream, she was lying in bed and it was dark. Children's voices, singing, came from the field outside:

> *Corky, Corky, Corky wants to see ya*
> *Corky, Corky, Corky wants to be ya!*

The dream Alice sat up, hearing a noise on the landing. It was a scritch-scratching sound, like straw rustling, which could mean only one thing. Corky was inside the house. With one quick movement, she was at the bedroom door, relieved to find it closed. On the landing, the rustling grew louder and she pulled a chair in front of the door, wedging it under the handle, hoping it would hold. The rustling stopped and there was silence. She leaned closer, then stifled a scream as the door handle began to turn. She pushed the chair hard against the doorknob, nerves taut, pulse thumping in her ears.

It was no good. Twig-like fingers curled around the door, pushing it open, and she screamed, waking suddenly, finding herself in bed.

She clutched the bedclothes, straining to see through the darkness. Her door stood ajar. Summoning all her strength, she ran across the room, closed it tightly and propped a chair beneath the handle. Now, no one could get in. She scurried back to bed, something rough on the floor catching between her toes. She bent down to pull it out and felt weak. It was a piece of straw.

With one leap, she reached the bed, diving under the bedclothes, holding them around her, wondering what to do. If Corky was on the landing, perhaps she could escape through the window. Now, she was aware of rain lashing at the windowpane and wind gusting around the house. Fingers shaking, she pulled back the curtains, seeing a flash of movement at the window. It was Corky, evil face grinning at her, rainwater running down his mottled head.

She must have fainted because next thing she knew, Granny was shaking her shoulder.

"Wake up dear, you've had a long sleep. I've brought you a cup of tea."

She set a mug of tea on the bedside table and Alice stared at her, eyes wide.

"Corky was here. In the night. He was in my room. And when I tried to get out of the window, he was there, looking in."

"Sounds like a bad dream to me, sweetie. He's just a scarecrow. How could he get into your room? Try and forget about it. He's scaring you more than the birds."

Granny looked out of the window.

"It's a lovely day. Come downstairs and we'll decide what to do. You've only a couple of days left, then it's time to go home."

She left Alice sipping her tea. As soon as she'd gone, Alice looked out over the field. Corky was nowhere to be seen. He wasn't in the field and she couldn't see him behind the trees. She looked on the bedroom floor, half expecting to see pieces of straw. But the carpet was clean. She let out a sigh of relief. It had been a continuation of the dream. Lucid dreaming, her brother called it. You thought you'd woken up, but you were still asleep, having the same dream. That scarecrow was certainly getting to her.

She pulled on her clothes, thinking what they could do with the day ahead. A trip to Warwick Castle? The children's adventure park? A picnic by the river?

She opened the window and a gentle breeze blew in. She pushed it further open, inhaling deeply, then jumped back as something fell onto the bed. Was it alive? It didn't move and she picked it up, placing it in her palm of hand, then staring in horror as she realised what it was. In her hand was a small piece of mouldy carrot.

Just out of vision, further down the field, Corky stood in the hedgerow, scarf fluttering in the breeze, smiling wider than ever. His turnip head had sunk in, creating a seeping cavity, and his nose was lacerated and pitted. A rotting, fetid odour hung around him. Time was running out for Corky.

Another idyllic day was over all too quickly and, once again, Alice walked up the stairs to bed. This time, she made preparations. She propped a chair under the doorknob and tied the window handles together with nylon twine. Neither the door nor the window could be opened. No one, scarecrow or otherwise, could get in.

Sleep came eventually and then she was dreaming, flying over the field beyond the garden, passing over the brown earth, where small green seedlings were pushing through, the full moon casting a bright light over the furrowed soil.

She flew to the far side of the field, seeing the other scarecrows silhouetted, looking for Corky but not finding him. She glanced back at her grandparents' house. And then she saw him, looking out of her bedroom window.

Panic stricken, she thought of her sleeping body inside the room. Time slowed as she tried to get back, aware she'd left her body vulnerable and unprotected. With one huge mental push, she willed herself back into the bedroom. There was a popping sensation and she was back in bed, opening her eyes in relief, looking straight into the coal black eyes of Corky.

She tried to scream but no sound came, and she inhaled his fetid, mouldering stench as his smile got closer. The scritch-scratching straw rattled in her ears and her eyes opened wide in terror.

Next morning, Alice opened her eyes, feeling the warm sun on her face, wondering why her arms were stretched out on either side. She looked down and saw the brown furrowed field beneath her feet. She was wearing old brown, muddy boots with the soles flapping loose.

In Alice's bedroom, Corky opened his eyes, luxuriating in the soft sheets and feeling the pillow beneath his head. Slowly he bent his arms and flexed his fingers, enjoying the unfamiliar movement.

There was a knock at the door and Granny came in, carrying a cup of tea.

"Better not get in the habit of having tea in bed," she smiled. "Your parents won't be doing this when you go home."

Corky smiled, drawing back his lips to reveal a row of perfect white teeth.

Outside in the field, arms stretched wide, Alice was aware of ethereal, shimmering children dancing around her in a ring.

They were singing:

Corky, Corky, Corky wants to see ya
Corky, Corky, Corky wants to be ya!

Get out of my house

Get out of my house, you don't belong
It's where I've lived for, oh, so long.
The old stone step scrubbed till it shone
My hands red raw in days long gone.

In blackened hearth the fire burned bright
It's where I sat night after night.
Sewing, mending, making do
Boiling up some rabbit stew.

The Great War took my boy away
Shot at Ypres, I rue the day.
Maiden, mother, wizened crone
My children gone, I sit alone.

Washdays Mondays, scrubbing hard
Hanging clothes across the yard.
Turning the mangle, wringing out
Feeling tired, plagued by gout.

Winter nights, feeling cold
Chilblained toes, getting old.
I died upstairs in the iron bed
Mad as a hatter, soft in the head.

Now, from room to room I roam
It's still my house, it's still my home.
Alive or dead, I'm never free
It's where I live, though ceased to be.

Many have come year after year
Some leave in fright, some leave in fear.
And now you're here, changing old for new
You can't see me, but I see you.

You wonder why the lights go out
The doorbell rings, you hear a shout
You feel a tug upon your sleeve
In bed at night you hear me breathe.

Listening hard, aroused from sleep
Beyond the door you hear me weep.
Get out of my house. You don't belong
I'll carry on haunting until you're gone.

A teenage girl uses an ancient technique
to bring an imaginary friend to life…

The Tulpa

I'm writing this because it is a true story and I want it to be recorded. There will come a time when I cease to exist. I'll look the same and sound the same. But it won't be me. And you need to know how this came about. Why I'm not responsible for my actions…

"What's that you're reading?" my sister asked, looking over my shoulder.

"'Mysterious Worlds' by Dennis Bardens," I answered, reading from the dust jacket, "A remarkable investigation into witchcraft, telepathy, second sight…"

It was the mid-seventies. I was sixteen years old and fascinated by the supernatural. The occult, the dark arts, ghosts, spirits, Alistair Crowley, all beckoned with the lure of the unexplained, something that was beneath the surface of polite society, making it all the more attractive to a disaffected teenager who was struggling to fit in.

At school, we experimented with levitation during lunch hour. One girl would lie on the floor of our Portacabin classroom and six others would kneel around her: one at the head, one at the foot and two each on either side. We would place our second and third fingers beneath the girl on the floor, so that we were supporting her, close our eyes and concentrate intensely. The goal was to make the girl rise a few inches.

Inexplicably, it worked every time. The girl would rise into the air, quite weightless, and we would hold her there, effortlessly, for a few seconds. We didn't think it was particularly strange. We believed it was the power of our collective thought. And maybe it was. A group of adolescent girls, with expanded energy fields, all producing powerful electric impulses. They say the presence of adolescents often explains the existence of poltergeist activity. Maybe this was the same: a manifestation of our combined adolescent power.

We also experimented with the Ouija board. Not the official one that used to be sold as a game. We did glass tipping. There were usually four or five of us. We'd create a circle made up of the letters of the alphabet, written on squares of paper placed in random order on the surface of a table. They were face down, so we couldn't cheat, ensuring any results were authentic. We wrote 'yes' and 'no' on two other squares placed inside the circle. We'd pull the curtains and turn on a lamp at one side of the room, so it was dim and creepy. Then, we'd place our index fingers on an upturned glass in the middle of the table. Someone would ask a question and we'd wait for it to move.

It always did and we took great delight in testing it to make sure it was working.

"Janey, decide what you want to be when you leave school, then sit in the room next door and concentrate on the word."

Janey, or whoever was the 'control', would leave the room and go next door.

"Okay, everybody, fingers on the glass. Tell us what Janey wants to be when she leaves school."

The glass would start to move, slowly at first, gradually picking up speed until it was fairly flying over the surface of the table. One by one, we'd turn over the letters it touched.

"P…S…Y…C…H…I…A…T…R…I…S…T…. Psychiatrist!"

"Come back in, Janey. What d'you want to be?"

"A psychiatrist! Is that what you got?"

"Yes! That means it's working. Let's carry on."

We'd ask who we were talking to, half believing we could summon long dead spirits, but to avoid it becoming too scary, always attributing our success to the power of our collective thought.

"Is anybody there?"

"It's going to 'yes'."

"Who are you?"

"It's spelling a name. What is it?"

"William Smith…"

"Have you passed over, William?"

"Yes…"

"When did you pass over?"

"1899…"

And so it would go on. It was a good game and kept us amused for hours.

It was around this time I found Dennis Bardens' book. From its pages, I learned about telepathy, dreams that foretold the future, loved ones who appeared at the point of death, and remote viewing, a technique employed by the CIA to learn about enemy territory.

I read about the power of the mind, and experimented with Zener cards, asking a friend to turn them over while I tried to guess, with limited success, which of the five designs was showing, thereby proving I was - or wasn't - telepathic. I read with fascination about astral projection and spent many a night trying to free my consciousness from my body, so I could gaze down from the ceiling on my prostrate form. I never quite achieved it, as panic usually set in at the thought I might not get back inside my body, and I was so terrified I'd end up sleeping with the light on.

"It's a load of rubbish," said my younger sister, looking at me with contempt. "I don't know why you're interested."

"Because it's unexplained. Because, maybe, there is an afterlife when we die and this is a way of proving it. Because I want to know more, I want to develop the power of my mind."

My sister raised her eyebrows pityingly. "Well, I don't. It's too scary."

"It's only scary because we don't understand."

"Whatever. I'm going to Youth Club. You coming?"

'No. I want to carry on reading."

I was addicted by the mysterious worlds that Dennis Bardens described, learning about witches' covens, apparitions, reincarnation, haunted objects, telekinesis and poltergeists. Then I extended my weird reading with anything I could get my hands on at the local library.

One story in particular took my fancy.

It was the tale of a French woman, Alexandra David-Neel, who travelled in Tibet, studying mystical techniques. She learned how to create an entity with the power of her mind. It was known as a Tulpa, an apparition that begins in the human imagination and eventually enters physical reality. She created a kindly, plump monk who was smiling and benign, similar to Friar Tuck in the tales of Robin Hood. She gave him a character, history and background and, through months of deep meditation and will power, brought him to life.

At first, he was shadowy and ethereal, appearing in her peripheral vision and summoned only when she thought of him. Gradually, he began to appear of his own volition and developed a physical presence. She described contact as like a robe rubbing against her or, once, a hand on her shoulder. Then she allowed him to live in her apartment as a guest.

Over time, his appearance began to change. His face took on a sly, malignant look and he became thinner and bolder. When she went on an expedition, he went with her, unbidden, and friends began to ask about the stranger in their camp. She realised he had escaped her control and was becoming increasingly malevolent, posing a threat to anyone who crossed his path.

There was only one solution. She had to reabsorb the creature into her mind, where it would fragment and eventually cease to exist. As a Tibetan lama and committed

Buddhist, she knew the technique required to banish the Tulpa, but hadn't realised how difficult it would be. The creature was determined to cling on to its existence and the battle proved difficult.

After six months, she brought it under control and succeeded in destroying its physical form, drawing it back into the realms of her imagination, before obliterating it. It was a long and tortuous process that left her emotionally drained, highlighting the dangers of bringing a Tulpa into the physical world.

I was transfixed by the story and couldn't get it out of my mind.

Around this time, an argument with my friends led to a lasting rift, causing me to experience long periods of solitude and loneliness. I spent hours alone in my bedroom, lying on my bed, thinking about the unknown world beyond.

The social isolation, combined with the turmoil of adolescence and the growing feeling of being an outsider in my peer group, led to me making a decision. I would create my own Tulpa, a friend who would embody all that I was looking for in a companion, someone who would be likeable, trustworthy and loyal, who would be there for me whenever I needed her. But unlike the woman in the story, I would keep control of my Tulpa. At the first sign of subordination, I would exert my willpower, drawing the Tulpa back into line, where it would remain, obedient and biddable.

And so Triff-Traff was born.

Triff-Traff was sixteen. She was slightly shorter than me, with a boyish build. She had long dark hair and pale skin, a small pert nose and big eyes that lit up her face. Cool and edgy, she dressed in black and wore Doc Martens. She was excitable and spoke with a quick, animated delivery. She enjoyed living on the periphery of society and didn't give a damn about social convention.

She had strong opinions about my former group of friends and took great delight in bringing them down, seeing through their superficiality with sharp character assassinations.

"Did you see Janey's new hairstyle? Really trendy… If she was 75."

"I would say Margaret's a cow, but that gives cows a bad name."

"As Fiona proves, you can put lipstick on a pig, but it's still a pig."

"Sandra is so boring, I fall asleep just saying her name."

I spent many long hours alone in my bedroom, meditating, giving Triff-Traff form and substance, fleshing her out and making her real.

She came from a broken home. Her parents had divorced when she was small and she lived with her mother, a well-known TV actress, who was more interested in her career than her wayward teenage daughter. Her father lived in America and was a famous TV producer. She rarely saw him, but he did give her a generous monthly allowance. She'd had a boyfriend for six months but had dumped him on the grounds that he was boring and juvenile. She said she was waiting for someone with attitude and authenticity to come along, and together they would discover the world. Until then, she was happy to be on her own. 'Attitude' and 'authenticity' were words she used a lot, along with 'non-conformist' and 'free spirit'.

She told me not to worry about not fitting in. She said we didn't need anyone, as long as we had each other and stayed true to ourselves.

Triff-Traff didn't believe in kowtowing to anyone. If someone crossed you or picked an argument, you disowned them. It was their loss. You turned away and didn't look back.

It was an attitude I liked and, over the next few months, Triff-Traff became more real, not just a voice in my head and an idea in my imagination.

I began to see glimpses of her in my peripheral vision. If I glanced across my bedroom, I'd see her, briefly, sitting on my bed, her back against the pillow, knees up, big eyes watching me. Just as quickly, she'd be gone, but she was beginning to enter the physical world. Sometimes, I'd enter my bedroom and I'd hear her singing. It was faint and insubstantial, but it was there, the words hanging like mist in the air.

It made me feel happy. I wasn't alone. I had a friend.

I told her she was welcome to stay in my bedroom whenever she wished, that she didn't need to wait for me to invite her or conjure her up. She didn't like the phrase 'conjure her up'. That made her angry. She wasn't dependent on me, she informed me. She didn't need me to give her permission to exist.

I backed down instantly.

"No, of course. I know it's not up to me. You're your own person. That's why I like you."

After that, she was in my room all the time. When I put on my make-up, she'd be sitting next to me, trying on a different a shade of eyeshadow and lipstick, backcombing her hair to give her a grunge look. I copied her and we sat there, looking at ourselves in the mirror, like twin sisters.

"Who are you talking to?" my sister demanded, knocking loudly on the door. 'I thought you were on your own."

"No. I've got a friend round. Leave us alone. Go and play with your toys."

Triff-Traff laughed. She didn't like my sister, thought she was a waste of space. Young, annoying and unformed, she said.

Then Triff-Traff left my bedroom and made the house her own. I was cleaning my teeth in front of the bathroom mirror when I saw her sitting on the bath behind me, watching. For a brief second, our eyes met. I turned round but she'd gone. That was a bit unnerving. It had been easier when she'd been confined to my bedroom. Now, I realised, she could turn up anywhere, as she did later that night when I was watching TV in the lounge. I glanced over to the sofa and there she was.

"Probably best if you stayed upstairs," I suggested.

She looked at me determinedly. "Why should I have to stay in your room? How would you like to be stuck there all the time?"

"Not much, I suppose. It may get awkward if my family sees you, that's all."

"It'll be cool. Don't worry. Just introduce me as your new best friend. Which I am, aren't I?"

"Of course. It's been brilliant since you arrived."

"There you go. Chill out. I'm here to make life better, not worse."

My mother popped her head around the door.

"Who are you talking to? I heard voices."

I looked at the sofa. It was empty.

"It was probably the TV. I had it on loud."

"I don't mind if you bring someone back," said my mother. "It's been ages since any of your friends came round."

"Yeah, well, I'm not really friendly with them anymore. I go round with other people."

"So, why don't you bring them round?"

"Yeah. Maybe."

She closed the door and, instantly, Triff-Traff reappeared.

"She wants to meet me," she said triumphantly.

Next day, Triff-Traff was at the bus stop, waiting for me. When the bus came, she sat next to me on a seat near the back. I don't know if people could see her, but no one sat next to me, despite people having to stand up.

At break, one of my former friends spoke to me.

"Who were you with on the bus? You two looked cosy together."

"Oh, just a friend who's come to stay for a while," I answered, secretly pleased. Now they'd know I'd moved on. I didn't need them any more. I had a new friend who was cool and edgy.

"There's a party at Jenna's Saturday night. Why don't you both come along?"

"Okay, thanks. We might. Depends what we're doing."

I smiled inwardly. Life was looking up, thanks to Triff-Traff.

That night, we sprawled on the floor, listening to music, chatting, hanging out. She was real. She was there. In my bedroom. In my life.

In the end, we didn't go to the party. It was nice to be asked, but I wasn't sure how Triff-Traff would fare with loud music, drinking and boys. She was still forming and I felt it would be too risky.

"I saw you walking back from the bus stop with someone," said my mother a few days later. "She looked nice. Who is she?"

"Her name's Triff-Traff. She's at my school, lives a couple of roads down."

"That's nice for you. I'm glad you've found someone. I was getting a bit worried about you spending so much time alone."

"Yeah, she's great. Much better than the other girls I used to hang out with. She's really nice. I can totally depend on her."

Which was sort of true and sort of not.

It had been six months since I'd created Triff-Traff and she now came and went as she pleased. Sometimes it was great. She was there when I needed company and we'd hang out, laughing and joking. Other times, it wasn't so good. She'd disappear and I wouldn't know where she was. When she reappeared, she'd be secretive and withdrawn, as if she had a secret life that didn't include me. She took great pride in asserting her independence.

I suppose it was natural she'd rebel against me occasionally. I was her creator and, like a child cutting the apron strings from its parent, she needed her own space. But I'd created her to be my companion, and I wasn't happy that she wanted to do her own thing.

She could also be very jealous, demanding exclusivity, and getting angry if I became too friendly with anyone else.

"What were you saying to that girl yesterday?"

"Which girl?"

"The one in the newsagents."

"We were talking about a magazine. Anyway, you weren't there."

"I was. You just couldn't see me."

"You were spying on me?"

She shrugged and gave me a peculiar little smile.

I realised she was slipping out of my control. Then three things happened, one after another, convincing me she was turning into a monster.

The first concerned my sister. I'd known for some time she didn't like Triff-Traff. She saw her frequently and always complained.

"Why's that girl here again? She's always hanging round. Tell her to get a life. She's creepy."

The dislike was mutual. Triff-Traff detested her.

"Tell her to do one. She's the one that's always hanging around."

"It is her house."

"And it's not mine?"

"Well, technically, no."

A couple of days after this exchange, my sister was coming down the stairs. I was below, in the hallway. Too late, I saw Triff-Traff's dark form appear at the top of the stairs, and watched in horror as she gave my sister a quick shove. My sister fell forward, but my reaction was quick. I bounded up the stairs and caught her half way, breaking her fall.

"It's okay, I've got you. You tripped, that's all."

"Are you sure? It felt like somebody pushed me."

I glowered at Triff-Traff, looking down at me from the landing and she gave me a self-satisfied smirk. Mum took my sister to A & E, just in case. It turned out she'd broken a bone in her foot and she came home in a plaster cast. I told Triff-Traff there'd be serious repercussions if she did anything like that again, with my sister or any member of my family.

The second thing happened a couple of days later. I was at the bus stop in my local town, alongside some of my former friends. They were giggling and talking, making me feel bad. I was convinced they were laughing about me behind my back and felt my cheeks flame red. I willed the bus to come, but it was late. So I stood at the back, by the wall, wishing more than ever I had a real friend, not a shadow friend that I'd summoned up myself. I didn't know where Triff-Traff was.

Suddenly, the bus appeared, approaching quickly to make up for lost time. As it neared the bus stop, everyone crowded forward and I saw Triff-Traff move swiftly behind Janey, the ringleader. She gave her a short, sharp push, causing her to stumble forward into the path of the bus. Luckily its brakes were good and, with a horrible screeching, it came to an abrupt halt. Janey had a lucky escape, no broken bones, just some bruising and bleeding.

She got to her feet, looking shaken, and turned angrily on her friends.

"OK, who pushed me?"

Her friends looked white and shaken, like they'd seen a ghost. Which I suppose in a way they had.

"We couldn't see," said one. "There were too many people. It wasn't one of us."

"Well, whoever it was, it's not funny. I could have been killed."

They wanted to call an ambulance, but she said she was okay. I looked to one side and there was Triff-Traff, a self-satisfied smile on her face. I ignored her and got on the bus. She didn't follow.

Later, at home, she was there in my room.

"This is getting out of hand," I said. "If you carry on like this, I will have to get rid of you. You can't hurt people."

"But they were being horrible to you. I did it for you."

"I don't need protecting, Triff-Traff. I created you for company, not as some kind of killer bodyguard. Just back off, okay?"

I brushed my hair in front of my dressing table with long, deliberate strokes and when I turned round, she'd gone.

After that, I didn't see her for a few days and, to be honest, I was relieved. She'd become needy and jealous, the opposite of what I'd initially created. I secretly hoped she wouldn't come back.

Then, the third incident happened.

A local boy asked me out. I'd always fancied him but thought he was way out of my league. We spoke outside the newsagent's and, next thing I knew, we were arranging to meet.

I arrived home on cloud nine and studied my face in the mirror. If I put my hair up, I was quite pretty. It emphasised my eyes. And I could experiment with that new smoky grey eye shadow I'd bought the previous week.

Then I saw her, reflected in the mirror, sitting on my bed.

"You're looking pleased with yourself," she said, not smiling.

I decided to tell her. Better than her finding out later.

"I've got a date," I said. "I'm meeting him tomorrow at the café in town."

"Great," she said, without conviction. "D'you mean the one on the High Street?"

"Yes, I'm seeing him at 4 o' clock. Oh, Triff-Traff, this is what I've dreamed of. I never thought anybody would find me attractive."

She gave me that funny, fixed smile, but didn't say anything. Then she disappeared.

The next day, just before 4 o' clock, I walked along the High Street. I saw the blue lights of an ambulance and a crowd standing round and experienced an immediate sinking feeling in my stomach.

"What's happened?" I asked a man standing near.

"Young chap got knocked off his bike," he answered. "Doesn't look good. He's in the ambulance."

As he spoke, it drew away, lights flashing. On the pavement, I saw a bicycle, a mass of mangled metal and misshapen wheels.

I didn't go into the café. I didn't need to. I knew what had happened. As the ambulance left, I saw her standing in the shadows. She looked dark and malevolent.

I knew then I'd got in too deep. Triff-Traff wasn't a friend. She wasn't even human. She was an entity I'd created out of my own emptiness and need. The only emotions she understood were loneliness, isolation and humiliation, because that's what she'd learned from me. She'd been born out of unhappiness and that's all she could relate to.

Now, she was malicious and murderous, and I knew what I had to do.

I had to reabsorb her into my consciousness, take away her power and render her harmless, then fragment her into a million pieces, so she could never manifest again. It would take time, but I had to do it, or take responsibility for the consequences.

The next day, I found out the boy on the bike was in intensive care. He'd sustained serious injury, hovering between life and death for some days, before finally rallying. I didn't contact him. It would have been too dangerous.

At home, I began to meditate every night, concentrating on creating a magnetic pull and drawing in Triff-Traff, anchoring her to me with thick, unbreakable cords. It was a long process and took every ounce of mental energy I could summon.

Sometimes, I could feel her pulling against me, trying to escape my control. But I persevered and after six months, I felt her power diminishing. She had less form now, just a dim shadow that appeared in the corner of the room. She didn't appear outside or anywhere else in the house. She didn't say anything and I began to hope she would soon be gone.

Around this time, I left to go to university. It was a miracle I managed to get the necessary 'A' level grades, given the amount of time and energy I was devoting to Triff-Traff. But I did, and accepted a place at Birmingham University to study History.

Triff-Traff came with me. She had to. She was now firmly entrenched in my subconscious.

A couple of weeks after I arrived at university, I knew the time had come. Triff-Traff was faint and insubstantial, nothing more than a flimsy wraith on the edge of my imagination, and I knew it was time to blast her to oblivion and rid myself of her forever.

It was with sadness that I approached the task. After all, she was my creation. I'd given her life. And now,

I had to take it away. But my life was moving on and she'd become dangerous. She had to go.

It was a Sunday evening when I sat in my study bedroom, preparing to go deep into meditation. My focus now was not on drawing in Triff-Traff, but on casting her out, scattering her into a million pieces, like psychic confetti. I wasn't sure how to go about the fragmentation process, but hoped it would come to me instinctively at the right moment.

I was way out of my depth, but hardly dared admit it to myself.

I felt myself go deeper and deeper into a relaxed state of mind, aware of nothing but my desire to be rid of Triff-Traff, the Tulpa.

Gradually, all went dark and I knew no more.

It was morning when I awoke. The sun was streaming through the window, its bright rays shining on my face, waking me and making me squint. I wondered why I'd forgotten to draw the curtains.

I realised I was lying on top of the bed sheets, fully clothed, and that something didn't feel right. I flexed and opened my right hand. It hurt. My knuckles were red and swollen and I saw dried blood on the back of my hand and cuff.

Cautiously, I sat up, feeling bruised and stiff. I saw I was still wearing my boots and they were covered in mud. I put my hand to my head and pulled dried leaves from my hair.

What had happened the previous night? Where had I been? Had I been successful in destroying Triff-Traff? I resisted the urge to summon her, to see if she was still around. First, I needed to clean up and clear my head.

I showered, feeling the hot water wash away the tension, breathing slowly to compose myself. I put cream on my sore knuckles and dressed. I needed fresh air and coffee, so made my way from the student accommodation to the main campus, heading for the refectory.

On the way, I passed a group of boys, fellow students.

"Hey, Triff-Traff, how are you this morning?"

They all laughed.

I walked past them, not answering, looking down at the pavement.

"That was some fight,' one of them called after me. "She won't cross you again. You gonna visit her in hospital?"

My breathing was shallow and fast, and I felt cold and clammy. The world closed around me to a tiny pinpoint. I sat on a nearby bench, away from the boys, my mind working overtime.

Triff-Traff? Fight? Hospital? The words were ringing in my ears. What had happened last night?

Two realisations hit me simultaneously. I'd been successful in drawing Triff-Traff back into my subconscious, but I'd been unsuccessful in fragmenting her.

She was too strong. And now she had a hold.

The Tulpa was clinging on to its newfound existence and I had neither the ability nor skill to destroy it. Only now, rather than exist as a separate entity, Triff-Traff was operating through me, and there was nothing I could do to stop her.

The Tulpa was taking over. I was becoming Triff-Traff.

On 25th November 1979, Amy Mortimer, aged 20, a student at Birmingham University was arrested on suspicion of murder.

Initially, she pleaded insanity, citing a split personality condition, but psychiatrists declared her fit for trial. The court case lasted six weeks, with the prosecution presenting insurmountable evidence against her.

After just five hours, the jury reached a unanimous verdict. Mortimer, also known by the nickname Triff-Traff, was found guilty on three counts of first-degree murder and two counts of attempted murder, thereby bringing to a close the case of the Campus Killer.

Throughout, Mortimer showed no remorse, smiling in a detached manner, as if she found the whole business to be an entertaining diversion.

She received three life sentences, to run concurrently. It is doubtful she will ever leave prison.

Does love transcend death?
A wife and son reappear after their death…

Can't let go

Ben Barton began seeing his wife and child three weeks after they'd been killed in a car crash.

It first happened late one night after he'd turned off the television. He'd watched a comedy show, barely taking it in, too traumatised by the horrific turn of events that had wrecked his life. Slowly, as if on autopilot, he'd clicked the 'off' button on the remote control and watched as the image on the screen disappeared and the system shut down.

Like a light going out, he'd thought to himself, like a life being extinguished.

It was a week since their funeral, when he'd watched their two coffins lowered into the ground and he'd thrown a rose on top of each, red for Rebecca and white for Toby, followed by a handful of earth. Earth to earth, ashes to ashes. The two people he loved most in the world gone in an instant, lying dead beneath the soil.

Now, he went into the kitchen to make a cup of tea, carrying it back into the lounge and wondering if he should start the new paperback his sister had given him. It was a thriller, his favourite type of book. But would he be able to concentrate on the plot? Could he even focus on the words? He doubted it. He couldn't keep his mind still. It was like a grasshopper, jumping from one thing to the next, without taking anything in properly.

As he walked into the lounge, he was aware of movement on the sofa. And there they were. Rebecca sitting next to Toby, holding the remote control, and the television was on. They were watching a documentary and Toby was asking a question, just as he always did.

"What does that mean, mum? I don't get it."

Rebecca smiled indulgently. "It's politicians being politicians. Who knows what it means? I don't think they know themselves. It's a mess."

"I knew we should have remained. Everyone at school wanted us to remain. It's just old people who voted for Brexit."

Ben stopped and stared, wondering if he was hallucinating.

"Rebecca?" he asked, his voice catching in his throat.

She turned.

"I see you've made a cup of tea for yourself. Typical. What about me?"

Ben absently ran his tongue over his lips that had gone strangely dry.

"You want a cup of tea?" he asked stupidly.

"Duh?" Rebecca mocked him, grinning widely. "Don't I always?"

"What about me?" asked Toby.

Rebecca looked at her watch. "No. It's past your bedtime. You've school in the morning." Then relenting. "Tell you what, get ready for bed and I'll bring you a cup of hot chocolate. Go on, up you go."

Ben watched, eyes wide, as his son slouched past him towards the lounge door.

"Night, Dad."

"Night, son."

'See you in the morning."

"Yeah," he answered doubtfully. "See you in the morning."

Toby disappeared through the lounge door and Ben heard the stairs creaking as he went up to bed.

Ben turned and stared at Rebecca. She was just as beautiful as he remembered, dark hair falling glossily around her shoulders, flawless ivory skin, small dimple on her cheek, big green eyes. Not how she'd been when he last saw her, cut and bleeding, her face so swollen he hardly recognised her.

"What are you staring at?" she asked.

"Nothing," he mumbled, "just thinking how beautiful you look."

"Are you feeling all right? You look like you've seen a ghost."

He flinched at her words and forced himself to laugh. "No, I'm fine, just pleased to see you. Surprised, but pleased."

"What are you talking about? We live here. Have you been on the beer?"

He thought back to that dark, rainy night three weeks ago, when Rebecca had gone out to collect Toby from Scouts. Normally, that was his job, but he'd had to prepare a report for work.

"D'you want me to go?" Rebecca had asked.

"D'you mind? It would really help."

"No problem. See you in a few minutes."

Only he didn't. That was the last time he saw her. After she'd collected Toby from Scouts, she took a short cut, driving along a narrow country lane known as Primrose Hill, heading for home.

For whatever reason, maybe she'd been tuning the radio, maybe she'd been chatting to Toby, asking him about Scouts, she never saw the tractor ahead, waiting to turn right. She'd slammed straight into it, without even braking. Irresistible force meets immovable object: one small Mini against two tonnes of industrial steel.

They hadn't stood a chance. The car concertinaed and they were both killed instantly. No one to blame. Just one of those unfortunate accidents: wrong place, wrong time.

Two lives gone, one life ruined forever, left behind to contemplate a lonely future.

He'd been working at his desk, unaware of time, glancing at his watch and realising it was over an hour since Rebecca had left. He'd called her mobile but it went to voicemail. Panic rising, he'd run out of the house and jumped in his car.

The Scout Hut was empty, so he'd headed up to Primrose Hill, knowing something bad had happened as soon as he saw flashing blue lights. A policeman flagged him down.

"Sorry, sir, the road's blocked. You'll have to go another way."

"What's happened?" he'd asked, hearing his pulse thump in his temples. "Is it an accident?"

"Yes, sir. The emergency services are there now."

"It's my wife," he'd shouted. "She should be home by now, but she hasn't come back."

"What car was she driving?"

"A red Mini Cooper, with a stripe on the bonnet."

He'd known by the policeman's expression that it was the car involved in the accident. Not waiting to hear more, he'd opened his car door and, ignoring the policeman's shouts to come back, had run down the lane towards the blue lights.

It was Rebecca's car, what was left of it. The bonnet was completely buckled, the whole car compressed into an alarmingly small shape against the tractor. A fire engine was there, cutting Rebecca and Toby out. But he knew, even then, it was no good. The crash was not survivable.

Now he stared at Rebecca, put his hand out to touch her cheek. She was soft and warm, just as she'd always been.

"You're beautiful," he said, looking into her eyes, feeling warmth spread through his body.

She laughed. "You've definitely been on the beer. You're acting very strangely."

"Where have you been?" he asked. "I was missing you."

"I went to get Toby from Scouts. You know where I was. You wanted to write your report. Is it finished?"

"Yes," he answered, glancing at his watch, at the date and time.

It was three weeks to the day since the accident, and it was 9.30pm. Exactly the time she should have been home with Toby on that fateful day.

"How was Scouts?" he asked, watching her carefully.

"Toby said it was pretty boring. They were supposed to be making a campfire outside but it was too wet, so they played games in the hall instead."

"I see," said Ben, trying hard to understand what she was saying. "And you got home okay?"

"Yes," she answered, regarding him curiously, "apart from going down Primrose Hill, which was a mistake. The farmer was driving his tractor in front of us. I thought he'd never get out of the way. We'd have been back sooner, otherwise."

Ben's rational brain was trying to understand, but his emotional need was greater. They were back. The wife and child he thought he'd never see again were here, at home. And he was questioning it?

"I'll make you a cup of tea," he said.

"That would be nice," she said sarcastically, snuggling back into the sofa. "It's a pig of a night out there. I'm glad we're back."

He carried the cup of tea into the lounge, wondering if she'd still be there. She was, snuggling under the fluffy white throw on the sofa.

"Lovely, thanks," she said, taking the tea. "Did you make Toby some hot chocolate?"

"Yes. I'll take it up," said Ben.

He carried the hot chocolate upstairs to Toby's room. Toby was sitting on his bed, wearing his red Wolverine pyjamas. He was typing on the keyboard of his laptop. Ben hadn't touched anything in his room since the accident, so everything was just as he'd left it, bed unmade, piles of clothes on the floor, paper and pens on the desk. Ben placed the drink on the bedside cabinet.

"Thanks, Dad. Is there a problem with the Wi-Fi? I can't get a connection?"

Ben thought fast.

"The server's probably down. Don't worry about it. I'm sure it will be up tomorrow. How are you feeling?"

Toby looked at him strangely. "Fine. Why?"

"No reason. Just checking."

"Okay. I'm going to give Kev a quick call, if that's okay."

"Yes, of course," he answered, watching as Toby picked up his mobile phone and speed-dialled a number.

He left the room and closed the door, hovering on the landing, listening to Toby speak.

"Hi, Kev. It's me. How ya doin'? Yeah, just back from Scouts… No way, you're kidding…"

Was this a massive hallucination brought about by grief? Was he in some kind of time warp or alternate reality? He had to get hold of Toby's phone and find out if he was really talking to Kevin.

He went downstairs and joined his wife, still sitting on the sofa, watching television. He couldn't help but sneak glances at her every few minutes, convinced she was a figment of his imagination and would disappear in front of his eyes.

"Will you stop looking at me," she laughed, "you're freaking me out."

Ben smiled, too nervous to ask about the accident, wondering if he was losing his mind, whether it had actually happened or he'd imagined everything. He'd been working hard recently, putting in long hours. Maybe his mind was playing tricks.

He resolved, in the morning, to look online for reports of the accident and confirm that it had actually happened. Once he had a reference point, he could think more clearly.

For now, he was content to relax in her company, forget the events of the last three weeks, and make believe life was going on as normal.

That night, he crept into Toby's bedroom, seeing his son lying on the bed, watching him breathe. He put his hand on the boy's cheek, feeling it soft beneath his fingertips. Ben's throat constricted with emotion. Last time he'd seen Toby he'd been bruised and cut, fatally injured, covered up and taken away in an ambulance. He never thought he'd get to touch him again and feel the soft warmth of his skin, inhale the sweet smell of his breath.

"Oh, Toby," he whispered, "are you real? I thought I'd never see you again."

A sound from the door attracted his attention. It was his wife.

"Are you coming to bed, Ben? You've been in here for ages. What are you doing?"

He turned. "Yes. Just thinking what a fine young man Toby is and how lucky we are to have him."

"We are indeed," she said, "now, come on. We have to be up in the morning."

As he slipped beneath the duvet, he felt her body soft and pliant next to him, felt her fingers pulling him towards her. His mouth found hers and he was lost in the embrace, luxuriating in a sensation he thought he'd never experience again. He touched her skin as if for the first time, feeling its soft downiness beneath his fingertips, trying to hold back the emotion that threatened to choke him. He didn't know how this was happening, only that it was.

He held her tightly, never wanting to let go, aware this might be his final goodbye.

Although he tried hard to stay awake and savour every minute, sleep claimed him and he dreamed of the past, when times had been happy and tragedy unknown, a distant memory somewhere on the horizon.

When he awoke, he was alone.

"Rebecca!" he called, hoping for an answer but knowing instinctively there wouldn't be one.

"Rebecca!" he called again, running on to the landing and shouting down the stairs. His voice echoed through the empty house. There was no one there.

He ran into Toby's room but the bed was empty. The cup of hot chocolate sat cold and untouched on the bedside cabinet.

Ben dropped to the floor, head in hands and let the tears flow, feeling the fresh blow of grief hit once again. This time, it was all the more painful for the unexpected reprieve he'd had the night before.

"I must be losing my mind," he whispered to himself. "They were so real. They were here. I felt Rebecca's arms around me. It happened. I couldn't have made it up. It was too intense. Too physical."

His mind went to his son, how he'd watched him sleep, seeing his chest rise and fall, how he'd heard him talking on the phone. The phone! He'd been talking to Kev. He had to see if it had really happened. He seized Ben's phone on the bedside cabinet and switched it on, hope building as it flickered into life. He went straight to the call log, looking for the last call Toby had made.

It was three weeks ago, when he'd called his mum from Scouts to say he was ready to come home. He hadn't spoken to Kev the night before. It had never happened.

Downstairs, in the lounge, he found Rebecca's cup of tea. It was cold and untouched.

As if in a dream, Ben went through the motions of showering, having breakfast and driving to work. He was a computer programmer at the local council, a humdrum job with little variety.

Today, thankfully, there were no meetings scheduled. He slipped into his booth, nodding a quick good morning to work colleagues, and settled down to his daily routine. The day dragged on as he found himself unable to focus, his mind continually going back to the night before, reliving conversations with Toby and Rebecca, experiencing all too vividly the feel of her body next to his.

He told no one what had happened, the experience too private and too unbelievable to share with anyone. Colleagues found him distant and remote, but that was only to be expected, given the tragedy he'd been through.

At 5 o'clock he drove home, letting himself into a house he knew would be empty and cold, remembering how once there'd been the sound of Toby running upstairs, his school blazer draped over the kitchen chair, Rebecca making the dinner, a quiz show blasting noisily from the kitchen television.

Now it was silent. No chatter, no noise, nothing.

He poured himself a beer, savouring the cool liquid as it slipped down his throat, soft and anaesthetising. Alcohol was the only thing that helped, dulling the emotions, taking the edge off the cutting, raw grief.

By 9.30, he'd eaten a tin of beans and drunk too much. He went into the kitchen to make a tea, looking up as he heard sounds from the lounge. The television that he'd just turned off was on again.

And then it was ground hog day.

He walked into the lounge and there they were, just as before. Rebecca was sitting next to Toby, holding the remote control, and the television was on. They were watching a documentary and Toby was asking, "What does that mean, mum? I don't get it."

Rebecca smiled. "It's politicians being politicians. Who knows what it means? I don't think they know themselves. It's a mess."

"I knew we should have remained. Everyone at school wanted us to remain. It's just old people who voted for Brexit."

Ben stopped and stared. "Rebecca?"

She turned. "I see you've made a cup of tea for yourself. Typical. What about me?"

It was the same script, word for word. He was going through the same experience as the night before, only now he knew what to expect.

"You want a cup of tea?" he asked.

"Duh?" Rebecca mocked him, grinning widely. "Don't I always?"

"What about me?" asked Toby.

Rebecca looked at her watch. "No. It's past your bedtime. You've school in the morning." Then relenting. "Tell you what, get ready for bed and I'll bring you a cup of hot chocolate. Go on, up you go."

Toby slouched past Ben, heading for the lounge door.

"Night, Dad."

"Night, son."

'See you in the morning."

"Yeah. See you in the morning."

Ben fell easily into the script, knowing the words he must speak, knowing in advance the response he'd get.

Once again, he took up a cup of hot chocolate to his son, heard him speak to Kev on his phone then settle for bed. Once again, he watched the soft inhalation and exhalation as his son slept, and once again, he went to bed with the wife he knew in reality lay dead and cold in the ground.

In this alternative universe, she was soft and yielding, warm as she'd ever been. He didn't understand it, but why question? It was an unexpected gift and as long as it was there for the taking, he'd receive it gratefully.

Night after night he went through the same experience. Always at 9.30, always the same words, relishing every second, secretly wondering how long it would go on for.

Colleagues noticed a difference. There was a spring in his step, a light in his eyes and a cheer to his voice. The haunted, empty person who'd sat silently at his desk had gone. If anything, he was too chatty, too friendly, his cheeriness almost manic. But it was an improvement and so they said nothing.

Then two weeks after Rebecca and Toy had first appeared, it all changed.

At 9.30, he heard sounds from the lounge and knew they were back. He walked in, a smile on his face, prepared to speak the well-rehearsed words.

They sat on the sofa, but this time they looked different. They were faded somehow, as in an old photograph. Their figures were hazy, their outlines blurry and indistinct, and it was hard to hear what they were saying.

"You want a cup of tea?" he asked, trying to keep the script flowing.

But this time, Rebecca just looked at him sadly and he knew it was coming to an end.

"Life moves on, Ben," he heard her saying. "Good things never last forever. Time for us to go."

"No," he cried, moving towards her, willing them to stay.

She became more hazy as she spoke and he realised they were disappearing before his eyes. "Stay a bit longer," he pleaded. "I'm not ready to let go."

She smiled sadly, green eyes full of tears. And then they were gone. He was looking at an empty sofa.

"No," he screamed. "I'm not ready. Come back!"

But the room was empty and the television silent.

He dropped to his knees, his world ripped apart once again, only this time it was final. This time there would be no long, lingering embrace as he went to sleep, no fond look at his sleeping son.

They were gone and he was alone.

Somehow he went through the motions of going to bed, dropping into a dark, dreamless sleep, before waking to the fresh, awful realisation that he was truly on his own.

"Why did you come back?" he shouted to the empty house. "I could cope with losing you once, but not for a second time. It's too much."

He sat on the bed, head in hands and knew what he must do.

After a few days of not coming in to work, questions were asked and the police sent to the house to investigate.

They found Ben sitting on the sofa. He'd been dead for two days.

That night at 9.30 sharp, the television switched on.

* * *

A year later, the house was sold and another family moved in, a couple with their teenage son. They knew of its history, but times were hard and they'd snapped it up for a bargain. Besides, they were people that lived in the 'here and now'. Past tragedy didn't bother them.

"Zach, I thought I told you to turn off the television."

Upstairs in his room, Zach heard his mother call from the kitchen.

"You need to get some revision done. GCSEs start tomorrow. If you're watching another reality TV show, there'll be trouble."

"I did turn it off, mum. I'm upstairs."

"Then who turned it on? Your dad's at the pub."
She looked at her watch. It was 9.30.

In the lounge, Rebecca, Toby and Ben settled down to watch TV. A group of politicians were discussing Brexit.

Love Lost

She sits among the gravestones
Features etched in pain
Tears run down in rivulets
She seeks her love in vain.

The wind bites cold and chill
Cutting to the bone
A fitting testimony
For a heart that's made of stone.

She never got to marry
Her ring finger is bare
She knows not where to find him
So she waits to see him there.

They once danced close and still
Two hearts that beat as one
About to tell their story
A coupling just begun.

But war rose up between them
And he took up his gun
Exchanging love for death
At the going down of the sun.

Long nights awake she sat
His locket in her hand
Thinking of a future
Without a wedding band.

She turned away from God
Grief broke her heart in two
She couldn't live without him
She knew what she must do.

A shining blade of silver
She plunged into her breast
And there among the gravestones
She laid herself to rest.

But peace slipped through her grasp
And so she walks and sighs
In search of what was taken
A love that never dies.

Then, faint on the horizon
A misty figure shines
A lone solider comes walking
Away from battle lines.

He comes among the gravestones
Seeking his lost bride
Crying tears of heartache
From which he cannot hide.

In life they could not marry
Their tale lost in the past
But love sustaining love
In death they meet at last.

They sit among the gravestones
Their hands and arms entwine
The soldier and his bride
Together for all time.

*An ancient find unleashes a violent past,
with a dark, dangerous legacy…*

Magnet Fishing

"Dad, can we go magnet fishing?" called out Harry.

He'd been watching Midlands Today on television and at the end of the programme they'd done their usual human-interest story. Harry had been glued to the screen, his eyes big with excitement.

"What's that?" asked dad, coming into the room.

"It's where you go fishing with a magnet in rivers and canals and you catch metal things."

"It the new craze," explained Harry's mum. "People have been fishing with magnets in local canals and pulling out all kinds of stuff."

"Yeah, like guns and knives and really old things," said Harry, excitedly. "The people on television found a bag full of guns. They don't know where they came from. They handed them in to the police."

"I'm not sure I want to fish a bag of guns or rusty weapons from the local canal," said dad. "Anyway, knowing our luck we'd find a load of old rubbish."

"It could be treasure, dad, or something really valuable, like jewellery or coins. Can we try it? Please?"

"Well, I used to go metal detecting," answered dad. "I suppose it's not so different. We might find something interesting."

"Yes!" Harry shouted, in delight. "We're going to find treasure!"

"Don't get too excited," warned mum. "For every person that finds something interesting, hundreds more find nothing. But it'll be nice for you two to spend time together.

A week later, Harry and his dad were fully equipped. Dad had Googled 'magnet fishing' and they now had a heavy duty Neodymium magnet, a super strong polycord rope securely attached to the eyebolt of the magnet, gloves to protect their hands and a bag for holding their finds.

"We'll take a wallpaper scraper as well. For scraping bits of metal off the magnet," explained dad, who had researched the subject extensively on YouTube. "Most of what we find will be old and rusty and will stick hard to the magnet. We don't want to be pulling that off with our hands. We'll take scissors as well, so we can cut the cord if it gets tangled up."

"Where shall we go?" asked Harry.

"How about we start at the old Pack Horse Bridge?" suggested Dad. "It was built in the seventeenth century. You never know, we might find some old coins."

"Oh yes!" said Harry, thinking of all the fantastic items they were about to find.

Mum made them sandwiches and they set off. They couldn't have asked for a better day. It was early autumn, the sun was shining and the sky a brilliant blue, perfect conditions for finding hidden treasure. Harry felt sure they were going to find something really exciting.

They reached the Pack Horse Bridge and stood on the old stone parapet, looking over the side where the water was deepest.

"I'll throw it first so you can see what to do," said dad. "I don't want you throwing yourself in as well."

Harry watched as his father threw the small magnet into the black water. It disappeared instantly, pulling the bright green cord after it. Harry shivered. The water looked scary and deep. Who knew what was lurking down there on the riverbed? Slowly, his father began to pull up the rope. After a minute or so, the magnet appeared.

"It's got something," said Harry, excitedly, leaning forward. "What is it?"

"Just a bit of old metal. Part of a bike, I think."

Dad removed the metal object, rusty and covered in weed, and dropped it onto the bridge beside them.

"Yuk, that looks disgusting," said Harry, in disappointment.

"Let's try again," said dad.

He threw the magnet a bit further this time. It made a loud splash as it entered the water and sank rapidly. Dad pulled the cord in slowly, until the magnet reappeared. There was nothing attached. They threw it in again and, once more, there was nothing. Then they moved to the other side of the bridge and tried again. This time, it attached to something very heavy. Dad pulled hard on the rope, giving it a sharp tug.

"I think it might have snagged on something," he said. Whatever it was came loose with a jolt, causing dad to lurch backwards. He laughed and pulled hard on the magnet. It appeared, carrying a square object about 20 cm across, discoloured and dripping with dark, slimy mud. Dad reached down and grabbed it, placing it on the bridge.

"It's an old manhole cover," he declared.

For the next three hours, they moved up and down the riverbank, taking turns to throw the magnet into the water and reel it in. By lunchtime, they'd accumulated a motley collection of objects: the man hole cover, a can top, a length of piping, a bike lock, some rusty nails, various pieces of unidentifiable rusty metal and even a discarded hard drive. Harry could hardly hide his disappointment. He'd been so sure they'd find something good.

They sat and ate their sandwiches.

"Why don't we try a different location?" suggested Dad. "How about the old millrace?"

They walked along the riverbank for half an hour, until they reached the disused mill. The footpath led onto a wooden bridge that crossed the river where the weir had been built. Harry looked over both sides of the bridge. On one side there was the millpond, its surface still and unmoving, covered in bright green duckweed; on the other, the weir, water gushing furiously, leading towards the old mill.

"See how the water's being forced into a narrow channel?" pointed out dad. "That's the millrace. The current is strong and powerful, so it can turn the water wheel."

Harry looked towards the disused mill, where the old water wheel stood, rusted and unmoving. He felt uneasy. There was a strange feel to the place. It felt lonely and neglected, a place of secrets and sadness, and danger, especially given the deep water and strong current.

"I don't like it here," he said. "It's creepy." He wasn't sure which was more scary, the still waters of the millpond or the rushing torrent of the millrace.

"Well, now we're here, we might as well have a go," said dad. "Let's try the pond."

He threw the magnet into the millpond and it landed with a splash, scattering the green duckweed and sinking out of sight. Dad pulled it back towards him.

"Looks like we have something," he said, as the magnet appeared. He scraped a piece of metal off the bottom of the magnet.

"A bit of old machinery, I think. Could be something to do with the mill."

Harry shivered again, noticing the sun had disappeared behind a bank of grey cloud and the temperature had cooled. The water beneath them looked black and cold, contrasting with the white spumes of spray where it passed over the weir.

"You have a go," said dad, handing the magnet to Harry. "Give it a good throw."

Harry threw as hard as he could into the millpond, waiting for a minute or so until the magnet sank, then he tugged hard. It wouldn't budge.

"It's stuck, dad."

He pulled again and it gave a little.

Dad took over, gathering in the polycord. Harry waited anxiously for the magnet to appear, experiencing the thrill of anticipation that this time they may have found something interesting.

"There's definitely something attached," he said.

The magnet appeared, bringing with it a long, pointed object dripping with dark, wet mud and covered with duckweed. As he swung it over the railing, Harry grabbed it.

"It's a sword," he gasped. "A really old one."

Instantly, he felt a coldness spread up his arm. He shuddered and drew back his hand, dropping the sword onto the bridge floor, but not quickly enough. A bad feeling went through him and, momentarily, he was filled with an inexplicable dread.

Using his foot as leverage, dad pulled off the magnet and began cleaning away the mud and duckweed. He picked up the sword. It was about three feet long, possibly with an ornate handle, although it was hard to see beneath the mud and rust.

"Looks quite old," he said. "We'll take it home and clean it up. Then we'll take it to the museum and see what they say."

Large spots of rain began to splash on the surface of the bridge and dad glanced up at the sky. It was brooding and dark. They'd been so intent on magnet fishing, they hadn't noticed the clouds building up.

"We'd better get home before this bad weather sets in," he said, coiling up the polychord. "Not bad for a first day's magnet fishing, though."

"Dad, there's somebody watching us," said Harry, looking towards the far side of the millpond. "Over there."

He pointed at the outline of a dark figure, shadowy and indistinct. It looked like a man, but it was hard to see in the fading light. Dad peered where Harry was pointing.

"Can't see anything, Harry."

Harry glanced at dad and when he looked back, the figure had gone.

"Probably a trick of the light," said dad. "Looks like a storm's coming. The light is very strange."

Harry had a strong and sudden urge to leave the place. It was as if something was saying to him: *'Get out. Get out. Now!'* The air felt heavy and charged with static. From nowhere a strong wind gusted across the bridge, whipping up the dead leaves and bending the saplings on the riverbank almost double. The rain fell harder, as if the clouds above had suddenly burst, dispelling their contents like water from a bucket.

"Come on, Harry, let's go," said dad, packing everything into the carrying bag.

"The sword's too big for the bag. D'you want to hold it?"

Reluctantly, Harry took the sword, and the same feeling of coldness swept through him.

"You carry it, dad," he said, handing his father the sword.

As they walked back on the footpath, Harry looked back and could have sworn he saw the dark figure. Only now it was on the bridge. Quickly, he hurried after his father.

By the time they reached home they were soaked. Dad put the bag and the sword in the garage.

"We'll sort this out tomorrow," he said, surprised when Harry readily agreed. He'd thought the boy would want to clean up the sword straightaway, but he was obviously tired. The sword certainly didn't look quite as exciting now they'd brought it home, just a long piece of mottled, muddy, rusted metal.

Harry was subdued during the evening, hardly touching his favourite dinner of spaghetti bolognese.

"Are you alright, Harry?" asked mum. "I hope you haven't picked up any germs from those objets you found in the water. Who knows how long they've been down there, or what kind of stuff you've disturbed dragging them up."

'What kind of stuff you've disturbed…' The phrase echoed unpleasantly through Harry's head, making him feel squirmy and afraid. What if they had disturbed something? What if the dark figure wanted his sword back? Once or twice, as they'd walked home along the riverbank, he'd turned to look back, sure he could see the dark figure some distance behind, concealed in the trees, following them.

He had a sudden desire to take the sword back to the millpond and throw it into the water as far away as he could. It wasn't theirs and they shouldn't have taken it.

That night, he left the light on, not wanting to risk the dark figure appearing in his bedroom. He slept fitfully, his dreams fractured and broken. He and dad were on the bridge pulling the sword from the water. But instead of old and rusted, it was gleaming and bright, the handle decorated with ornate metal work delicately fashioned into complex twists and turns, surrounding a large red jewel.

Harry held the shining sword, feeling powerful and strong, its energy coursing through his system. But no sooner had he picked it up, than the dark figure was there again on the far side of the millpond. Only now, it was walking towards him, across the water. It was actually walking on the water!

As the figure approached, Harry could see it was a man with long, matted hair and a huge black beard. He was wearing a dark cloak, held up at one side with a decorative pin. Harry could see the pin clearly, noticing its sweeping curved design, and the shining red jewel at its centre, matching the stone in the sword. The figure held out his hand, reaching up for the sword.

For a moment, he disappeared from view beneath the bridge and Harry could hear him climbing up. Harry stood, rooted to the spot, unable to move, the sword still in his hand. Then through the railings, the man's head appeared and Harry saw with horror that he had no eyes, just empty, blood-rimmed sockets. A hand shot through the gap in the railing, clutching Harry's leg and a smell of rotting flesh filled the air. Harry screamed and kicked at the hand, seeing lumps of skin fall away, revealing the bones beneath. He screamed again, and felt somebody holding his shoulders.

"Harry." He heard a soft voice.

He opened his eyes and there was mum, holding him tight, drawing him towards her. He inhaled the scent of her freshly washed hair, his heart thumping wildly against his ribcage.

"It's okay, Harry. You had a nightmare."

"We have to take the sword back, mum. It isn't ours. The man wants it back."

"It's only a dream, Harry. There's no man. Tomorrow you and dad can take the sword to the museum. I'm sure they'll be very excited with your find."

"I hope so," said Harry, feeling doubtful.

"Come on, have some Calpol, that will calm you down." Mum poured some of the pink liquid onto a spoon and popped it into Harry's mouth. The sweet taste was instantly calming. His mother sat with him for a while, gently stroking his forehead until sleep claimed him. This time he slept calmly, unaware of the dark shadow watching from the corner of the room.

The next day, while dad was upstairs, Harry opened the door leading from the kitchen into the garage, determined to confront his fear and take a look at the sword. The carrying bag sat on the floor in the middle of the garage where dad had left it, the sword alongside. Harry gasped and stared. He'd expected the wet mud to have dried out, but instead, the sword was soaking wet, lying in a pool of brackish water, glistening in the rays of sunshine coming through the garage windows, flecks of green duckweed still covering its surface.

Harry slammed the door shut.

"Dad!" he called out. "Dad, come quick!"

His father appeared in the hallway. "What's the matter, Harry?"

"The sword's wet. It's lying in a pool of water. The man wants it back, I know."

Dad held up his hand. "Calm down," he said. "Let me have a look, okay?"

Harry nodded and stood to one side, as dad opened the door to the garage and peered inside.

"What d'you mean it's still wet?" he laughed, stepping into the garage and picking up the sword. "It's dried out, look." He held up the sword, covered in dry mud, now a pale brown colour, with a few flecks of dark green, dried-out duckweed still attached.

"There was water there," said Harry. "I saw it."

"Well, it's not there now," said dad. "And the man was just in your dream. Mum told me you had a nightmare. You've always had a vivid imagination. This afternoon, we'll take the sword to the museum and see what they say? Okay?"

"Okay," said Harry.

Dad went back into the kitchen, but Harry stayed in the garage, staring at the sword. It didn't look much, lying there on the concrete floor, not half as impressive as when they pulled it out of the water.

On impulse, he reached down and picked it up. It felt cold and rough, but he didn't get the same feeling of dread that had filled him before. He scratched the surface of the handle with his nail, clearing away some of the dried mud, looking to see if the red jewel in his dream was there.

To his amazement, a small circular area in the centre of the handle felt smooth beneath his fingertip and as he cleared the mud, the jewel was revealed, just as he'd seen in the dream, although now it was dull and dirty. Harry dug in his nails, trying to dislodge a lump of dirt, and to his horror, the jewel came loose, falling into his hand. He wet his finger with his tongue and wiped its surface, holding it up to the light, marvelling at its clear-cut facets and deep red translucence.

Dad's voice sounded behind him, making him jump.

"Harry, mum's looking for you."

He quickly put the jewel in his pocket. He wasn't sure why, it was just an impulse.

"Coming," he called, placing the sword back on the garage floor.

That afternoon, Harry and dad walked up the steps to the museum and asked to see the Curator. They were told he wasn't available, but the Information Officer would see them. A man with a ponytail, casually dressed in shirtsleeves and jeans, appeared on the central staircase, walking down to where they waited in the colonnaded entrance hall.

"I hear you've found something you wish to show us," he said to dad.

Dad opened the bag and took out the sword, carefully wrapped in a towel. He gently loosened it so the man could take a look.

"We pulled this sword out of a disused millpond," he said. "We thought it might be old."

"I see," said the man, examining the sword. "It's hard to say while it's in this state. I wouldn't like to hazard a guess. We'll need to clean it up before we can date it. Why don't you leave it with me? I'm sorry I can't chat longer, but I have a group booked in to see our Egyptian exhibits. Fill in a form, letting us know when and where you found it, and we'll let you know when we've had a look."

He addressed Harry. "Don't get too excited, young man, we get lots of things brought in and very rarely are they of historical interest. I don't want to raise your hopes. There again, you never know."

He winked and grinned.

Harry was disappointed. He had thought the man would be able to tell them something straight away. In his pocket, he felt the smooth surface of the jewel between his thumb and fingers. Now was the time to hand it over and explain what had happened. But, embarrassed, he remained quiet.

Next thing he knew, dad was filling in a form, giving their details. The man took the form and the sword, and disappeared back up the stairs, promising to be in touch. Then he and dad were leaving the museum, and the jewel was still in his pocket.

They didn't hear from the museum until two days later, when dad took a telephone call.

"I see," he said. "Really! Is that so? Well, I never. How amazing. Yes, we'd certainly like to come and watch."

Harry hopped from one foot to another. On the one hand, he wanted the sword to be old and valuable. On the other, he didn't, because that would mean he'd damaged it when he removed the jewel, and they might be angry with him.

"Wow," said dad, hanging up. "They think the sword is very old, possibly pre-Viking. Which would make it thousands of years old. Tomorrow, they're going to send a team armed with metal detectors and magnets to the millpond, to see if they can find anything else. What do you say to that, Harry?"

Harry squirmed uneasily, thinking of the jewel, now upstairs in his bedroom, hidden in a secret place beneath the floorboard.

"Very exciting," he said, uneasily. "Are we going to go and watch?"

"You betcha," said dad. "Of course we'll be there."

Harry thought about the dark figure he'd seen watching from the other side of the millpond and then the bridge. The man didn't want them to have the sword, he felt sure. And now, the most precious part of the sword was hidden upstairs in his bedroom. The man would not be happy about that, he was sure.

That evening, Harry sat in his room, drawing on his sketchpad. He drew without thinking, letting images from his dream the night before find their way onto the page. At bedtime, mum came upstairs, with a cup of hot chocolate.

"What's that?" she asked, looking at his pictures.

"That's the man who the sword belongs to," said Harry, pointing at the dark figure he'd drawn on the edge of the millpond

His mother looked at the picture of the big, wild-haired man, holding a sword, wearing a black cloak fastened at one side.

"That's the cloak he wears and that's the pin that holds it up," explained Harry, showing her another picture in which he'd drawn a close-up of the decorative pin. It was golden and had a long clasp, curling under at one end, fashioned into a circular frond.

"It's beautiful," said mum. "Is that a ruby at the centre? Like the one you've drawn in the sword?"

"I'm not sure," said Harry, suddenly uncomfortable. He took the pictures back from her.

"They're very good, Harry," said mum. "If the sword is as old as they think, its owner may well have looked like that."

Harry looked at his mum. "No mum," he said. "That *is* what the man looks like. I dreamed about him last night. He's not happy. I don't think we should have taken the sword from the millpond. He wants it back."

More than ever he wished he hadn't taken the red jewel.

"How can he want the sword back?" laughed mum. "He must have died hundreds or even thousands of years ago."

It was a thought that didn't make Harry feel any better.

"Can I sleep with the light on again, please?" he asked mum. "Just in case the nightmare comes back?"

"Of course," she assured him. "I'll leave the nightlight on. Don't worry. The nightmare won't come back. Think about tomorrow and how exciting it will be. Goodnight, Harry."

That night, the man came again. Only this time, he wasn't at the bridge. He was in the house. Harry dreamed that he'd woken up, his sleep disturbed by a strange noise. Sitting upright, senses on high alert, he tuned in to a strange shuffling sound. Somebody big and cumbersome was coming up the stairs and that could mean only one thing. Before Harry had time to move, the sound had reached his bedroom door and, in the dim light, he saw the doorknob turn. Slowly, the door creaked open and the man was there, his huge frame filling the doorway. Harry shrank to the back of the bed, pressing himself against the wall, not wanting to look, but unable to take his eyes off the cloaked figure before him.

The man shambled into the room and Harry saw why movement was so difficult for him. He was badly wounded, his left leg dragging behind him, his face bloody and battered. A damp, dank smell filled the air. The man got nearer and Harry could see he was dripping wet, like he'd just come out of the millpond. Again, Harry saw the decorative pin, fastening his cloak to one side of his neck.

The figure raised a hand and pointed at Harry, speaking in a cracked, rough voice:

'He who first touches the sword incurs the curse. Return it or bear the consequences!'

He leaned towards Harry, breath fetid, eye sockets sightless and bloody. It was too much. Harry began to scream. The suddenly, the man was gone, he was waking up and mum was there.

"It's okay, Harry, it's another bad dream. I'm here."

Harry's breath came in short, shallow bursts and his heart hammered.

"The first person to touch the sword is cursed," he cried out. "That's me, mum. I touched it first. We have to put it back in the water."

"Hush, hush," she said gently. "That sword is making you have bad dreams. There is no curse. You're quite safe."

She settled him back into bed and sat for a while, stroking his head, until he slept once again. Standing up, she tiptoed across the room, frowning as her bare foot encountered a wet pool on the wooden floor.

"Silly boy," she murmured, "He must have knocked over his water glass."

Reaching for the tissue box on the shelf, she quickly mopped up the pool of brackish water and left the room.

By morning, she'd forgotten about it.

The next day, Harry and dad stood on the bridge by the millpond, watching as six men in wetsuits, carrying metal detectors, waded in. A further two men motored to the centre of the millpond, where it was deepest, in a small dinghy. They carried two large fishing magnets.

Also on the bridge, alongside Harry and dad, stood the Information Officer they'd already met and a self-important, bespectacled older man, in a dark brown suit, who Harry instantly disliked. He introduced himself as the Museum Curator.

"Fabulous find," he said, shaking Harry's hand. "I believe you were the young man who found it?"

"Yes," said Harry in a small voice, remembering the dark man's words from the night before.

"At first we thought it was a Viking sword," continued the man. "On closer examination, we think it pre-dates the Vikings. It could be from the 5th or 6th century BC. If so, it could mean re-writing the history books for this area, especially if we find anything else of interest. The sword is already creating quite a stir among archaeologists and historians. Once the conservation team has done its work, we'll have a better idea what the sword would have looked like. Although that will take time, possibly up to a year."

Harry nodded. He already knew what it looked like and who'd been carrying it. He'd drawn a picture of it.

The Curator continued: "I appreciate you not mentioning it to anyone else for the moment. It's important we keep things quiet for as long as possible. We certainly don't want hundreds of people turning up with magnets or metal detectors. It could compromise a very important historical site. We may have to close off this area to the public for some time."

For the next few hours, Harry and dad watched as the men searched. They brought up a number of metal objects, but nothing of note. Just old bits of farm machinery.

"Are you going to search below the weir and the millrace?" dad asked the Curator.

"Access is tricky," explained the Curator, "and it's doubtful we'd find anything. The constant motion of the water would have washed things away. Our best bet is the millpond. There's a lot of sediment at the bottom. That's where things may well be buried."

As he spoke, there was a shout from the centre of the millpond.

"Got something," shouted one of the men.

He started up the small outboard motor and the dinghy was soon traversing the millpond, nuzzling into the bulrushes to one side of the bridge. The man in the boat brought his find onto the bridge and presented it to the Curator.

Harry watched, half in dread, half curious. Ever since his dream about the curse, he'd been hoping they'd discover the sword was worthless, a rusty old toy that some child had dropped into the millpond in recent years. In that case, his dreams would be nothing more than nightmares and he'd be safe. But if they discovered more ancient relics, it would change everything. The curse would be real. Someone would have to pay the price for bringing up the sword, and that would be him.

"Looks like a decorative pin," the man from the boat was saying to the Curator, handing him the object inside a plastic specimen bag.

The Curator opened the bag and carefully took out the item, pouring water over it to remove some of the slimy dark mud.

"Indeed it is," he said. "Even in this state, before it's cleaned up, you can see the intricacy of the design. This would have belonged to someone important, a chieftain or king, a leader of the tribe. And look, it has a precious stone, in the middle. Could be a ruby. It's a little difficult to say until we can take a proper look."

"The interesting thing," added the Information Officer, looking closely at the pin, "is that the design is very similar to that of the sword. It would appear the sword, at one point, also had a jewel, considerably larger than the one in the pin, located in the centre of the handle. We think it came loose and is probably at the bottom of the millpond."

Harry looked at the decorative pin. It was exactly the same as the one he'd seen the wild-haired man wearing, as he knew it would be. Just like he'd drawn in his picture.

He felt his cheeks flush red. He put his hand in his pocket, feeling the jewel in his fingers. On a whim, he'd removed it from its hiding place under the floorboards and brought it with him. Now he thought of the warning the man had given him about the sword.

'Return it or bear the consequences.'

"We have to put the sword back," he said to the Curator. "The owner wants it returned. If he doesn't get it back, there'll be consequences. He told me."

The Curator glanced up at dad, an expression of annoyance crossing his features. "Does he have learning difficulties? He's getting rather over-excited. It's been a long day. Perhaps you should take him home."

"Yes," said dad, gripping Harry's hand in his. "Come on, Harry, your imagination is getting the better of you again."

"No," shouted Harry, in desperation. If they didn't put the sword back, he was the one who would bear the consequences.

"We'll invite you to come in to the Museum as soon as the pin and the sword are fully restored," said the Information Officer, kindly. "That's when we'll release the story. You're going to be famous, Harry, the little boy who pulled the sword from the lake. How about that? A modern day King Arthur! This find will give you a place in history."

"I don't want a place in history. I just want the sword to go back in the lake," sobbed Harry.

"Come on, Harry. Time to go home." Dad was pulling him from the bridge on to the footpath and Harry had no choice but to go with him.

As dad led him off the bridge, he heard another voice, silvery and faint, floating over the water towards him. It was a woman.

'Pass on the jewel, pass on the curse.
So speaks Nimue, Lady of the Lake.
Pass on the jewel, pass on the curse, Harry.
Save yourself…'

He turned round to see who might be speaking, but no one else seemed to have noticed. He looked back at the scene on the bridge and there he was, a dark, shadowy presence standing alongside the Curator, watching Harry. The Curator flinched, as if a cold draft had wafted across him, and Harry felt a cold stab of fear.

Now they'd given the sword to the museum, it would never go back into the water and there was nothing he could do about it. Who would ever believe his story about the curse? And now the museum was combing the millpond for further finds, it was stirring up things even more.

"Harry, come on," said dad, firmly.

"No!" he shouted, making a sudden decision. Why should he be cursed for something that benefited the museum? "I've got the jewel here. It fell out when I picked up the sword at home. It's here. You can have it."

Dad dropped his hand in surprise and Harry ran back to the bridge, pressing the jewel into the Curator's fat hand, who looked at the object in his hand with surprise. A huge smile broke across his features.

"The jewel from the sword. Well, I never." He looked sternly at Harry. "Did you steal it, boy? Damaging an ancient artefact is a very serious matter."

"The important thing is we have it back," said the Information Officer, looking wide-eyed at the ruby. "I think, under the circumstances, we may overlook the transgression?"

"That remains to be seen," grunted the Curator.

"Come on, Harry," said Dad, grasping his hand. "Time to go. Well done for handing in the jewel. I didn't even know you had it. You did the right thing. But it's definitely time we made ourselves scarce."

This time, Harry left without looking back.

When they got home, Harry went up to his room, pale and silent. He didn't know what form the curse would take or when it would happen. But one thing he knew, it would be bad. If the Lady of the Lake was to be believed, there was a chance it wouldn't happen to him. But maybe he'd made up those words in his head. Maybe the dark man would still come for him.

He sat on the bed looking at the drawings he'd done of the man, the gleaming sword and the ornate pin. The Curator had said the man must have been a chieftain or a king, so he must have been powerful. And that power had continued beyond his death, Harry was sure. So, what was his story? What had happened? Why was there a curse on the sword? Had it been used to kill the man?

He was so engrossed in his thoughts, he didn't hear dad come into the room.

"Harry, what are these drawings?" Dad's voice brought him back to reality.

"It's what I dreamed," said Harry. "I drew them yesterday. I told you the man wants his sword back."

Dad picked up the picture of the pin.

"But this is exactly like the pin they've just found. Or how I imagine it will look when it's cleaned up."

"I know," said Harry, impatiently. "The man used it to pin up his cloak."

"Who is this man you keep talking about?"

"The man who was watching us when we found it and who is in my dreams. He as in my room last night and he was there again today on the bridge. He wants his sword back and if he doesn't get it, he'll make the curse work."

"And what is the curse?" asked dad.

Harry repeated the words the man had spoken in his dream: *"He who first touches the sword incurs the curse. Return it or bear the consequences!"*

He looked up at his father.

"Dad, I was the first one to touch the sword. Does that mean he's coming for me?"

He purposefully didn't mention the Lady of the Lake's words about passing on the jewel, feeling suddenly guilty about passing on the curse. He didn't like the Curator, but he didn't deserve to have a curse on him.

His father sat down opposite him.

"Listen to me, Harry. I don't know what's going on here. I don't know how you managed to draw a picture of the pin before it was pulled out of the water. I don't know who this dark man is or about his connection to the sword. But one thing I do know, he's not real and he can't harm you. Maybe it's telepathy, maybe you've tuned in to something that happened in the past. But that's where it belongs. In the past. Do you believe me?"

Harry spoke in a tiny, timid voice. "I want to, dad. But I'm not sure. I'm scared."

That night, Harry's mother and father sat up discussing events. Harry was clearly troubled, but it was all in his head, surely?

"He seems to have tuned into something," said dad. "He said he drew the pin yesterday, before it was discovered. I saw the pin today. His drawing seems accurate."

"He has been having bad dreams," said mum. "He keeps talking about a dark man. He said the man was in his room last night. And on the way out, I stepped in a pool of water. I thought Harry had spilled it, but now..." She broke off, looking confused.

"He's always had an over-active imagination," said dad. "Maybe finding the sword has triggered something in his mind. He's certainly very scared."

"Perhaps we should take him to the doctor. Get him a referral to a psychotherapist."

"Or just let things run their course. I'm sure his imagination will settle down."

"You don't think the sword is really cursed?"

"Of course not. That's the stuff of horror movies. He's been feeling guilty about pocketing the jewel that was in the sword. He knew he'd done wrong and created a punishment for himself."

"Well, at least he handed it back."

"Exactly. I think the dreams will stop now."

"So, we do nothing?"

"No. We'll keep an eye on him. He'll be much better tomorrow, I'm sure."

Dad turned on television and they snuggled up on the sofa, watching a late night movie. The film finished late and it was way past midnight when they went up to bed. Mum softly opened Harry's door to check on him. Harry was asleep, looking peaceful and calm. No bad dreams seemed to be visiting him tonight. She smiled. It looked like his dad was right. He'd just been feeling guilty.

The next morning, dad was cleaning his teeth when he heard mum scream.

"He's gone. Harry's gone. He's not here."

Dad rushed to Harry's room, finding mum in a panic, opening the wardrobe doors, looking under the bed. He pulled back the curtains, flooding the room with light. Now they could see the big pool of water on the wooden floor. It wasn't clean water from a bottle or the tap. It was murky, brackish water, with small pieces of duckweed floating on the surface.

"The millpond!" shouted dad. "Come on, let's go."

In half an hour, they'd reached the millpond. Heavy clouds concealed the sun and a low mist hung over the water, giving it a mystical, eerie feel. They ran onto the bridge, their footsteps echoing. There was no sign of Harry.

"Oh my God. What if the curse was true?" cried mum. "What if he's in the water?"

Then dad pointed. "Over there, look! On the other side of the millpond."

They saw Harry, small and vulnerable, standing silently on the edge of the water, gazing through the mist.

"Harry!" screamed mum, running across the bridge and down to the water, hoping he wasn't about to do anything stupid. Dad followed.

Harry didn't seem to hear. He just carried on gazing across the millpond.

"Harry!" she screamed again.

This time, Harry looked at her, his eyes wet with tears.

"Are you okay, Harry?" she called.

"Yes, I'm fine," he answered in a small voice, his words swallowed up by the swirling mist. "But he's not."

They looked out over the water. Through the mist, they could just make out a figure in a dark brown suit lying face down in the water. It was the Curator of the Museum.

A soft, sweet voice sang quietly, its dulcet tones suspended in the misty air. They didn't hear it. But Harry did.

* * *

The site was now a crime scene as well as one of historical interest and, a few days later, it was decided to drain the pond to see what further secrets it held. No other artefacts were found, but they did find some ancient bones, buried deep in the mud. A paleoanthropologist examined them, discovering, after extensive testing, that they belonged to a large male and dated from approximately the same era as the sword and the pin. It would appear from a series of grooves on the bones that the unfortunate individual had died a violent death, his left leg almost severed in a frenzied attack. From what the experts could ascertain, the angle of the wounds correlated with the blade of the sword, leading to the supposition that the victim was killed by his own weapon, which was then thrown into his grave alongside him.

As for the Curator's death, that remained a mystery. Only one set of footprints led down to the water's edge where the Curator had entered the millpond. With a lack of motive for suicide, the Coroner declared a verdict of death by misadventure.

It was assumed the Curator had visited the site alone, early that morning, entering the water for some unexplained reason, where he had thence got into difficulties.

Harry knew otherwise, but wisely kept his counsel to himself. The dark man never visited him again and never again did he hear the voice of the Lady of the Lake. When the story of the sword hit the news, Harry was indeed famous. He became known as the boy who pulled the sword from the lake.

As Harry grew up, the find sparked an interest in ancient Britain that became a passion and later a vocation. After qualifying, he became the youngest ever Curator of the Museum, a position he held until he retired. The sword and the pin held pride of place in the main gallery, their red jewels glowing magnificently. Sometimes, when the Museum was closed and everyone had gone home, he would stand, looking into the main gallery, the sword and the pin never losing their fascination.

Sometimes, he could swear he saw the hazy figure of a man in a brown suit looking longingly into the display cabinet.

There again, the museum was full of shadows as darkness drew in.

An old hotel on the Yorkshire moors is no place for a mother and child to seek sanctuary...

Room 408

The weather was closing in as I drove onto the North York Moors.

The sky was inky black and a wind was picking up. The dramatic landscape I knew so well appeared alien and forbidding. The hills, usually purple-clad with heather, were covered in a creeping blackness, and an unnatural darkness had dropped over the landscape like a veil, so that land bled into the sky, with no discernible horizon.

"I don't like it, mummy," said my daughter, from the back seat. "How long before we get there?"

"It's a long way yet, Grace," I answered. "Are you still watching your DVD?"

"No, it's finished. I don't want to watch another. I just want to get there. I want daddy."

A sudden bolt of lightning forked down on to a nearby hillside, momentarily lighting up the landscape. Grace screamed.

"It's okay. Don't worry. We're all right as long as we stay in the car," I said, wondering if that was true. Was it better to stay in the car or get out when there was a storm? My rational mind had stopped working.

Now, large raindrops hit the windscreen, landing with ferocity, as if we were being pelted with stones by an angry mob. The rain grew heavier and within a couple of minutes, it was torrential. I turned the windscreen wipers to their maximum speed, but the torrent was so heavy, I couldn't see anything. The temperature had dropped, I noticed, and an icy chill hung in the air, as if the god of the hills had exhaled a massive, freezing breath.

I thought of the story the locals told about these parts. We'd passed the Hole of Horcum a few miles past, a massive crater in the landscape, some 400 feet across, no doubt made by geological movement. According to legend, a Saxon giant, known as Wade, had caused it, scooping up a massive handful of earth to throw at his wife during an argument.

An angry giant stamping over the hills was not an image I wanted in my head right now. I needed to concentrate on the here and now, and cope with the horrendous driving conditions.

It wasn't just my safety at stake. The life of my seven-year old daughter was in my hands. I didn't want to plunge off the road and risk life and limb, or at the very least spend a night stuck on the moors. There were no other cars about. No one else stupid enough to risk coming out in these conditions, I thought bitterly. And yet, it had been such a nice day when we set out from our home in the Midlands. No warning of the treachery that lay ahead. There again, I'd been playing music in the car. I hadn't been listening to the radio. Maybe there had been weather warnings.

But what to do? That was my immediate problem.

Another bolt of lightning forked down from the dark heavens, its white light stark against the black backdrop. Grace screamed again, but her voice was drowned out by the huge thunderclap. There was no gap between lightning and thunder, which meant the storm was overhead. That meant we were at risk. My head told me it would be safer to stop, that rubber tyres would earth the car, but fear made me press on. I wanted to see the twinkling lights of habitation and feel safe. It felt very alone up there on the moors.

"Mummy, can't we stop somewhere?" cried Grace. "I'm frightened."

"Okay, let's see what the sat nav says. If there's a pub or hotel near, we'll stop for the night, I promise. There's no point carrying on in this weather."

I pulled over to the side of the road and turned on the sat nav system, selecting 'local points of interest'. I could see where we were, a small dot on a lonely road crossing a vast expanse of moorland. Ahead, I saw a small circle and the word 'hotel'.

"It's okay, Grace," I told her. "There's a hotel coming up. We'll stay there. When we get there I'll call daddy and tell him we'll see him tomorrow."

"All right," she said in a small voice, and I could tell she was petrified, never before in her young life having experienced the raw, undiluted force of Mother Nature, or the realisation that her parent was powerless against it.

"Hang on in there. It's not far," I said, pulling onto the road and edging the car forward, driving slowly to make sure we maintained our course.

Huge hailstones, as big as the proverbial golf balls, began to hit the screen. The god of the moors was giving full vent to his anger. According to the on-screen map, we were nearing the location of the hotel and, at just the right time, a sudden bolt of lightning provided illumination. I saw a high brick wall running alongside the road to our right, giving way to a massive pillared entrance, with a stone stag standing proud on top of the lintel, his antlers huge and impressive. A sign announced: 'North Anger Abbey. Hotel and Conference Centre.'

"Someone liked Jane Austen," I thought. "Or maybe the name came first. Abbey implies something very old. Maybe that's where she got the idea."

I didn't like the fact they'd used 'Anger' as a separate word. It didn't look welcoming.

I turned the car, passing through the columns and onto a long, imposing avenue, flanked by large, evenly spaced trees. Within the estate walls, it was calmer and the weather less threatening. We were less exposed than on the moors, sheltered by the planted woodland on either side of the avenue of trees.

"It looks creepy," said Grace.

She was right. We'd been spared the ferocity of the weather, but hadn't found a friendlier alternative. The trees on either side of the road stood tall and fierce, like guards on duty, the woodland beyond wild and untamed, branches flailing like twisted limbs, gnarled tree trunks grimacing with contorted, agonised faces. Who knew what dangers lurked in the underbelly of the woods? I thought about the hotel in The Shining and wished I hadn't.

I took a deep breath and focused on driving, trying not to look to either side, imagining potential horrors. Too many late night movies, I chided myself. Get a grip. Be sensible.

I seemed to have been driving forever before the hotel came into view. It was a large, palatial establishment, possibly Victorian, although it was difficult to see in the darkness. I saw welcoming lights twinkling at the windows and breathed a sigh of relief. The setting might be creepy, but at least I'd found people and hopefully, a bed for the night.

I parked the car to one side of the main entrance, where a sign announced 'Reception'. I couldn't see any other cars. Maybe there was a larger car park to the rear.

"Stay in the car, Grace," I advised. "I'll pop in and see if they have any room."

"I want to come with you."

"No point getting out if there's no room. I'll be a couple of seconds. I promise."

I pushed open the car door and, battling against the wind and rain, made a run for the entrance, holding my coat over my head.

The front door was a massive oak affair, with ostentatious metal studs and rivets, but it moved easily when pushed. It opened into a dimly lit, plush-looking reception area, with a huge open fire roaring in a hearth to one side, surrounded by three formal sofas. Opposite, stood the reception desk, high-topped and mahogany, like something out of Dickens. The furnishings throughout were of a deep red colour, matching the crimson painted walls, on which hung a selection of large, gilt-framed pictures depicting hunting scenes, women in large crinoline dresses and dour, long-faced aristocrats. Large ornate vases were positioned in alcoves, and a marble statuette of a full-size, partially clothed nymph stood provocatively in front of a wooden panelled area.

"Not bad," I thought. "Old-fashioned and expensive, but who cares? As long as they have a room."

The reception area was deserted, any sounds of guests or people drowned out by the torrential lashing of the rain on the windowpanes. Sumptuous, floor-to-ceiling velvet curtains were partially drawn, affording me a glimpse of the wild, dark night and my car parked outside. I looked around for assistance, not wanting to leave my daughter longer than necessary. A small sign saying 'Please ring for assistance' had been placed in front of a push bell, and so I pushed it, hearing a distant ring somewhere to the rear of the reception area. Now I heard movement. Someone was coming.

A young woman came into view, buxom figure straining against a tight fitting, deep red dress. She had black hair, piled on her head, very white skin and red lips. She wasn't quite what I was expecting but she was smiling and that was a good start.

"Hello, can I 'elp you?" she asked in a Yorkshire accent, which somehow grated against the luxurious surroundings.

"I was wondering if you had a room for the night. My daughter and I were travelling over the moors, but the weather became too bad to continue. I don't have a booking, sorry."

I glanced around. It didn't seem busy. In fact, I got the distinct impression the hotel was rather empty.

"Aye, it's a bad night," said the girl. "You don't wanna be out on t'moors on a night like this."

She opened a large, hard-backed reservations book and ran her finger down a list of names and room numbers. Strange for this day and age, I thought. Where was the computer? Maybe it was in the back room. I didn't care, as long as they had a room.

"I'm afraid we're fully booked," said the girl, frowning. "We get a lot of walkers this time of the year."

"We'll take anything," I said. "Even a broom cupboard. I don't care. I don't want to spend another minute out there."

As I spoke, an enormous thunderbolt cracked through the sky, so strong it made the pictures and ornaments vibrate. The lights flickered off, and for the brief moment a flash of lightning lit up the interior, I saw it in ruins around me, the walls crumbling and blackened, the woman behind the reception desk a grotesque cadaver, decaying and rank, black matted hair hanging loose, mottled flesh dropping from her face.

I stepped back in revulsion, then the lights came on and all was back to normal, if such an establishment could ever be described as such. I exhaled sharply. The stressful journey was making my mind play tricks. I glanced out to the car, worried about my daughter. She would be terrified.

"Please. Anything. My daughter's in the car. I must go and get her."

"We do 'ave one room. Number 408." Her finger hovered over a number in the reservations book and I saw there was no name against it.

"We'll have that."

"We don't normally 'ave guests in there. The original occupant isn't too friendly."

"The original occupant?" I suppressed a smile. "I thought you were going to say it's too small or not properly furnished."

"Oh no. It's a good size and well furnished. It's got a beautiful bed, en suite facilities and lovely views over the grounds. In fact, it's one of our better rooms, it's just…"

She didn't have a chance to finish. The front door crashed open and my daughter, terrified and wide-eyed, rushed into reception.

"Mummy. You said a couple of seconds. You've been gone ages. The thunder came and I was all alone."

She stood white and shaking, with tears in her eyes. I cuddled her to me, chastising myself for leaving her in the car. What kind of mother was I?

"Sorry darling, it took longer than I thought. But guess what? They have a room. We can stay overnight."

I spoke to the receptionist. "We'll take it, thank you."

I had no idea what she meant about the 'original occupant' and, quite frankly, I didn't care. Anything was better than spending a night on the moors in a violent storm.

Room 408 was, as promised, very nice. It was large, dominated by an old-fashioned bed with a polished, mahogany frame and headboard, and a clean, white broderie anglaise counterpane. I pulled the dark red velvet drapes across the windows, closing out the night. A door to one side led to the en-suite bathroom, traditionally tiled in blue and white, with a large decorative basin, high level WC and stand-alone slipper-bath.

My daughter bounced up and down on the bed, lying back on the plumped out, down pillows.

"Nice comfortable bed," she declared approvingly. "I'll sleep well tonight."

Spying an old mahogany wardrobe on the other side of the room, she went to investigate. It was an ugly, fussy piece of furniture, with two large mirrored doors aside a centrepiece of small drawers and doors and a mirrored alcove. Decorative panels featuring entwined floral carvings added interest to the top, and two large drawers anchored it below. All doors and drawers were fitted with swinging brass handles, shiny against the dark wood.

"What's in here?" asked my daughter, opening one of the big, mirrored doors.

"Don't get too excited," I said. "It won't be Narnia."

"What's this?" she exclaimed, peering in.

I went over to see what had taken her interest. Hanging at the back of the wardrobe was an old-fashioned maid's uniform, comprising a long black dress and a starched white apron with ruffled edge and front bib. A pair of black lace-up shoes stood beneath.

"It's fancy dress," said my daughter, exploring further.

In one of the drawers, she found a couple of maid's starched white headpieces, edged with white lace.

"Do maids still wear these?" she asked, trying one on.

"Put it back," I instructed. "It's a bit old-fashioned, but maybe that's how they like their maids to dress in this hotel. I don't know."

I wondered vaguely if the clothing belonged to the 'previous occupant' and put the thought out of my mind.

"I'm hungry," announced my daughter, moving on to a more pressing subject.

"I'll see if they can bring something up to our room," I suggested, feeling too tired to encounter a formal dining room. A bowl of soup and bed was all I needed.

There was an old-fashioned dial phone on the bedside table and I dialled '0' for Reception. Grace was fascinated, never having seen one before. I waited while it rang out, but no one answered.

I took out my mobile phone and tried ringing my husband to let him know we wouldn't get to Newcastle that evening, but there was no service. Given the terrain and the atmospheric conditions, I wasn't surprised. I sent a text, advising him of our situation. Hopefully, it would transmit at some point. Then I set about going downstairs to find some food.

"I'll stay here," said my daughter, bouncing on the bed again.

I thought again of the 'previous occupant'.

"Are you sure? Why don't you come with me?"

"No. I prefer to stay here. I can unpack."

"No need. We'll be leaving first thing tomorrow. Come with me."

"No. I'll be fine."

With some misgivings, I left the room. I purposefully left the door unlocked, so she could escape if necessary, and took the key with me. It was a heavy, old-fashioned piece of metalwork, in keeping the rest of the hotel.

I walked along the red-carpeted corridor, passing numbered doors. It was very quiet, as if uninhabited. The receptionist had said the hotel was fully booked. If so, where were the guests? I looked at my watch. 10.30 pm. It wasn't late. Maybe I'd find more signs of life in the hotel bar or restaurant.

I walked down two flights of stairs, seeing no one, then descended the large, main stairway into reception. The fire was still burning fiercely in the hearth and I felt its warmth as I approached. As before, there was no one in reception.

I followed a sign to the 'Lounge Bar' and 'Restaurant', finding, to my disappointment, that the door to the restaurant was locked. The door to the bar was open and I went in, but again was disappointed. It was empty and cold.

Like the rest of the hotel, the bar area was luxuriously appointed, with comfy red Chesterfield sofas, low, lacquered coffee tables and sparkling, crystal chandeliers. A grand piano, shiny and black, stood at the far end of the room. Ashtrays had been placed on each of the tables, which I thought odd, given the smoking ban. I walked across the room to the windows, where thick red drapes were undrawn, and shivered as I looked into the black night. The storm had subsided but the darkness pressed solidly against the windows, and I had an overwhelming feeling of desolation. I turned back into the room. Beyond the piano, a generous circular bar offered a selection of optics, but it was closed, drink mats placed over the pumps. Feeling uneasy, as if something was out of kilter, I left, glad to leave it behind me.

As I walked towards Reception, I had the distinct impression I heard the low hum of people talking, a woman laughing, the chink of glasses and piano music playing. I retraced my steps and looked nervously into the bar, but as before, it was as silent as the grave. I shook my head. It had been an unpleasant evening and I was easily spooked. I thought of my daughter upstairs on the second floor. She seemed a long way from me. I needed to get back.

The receptionist was waiting as I went back into the main entrance hall.

"Everything all right?" she asked, her rough accent coarse and inappropriate.

Her skin seemed paler than ever against her red lipstick and black hair.

"Yes, fine," I answered. "It's very quiet. I thought the hotel was fully booked."

"It's late. They'll be asleep."

She glanced over to a large Grandfather clock at the far side of the entrance hall. I hadn't noticed it before. As I looked, it started to chime, both hands pointing upwards to twelve.

"It can't be midnight already, " I said, frowning. "My watch said 10.30 just a few minutes ago."

I looked at my watch. Both hands in its small face pointed to twelve.

"But that's impossible. I haven't been looking round for an hour and a half."

The girl looked at me blankly. "Were there anythin' else?"

"Er, yes. I wondered if we could get anything to eat."

"No," she replied. "Kitchen's closed up. Staff went a long time ago."

"Right, of course. No problem."

I was filled with a sudden, inexplicable dread. Something wasn't right here. I'd seen no evidence of guests anywhere, time seemed to be playing tricks on me and I'd left my daughter alone in a room where the previous occupant had been described as unfriendly. What had I been thinking of? For the second time that evening, I'd left her on her own.

"Sorry," I mumbled. "I must get back to my daughter."

Time seemed suddenly to weigh heavy, as if trying to hold me back. I tried to run up the main staircase, but my legs moved slowly. I made it to the landing and started on the next flight of stairs, everything around me unnaturally still.

Grace. I had to get back to Grace. Then I was running along the corridor, its carpeted length stretching endlessly before me. The harder I ran, the longer it stretched, our room at the end never getting closer. I closed my eyes and concentrated on moving forward. Then, at last, I was outside Room 408, turning the door handle, pushing on the door.

It wouldn't budge.

This wasn't right. I'd left it open. I know I had. I hammered on the door, pushing with all my might. The door was locked.

"Grace! Grace! It's Mummy. Open up."

There was no answer. Feverishly, I looked for the key, tipping out the contents of my handbag and, with trembling hands, placing it in the lock. Aware of my pulse pounding in my ears, I turned the key and opened the door.

Grace was sitting in bed, reading a book and eating biscuits.

"Hi, mummy. Where've you've been? You've been ages. I found these biscuits in your bag. Hope it's okay."

"Yes. It's fine. Are you all right?"

"Yes. Why wouldn't I be?"

"Well, I left you alone in a strange hotel room…"

"I wasn't alone."

My heart leapt. "You weren't? Who was here?"

"Annalise. She's really nice."

"Who's Annalise?"

"This is her room. She's really kind. She's letting us stay here for the night. She works here."

"Don't tell me. She's a maid and that's her uniform hanging up?"

Grace beamed at me. "How did you know?"

"An educated guess." I hesitated. "Was she a real person?"

"Yes. What else would she be? She's really pretty. And friendly. She kept me company while you were gone."

"And where is she now?"

"She had to leave."

My appetite had gone and I felt exhausted. I couldn't wait to get out of this strange place. I locked the door.

"Let's get ready for bed," I suggested. "We'll make an early start tomorrow."

"Okay." Grace jumped off the bed and began changing into her pyjamas, singing under her breath as she did so.

> *"My life is like the summer rose*
> *That opens to the morning sky,*
> *But ere the shades of evening close,*
> *Is scattered on the ground - to die!"*

"What's that you're singing?"

"It's Annalise's song."

A chill went through me. Whoever or whatever Annalise was, I didn't like her. But Grace seemed okay, so I let it go. "It's very nice. Do you want to use the bathroom first?"

"Okay."

I must have drifted off to sleep immediately, my body worn out with nervous tension, but now I was wide awake. It was dark in the room, impossible to see, but something had woken me. I could hear Grace's breathing, soft and regular, by my side. She was fast asleep.

But then I felt it, or rather heard it. Someone's face was close to mine. I could hear their breathing right above me and, as I inhaled, my own breathing fast with panic and fear, I smelt her breath. It wasn't unpleasant. It was sweet and warm, but too close. Her face was right above me. I pushed my head back on the pillow, squeezing my eyes shut, telling myself it wasn't real.

Putting my hand out to one side, I reached for the small lamp on the bedside cabinet. Instead, my fingers touched something solid. I moved them slightly, feeling fabric beneath my touch. It was a person. A woman. I was touching the outline of her thigh and she was wearing a long dress. I stifled a scream, not wanting to wake Grace, blind terror running through me. Was this Annalise? Was she a real person or a ghost? I pulled my hand back and lay frozen, feeling her breath on my face.

And now there was another sound in the room. The brass handles hanging on the wardrobe were moving, each one shaking, vibrating against the wood. I closed my eyes as tight as I could, not daring to open them for fear of what I might see. Then suddenly, she was gone. The pressure in the air above my face was lifted and the sweet smell of her breath vanished.

I opened my eyes, looking into the darkness. As I grew accustomed to the lack of light, I was aware of movement. A dark figure was walking across the room, past the foot of the bed, towards the door. It was impossible to see clearly, but I could make out the dim outline of a long black dress and white bib apron.

Next morning, there was no sign of the storm that had decimated the moors the previous night. I pulled back the curtains and surveyed the view. A low mist hung over the grounds, wraith-like and eerie, shrouding shrubs and trees with a thick mantle. I shivered and turned back to the room. Grace was waking up.

"Good morning. Did you sleep well?"

"Oh yes. Didn't wake once. I had a great sleep."

"Good. So did I. Let's get back on the road. We'll find breakfast where we can."

I couldn't wait to leave this strange hotel, with its lack of guests, time lapses and uninvited visitor to our room. On impulse, I opened the wardrobe doors. The dress and apron were gone.

We left quickly. I didn't see the pale-skinned receptionist. I didn't see anyone. I left fifty pounds on the counter. I thought that was a fair price for our overnight stay. The fire was still blazing in the hearth, logs burning merrily.

As we drove away, I looked in my rear view mirror. North Anger Abbey was disappearing from view, swallowed by the thickening mist. I drove as fast as the mist would allow, down the tree-lined avenue, reaching the main road in a few minutes and turning right to continue our journey where we'd left it the night before. Outside the walled estate, the mist was clearing and it was turning into a beautiful day. The sky was already a dull blue and the moors dusted with heather, purple-hued and beautiful. A brand new day was emerging from the ravages of the storm and I resolved to put the previous night behind us.

I glanced back at Grace. She seemed happy, wearing her headphones and watching a DVD. The strange night hadn't seemed to affect her at all. My experiences must have been down to extreme tiredness and an over-active imagination. Now, my main priority was to find breakfast and get to Newcastle as quickly as possible, where my husband awaited us.

On cue, my mobile sounded. I answered it hands free.

"Hello?"

"Hi, darling. It's me. Just picked up your text. I was worried sick what had happened to you last night, but I guessed you couldn't get a signal."

"There was a terrible storm, I couldn't drive. We stayed in a hotel on the moors."

"I'm glad you're safe. Where did you stay?"

"A big old place called North Anger Abbey, a bit weird. I wouldn't recommend it. But at least we had shelter from the storm."

"North Anger Abbey? Strange. I thought that place burned down years ago."

"Maybe they've renovated it. It certainly looked very luxurious. I'll tell you about it when I see you. For now, we just want to get some breakfast."

"Okay Drive carefully. I'll see you soon. Tell Gracie I love her."

A couple of miles farther on, we drove into a village and found a bakery. There was a small tearoom attached, serving served bacon baps. We ordered two each and ate ravenously, without speaking. Two cups of coffee later and I felt fortified enough to continue the journey. I paid and was about to follow Grace outside, when a thought occurred to me. Opening the car door with the remote, and telling Grace to get in and wait for me, I turned to the owner, a large, red-faced Yorkshire woman.

"Do you know North Anger Abbey?"

She frowned. "Oh, aye. I know that place all right. You don't want to go up there."

"Why not?"

"Well, for a start it's a ruin. Burned down years ago. But even afore the fire, it were a strange place."

I looked at her closely to see if she was pulling my leg, but she seemed serious.

"Burned down?"

"Yes. They used to keep a fire going in the entrance hall. They say a log rolled out in the night and set the furnishings alight. Nex' thing you know, the 'ole place went up."

A cold shadow passed over me and I shivered. "Why was it a strange place?"

"Funny things went on there. Some say it was the locals burned it down. To cleanse the place."

"What kind of funny things?"

"People disappeared. Some said it was inhabited by the undead. They say a maid 'ung herself in one of the upstairs rooms. Folks staying there saw 'er 'anging over the bed at night."

"Wearing an old-fashioned maid's uniform with a white starched apron?"

"Aye. I see you've been reading up on local folklore. Personally, I don't believe a word of it." Her face darkened. "But steer clear nonetheless. It's not a good place. Certainly, no place to tek a child."

Too late, I thought, a feeling of dread closing around me.

She wiped the counter with a cloth. "Right, best get on. 'Ave a good onward journey."

"Thank you."

I climbed into the car, feeling shell-shocked and numb. What had happened last night? My memory flashed back to the ruined entrance hall and the cadaver-like woman I'd seen for that brief moment during the lightning. Was that the reality? Had we stayed in a burned-out ruin that somehow our imagination had transformed into a luxury hotel? I couldn't make sense of it.

I drove fast, getting as far away as I could from North Anger Abbey, Annalise and the cadaverous receptionist. Then, without warning, a clear, sweet singing voice came from the back seat.

> *"My life is like the summer rose*
> *That opens to the morning sky,*
> *But ere the shades of evening close,*
> *Is scattered on the ground - to die!"*

I looked in the rear view mirror and froze. Instead of my fair-haired daughter, I saw a dark-haired girl in a black dress, with a white, bibbed apron and a starched white headpiece. Her head leaned awkwardly to one side, ligature marks around her neck.

I stifled a scream, my eyes locked into the grotesque vision in my mirror. Slowly, she straightened her head, looked right at me and smiled.

A car's horn sounded, breaking the moment. Another car approached at speed and, with a split-second to spare, I wrenched my car on to my side of the road, avoiding collision.

When I looked in the rear mirror again, it was my daughter who looked back at me, eyes wide and face white, scared at the near miss.

"Mummy, are you okay?"

"Yes. Sorry, I lost concentration. Watch your DVD. Everything's fine."

Only, it wasn't. As she turned back to her DVD, I saw something that made my blood run cold. On her neck were two small puncture marks.

Night Horrors

As you turn out the lights
We come out to play
We're creatures of darkness
Never seen in the day.

We hide in the shadows
We creep out at night
We've only one aim
To give you a fright.

We run over the bedclothes
We skim over your face
Deadly and dark
Light as fine lace.

We hang from the ceiling
Suspended above
Then when you sleep
We make our move.

As you draw in your breathe
And your lips open wide
We drop on a thread
And climb right inside.

You wake with a shudder
And let out a scream
Gasping and spitting
You think it's a dream.

There's stuff on your face
That makes your skin crawl
Clinging and cloying
A venomous caul.

As you blink in the darkness
Shaking and hot
Trying to work out
What's real and what's not…..

…we creep into the shadows
And hide in the cracks
But this time tomorrow
You know we'll be back!

On a hot summer's day, two girls disappear.
But who is really to blame?

The Green Man

Last week, a girl from the village went missing. She went into the woods and never came back, which can mean only thing. It's happening again. They've been searching ever since, but I know they won't find her. Because I know what happened to her, only they'll never believe me.

When I saw on the news that the villagers were going out to search for her, I got out my old black and white photo album and looked at the pictures, remembering a summer many years ago. It was a summer that marked the transition from innocence to knowledge, when we finally saw the world for what it is - a dark, dangerous place with evil lurking where you least expect it, waiting to ambush the unaware.

It was August 1952, a really hot month. The sun shone every day and there was a drought. The grass was scrubby and brown, and the earth dusty and dry. The plants on my mother's porch withered and died with no chance of survival. There was no breeze, just relentless heat, sucking every last drop of moisture from the air and making it difficult to breathe.

We escaped to the woods. There, at least, it was cooler, the mantle of the overhead trees creating a soft, green world beneath which the sun couldn't penetrate. I remember looking at the dappled light as occasional sunbeams found their way through, thinking how pretty it was. It was private and remote, our own secret place where we could be safe, away from the villagers, away from my father with his belt and his shouting.

There were five of us in the gang. My older brother was the leader. Tom was twelve, giving him two years' seniority over me, which he never ceased to remind me. It wasn't an easy relationship and I was always in his shadow, but although we fought and our arguments frequently ended in blows, the blood tie was strong and I would have defended him to the death if I had to.

I can see him now, riding his blue Raleigh bike along the woodland path, me behind on his old bike, another hand me down. We'd pick up speed as the path dropped steeply into the dip, giving us the necessary acceleration to climb the opposite side. It was an amazing feeling, the speed creating a breeze that whipped through your hair, the trees flashing past in a blur of green. I was followed by the other members of the gang, Wilf and Wally, the identical twins, and Scarface Al, so named because of the jagged red scar that ran down one side of his face, courtesy of a gunpowder-making experiment that went wrong. He was the hard man of the group, but by dint of age, my brother was leader.

This particular day, we were sailing down the path into the dip, in our usual formation, my brother at the head, Scarface bringing up the rear. This time, instead of climbing back up the other side, my brother braked sharply at the bottom, and I narrowly missed going into him.

"Whoa! What ya doin', idiot? Don't brake when I'm sharp behind."

The others applied their brakes, calipers squealing as they skidded to a halt on the dry dirt path behind me.

"What's up?"

"Why've we stopped?"

My brother pointed through the trees to an area on the left of the dip.

"Never noticed that before. Why don't we take a look?"

We left our bikes on the side of the pathway, wheels still spinning, and followed as he parted branches and climbed through the undergrowth.

It was a low, domed, brick structure that had attracted his attention, almost entirely concealed by ivy and creeping foliage, the tallest point maybe four or five feet high. At the front was a small dark opening, barely visible.

Surrounding the structure was a shallow ditch, giving the appearance of an overgrown moat, although as we got closer, we saw it had been filled with bricks, rubble and general rubbish. Someone had placed a wooden board over the moat in front of the entrance, making it easier to gain entry.

"What is it?" asked Wilf.

"I think it's an icehouse," answered my brother. "These woods are in the grounds of the old manor house. All big houses used to have icehouses. It was the coolest place to keep the ice."

Given the heat of the summer, the thought of being cool had a magnetic appeal, along with the curiosity of exploring an old, forgotten building. I must admit to feeling a little apprehensive, as it looked an eerie place, so still and forgotten in the woods, the dark entrance forbidding and mysterious. But I wasn't going to let the other see I was scared. I'd never hear the last of it.

I followed them over the rubbish filled moat, not wishing to put my foot on the wooden board in case it gave way beneath me, and jumping over. My brother had a box of matches and he struck one as we peered inside. There wasn't much to see, just a dark, dank, circular room, full of dead leaves. But, of course, we didn't see that. We saw something magical, a hidden den, a place to meet and call our own.

We went there every day, gradually transforming the old icehouse into our own private world. My brother and I went up into the attic at home, finding various items my mother no longer wanted. A couple of old tab rugs provided our floor cover, some ancient pictures of old buildings made the walls more interesting and a pop crate with a board on top was a table. We placed three old candlesticks on its surface, lighting three white candles we bought from the village stores, delighting in the way the flickering light made the den homely and cosy.

It was a good summer. We spent our time playing cards and jacks, whittling wood, making campfires and generally hanging out. Never once, in all the time we visited, did I place my feet on the big wooden board that covered the rubbish-filled moat. I jumped every time, and over the weeks, it became a superstitious ritual, like not standing on the cracks between the flagstones.

Naturally, word got around, and there were a couple of unwelcome visitors, boys from our class we didn't like and, with typical male aggression, they tried to oust us. We were good fighters and gave any intruders short shrift, sending them away with bloodied noses and hurt pride. It was our den. It belonged to us, the five founder members. Until the girls appeared and things changed forever.

One afternoon, late August, we were sitting in the icehouse drinking cider. None of us liked the taste, but it was a grown up thing to do and, more to the point, it was an act of rebellion. We heard girls' voices outside and froze.

"Stay here," my brother instructed and peered out.

Next thing we knew he was outside and chatting away, fuelled by the cider, no doubt. Not wanting to miss out, I joined him and found Eliza Long and Sally Sicksmith standing on the other side of the moat. They lived in the big houses at the far end of the village and went to a private boarding school. They were way out of our league, with their blond curls, white socks, and blue and white frilled frocks. But that, of course, made them all the more alluring. I hung back, letting my brother take charge.

"Is that your den?" Sally was asking.

Looks like fun," said Eliza, smiling prettily.

"Girls aren't welcome here," said Scarface, emerging from the icehouse entrance. "Go away."

"Ugh, what happened to your face? How did you get that scar?"

"Fighting an armed robber," answered Scarface, unable to resist the temptation to impress. "He came off worst. If you think this is bad, you should have seen him."

"Gosh, you're brave."

"You must be really tough."

The girls were suitably impressed and I watched with alarm as Scarface was won round by their compliments. Now the twins came out of the icehouse, looking disdainfully at the girls.

"Why don't you go away?" said Wilf.

"Yeah, go and play with your dolls or something," added Wally, trying to play the big man. It didn't work. The girls laughed and ignored them, focusing their attention on Scarface and my brother. I was tongue-tied and invisible.

"Can we see inside?" asked Eliza. "Looks like you've made it really comfy in there."

"Girls aren't welcome," said Wilf, standing his ground in front of the icehouse entrance.

"You could make an exception for us, couldn't you?" asked Sally, looking up through her eyelashes at my brother.

"I suppose so," he answered, pleased at being singled out as the decision-maker. "But just this once. You can't come back again."

"Wilf, we've gotta go," pointed out Wally, looking at his watch. "Mum said to be back at one and it's nearly half past."

"Yeah, all right." Wilf spoke sternly to my brother. "You can let them in while we're gone, but they can't come back. This is private property."

The twins left unwillingly, mounting their bikes and riding away along the woodland path.

"You don't say much, do you?" Eliza said to me.

I muttered something incoherent and looked down at the ground, feeling my cheeks flush red. But no one seemed to notice. The girls were too busy flirting with my brother and Scarface.

"Is it safe to step on that piece of wood?" asked Eliza, indicating the board across the moat.

"Yeah, it's totally safe," answered Scarface. "We cross it every day." He put one foot on it, to prove the point.

Sally, I noticed, had a white handkerchief wrapped around her hand and I could see bloodspots seeping through.

"What happened to your hand?" I asked.

"Oh, it's nothing," she laughed dismissively. "I cut it on some brambles."

To prove her point, she undid the handkerchief and tossed it away. I watched as it fluttered down and caught on a bramble. "Come on, Eliza, let's take a look inside."

"I wouldn't step on that, if I was you," I said, thinking how I always jumped over the wooden board. "We're not sure what's underneath…"

But she didn't hear. She grasped Eliza's hand and pulled her on to the board. Next thing we knew, it gave way with a cracking, splintering sound. Screaming loudly, both girls fell through the broken pieces, disappearing completely from view into the moat beneath.

For a split second, we looked at one another in horror, peering into the hole where the girls had disappeared, aware of the sudden silence.

"Where are they?"

"They can't just disappear."

"Is it some kind of old mine shaft?"

My brother took charge. "Quick, we need to pull out this wood and rubbish, see what's underneath. We can get them out."

He began tearing pieces of rubble and brickwork out of the moat. Scarface and I did the same, pulling away bits of masonry, breezeblock and rusty old metal objects.

Soon, there was a random collection of rubbish on the woodland floor behind us. We called out as we worked. "Sarah, can you hear us? Eliza, where are you?" But there was silence. The girls had completely disappeared.

We'd gone down maybe three feet, our T-shirts wet with sweat as we laboured to find the opening to an old mine shaft, anything that would explain where the girls had gone. Beneath the rubble we found a wide flat stone, around three foot square. We curled our fingers around its edges and, struggling, pulled upwards. It was very heavy and, at first, didn't budge. I had the distinct impression of something pulling against us in the opposite direction.

"Okay, one massive effort," directed my brother. "When I say 'heave', pull with all your strength."

As he shouted 'heave', we flexed our muscles, inhaled and pulled for all we were worth. With a horrible squishing, popping sound, the stone came away. None of us were expecting to see what lay beneath.

A huge green face looked up at us, filling the entire hole. It was a shimmering, hazy sort of green and the features wobbled slightly, as though cast in jelly. It reminded me of a picture in one of my childhood books, where the illustrator had drawn the sun with a big, beaming baby face in the centre.

As the stone came back, the eyes opened wide, taking us in, then the mouth pulled back in a wide grin. We stared, horrified, too shocked to move or make a sound.

"Well, hello," said the big green face, beaming up at us. "And what have we here? Oh, horrible! It's boys! Slugs and snails and puppy dogs' tails. Yuckety yuk. Girls are so much sweeter. Sugar and spice and all things nice."

"Where are they?" screamed my brother, screwing his face up in rage. "What have you done with them?"

The face raised an eyebrow.

"No need to get cross." Its plump cheeks puffed outwards as it grinned at us, looking jovial and self-satisfied. "We all have to eat. And it's been such a long time since my last meal. Fifty years or more. And then only one measly housemaid. I can't tell you how hungry I was."

"Where are the girls?" I shouted. "Have you eaten them?"

It let out a belch. "Oops, pardon me. No manners."

"How did you do it?" gasped Scarface, staring down at the face in bewilderment.

"How did I do it?" repeated the face. "Oh, I see, you want a demonstration. It's more a case of absorption than actual eating. Like so…"

The face opened its mouth wide and frowning in concentration, began to inhale. I can only described the sensation as like being in a strong wind, only instead of being blown off our feet, this was a sucking sensation that pulled us towards the open mouth.

"Hold fast," cried my brother, grabbing on to the large stone and anchoring himself. "Get out of the moat."

He levered himself over the lip of the moat and away from the terrible sucking breath. Scarface, too, broke loose and was able to pull himself up and away, collapsing next to my brother on the ground. But I wasn't so strong and I could feel myself being drawn towards the huge open mouth gaping beneath me. I've never felt fear like it. My body was rigid and I was cold as ice, preparing for imminent death. Would it be painful? Would I feel anything? I ground my teeth together, closed my eyes tight and awaited my fate. Then I felt two sets of hands grip my shoulders and pull me up, away from the menacing open jaws. Next thing I knew, I was out of the hole and lying on the grass beside the moat. My brother and Scarface had saved me.

"Run," shouted my brother.

I needed no further prompting. Hot on the heels of my brother and Scarface, I leapt clear. Finding our bikes in the undergrowth, we dragged them to the pathway and pedalled for all we were worth, desperate to get away from the woodland glade with its monstrous secret. Just as I got on my bike, something white and lacy fluttered past me. It was Eliza's handkerchief, spattered with spots of bright red blood. I grasped it and put it in my pocket. It was proof that the two girls had actually been there. It proved to be our undoing.

When we got back, we raised the alarm. We told them about the big green face in the moat, with its hunger and huge open mouth. Of course, it sounded ridiculous, a silly story from the overactive minds of three, soon to be teenage, boys. We went with them to the icehouse and showed them the location of the green face, where we'd last seen the girls. But the face was gone. In its place there was just a hole filled with bricks and rubble and rubbish. Then all they could focus on was the whereabouts of the girls. Where were they? What had we done with them? Where had we concealed the bodies?

We denied all their accusations but it didn't look good. And then there was the damning evidence of the handkerchief, bearing fresh blood that proved to be Eliza's, along with my fingerprints.

Of course, they never found the girls. As we knew they wouldn't.

Now, here I sit, watching television, looking at the very same woodland, hardly changed over the years, where a team of policemen, dressed in white, walk in formation and sift the ground, looking for another missing girl.

They won't find her. It's fifty years on. I know exactly what's happened to her.

I wonder if my brother and Scarface are watching the news. I haven't seen them in years. They kept us apart.

A key sounds in the lock and a nurse, dressed in a blue uniform, steps into the room. She carries a bowl and a syringe. It's government property. I can see the stamp on the side of the bowl. Broadmoor Hospital.

"Time for your medication," she says sweetly.

Two Brummie bachelors encounter an exotic Brazilian seductress with a terrible agenda...

Lileth

I see George across the bar. There's no mistaking his shock of red hair. He's a genuine ginger nut. Tall and gangly, with long, flailing limbs, like a four-legged spider. If anyone's going to knock over his pint, it's George.

He's never had much luck with women. He's a great laugh, always good fun, but lacking in the looks department. A combination of jug ears, florid complexion and large nose doesn't sit well together. He looks like a Picasso painting, with all the bits stuck on in the wrong place.

He sees me and calls me over.

"Have a seat. My round. What ya having?"

You can't fault George's generosity. He's always first to buy a round. Mind you, he's well off. Looked after his mum and dad until they died a couple of years back, then inherited the house. A nice, Victorian, red brick in a better part of town. Turned out his dad had been a dab hand on the stock market. Left stocks and shares worth over half a million, which meant George was set for life. Not that he gave up his job. He's a history teacher at the local comprehensive. It's something of a vocation with him. There are never any discipline problems in George's classes, despite it being a rough school. He brings the subject alive and the kids love him.

He looks different today. There's an excitement about him, something bubbling beneath the surface, a sparkle in his eyes. If I didn't know better, I'd say he's met somebody, but that's never going to happen for someone like George. He's like me. A confirmed bachelor.

"How's it going?" I ask.

Then, blow me, he tells me he's met someone.

"A girl?" I ask, incredulous.

"No, a bloody squirrel. Of course it's a girl."

"What's she like?" I ask, envy and interest rising in equal measure. I push away the thought she's plain and desperate. Or it's been a one-night stand.

"She's gorgeous," he answers. "Really pretty, long dark hair, big brown eyes. Here, have a look."

He scrolls down his phone and shows me a picture of himself with his arm around the most perfect girl I've ever seen. She's stunning. Exotic is the word that comes to mind. Slender and dark-skinned, smoky eyes full of promise, long black hair cascading over her shoulders.

"Wow," I say, for want of anything better. "How long's it been going on?"

"Three weeks," he says, with a glint of self-satisfaction and more than a touch of one-upmanship. It's a game I can't play. I can't even remember the last date I had.

"I met her in the bookshop, looking at new fiction titles. She picked up the latest bestseller. I asked her if it was any good and she said she wouldn't know, more of an Ian McEwan fan herself. I couldn't believe it. He's my favourite writer. That was it. We went for a coffee. The rest is history."

"Wow," I say again, genuinely stunned. This is the last thing I expected. "Do I get to meet her?"

"All in good time." George is suddenly defensive.

I suppose it's early days. Plus, he's clearly punching above his weight, obviously worried she might be tempted in another direction. I wonder what she'll think of me. She's way out of George's league.

"Go on," I say. "Give me the low down. What's her name? Where does she come from? Is it serious?"

"Her name's Lileth. She's Brazilian. Amazingly, she did a history degree, like me. Specialised in Aztec civilization. She's 28, works as an au pair for a local family. That's where she is at the moment." As an after-thought, he adds, "And yes, it is serious. I've asked her to marry me."

"Woah!" If I was surprised before, now I'm astounded. "Rewind that last bit."

He grins. "You heard right. I've asked her to marry me. Sometimes you just know when it's the right one."

Sometimes, I think, girls just know when the right mug comes along. Especially when it's one that's rich, available and easy to manipulate. This girl has gold-digger written all over her. I bet she's planning the divorce already. Then making a swift exit back to Brazil with a cool half-million under her belt.

Actually, that would have been okay. The truth is far worse than I could ever imagine. But I'm jumping ahead.

I get to meet her a couple of days later. It's a Saturday morning and I'm in the local coffee shop, sipping a flat white and reading The Guardian. I try to focus on the print, but George's words have knocked me off kilter. "I've asked her to marry me. Sometimes you just know it's the right one." I'm delighted, surprised, envious. I keep seeing her picture in my mind and fantasize what it must feel like to touch that smooth skin and look into those dark eyes, smouldering with desire.

I stare absently, lost in my daydream and, suddenly, there she is. My eyes snap into focus. The girl from the picture is sitting two tables away and George is with her. I hold up my paper, not wanting them to see me, wondering how I didn't notice them before. Perhaps they came in after me.

Peering round my paper, I watch. One of his hands is over hers on the table. He gazes adoringly into her eyes, murmuring something under his breath. It must be funny because she throws back her head and laughs. It's a loud, throaty laugh that attracts attention. I stare at her wide, open lips and perfect white teeth, wondering what he said. He's assuming the role of the self-assured lover effortlessly. Small eels of jealousy twist and turn in my gut.

I'm thinking, 'This is George. Gormless, gawky George. What's he got that I haven't?'

He moves his hand to lift his coffee cup, revealing her hand beneath. It's beautifully manicured with long, blood red nails and a huge diamond ring on her fourth finger. I gulp my coffee. So, it's official. They're engaged. I inadvertently lower my paper just as George looks across. He smiles and beckons me over. I've no choice. I join them.

George pulls back a chair and I sit down. He introduces me to Lileth.

"Charmed," I say and kiss her hand.

Now I feel like a fool. Why did I do that? Trying to show George I'm as big a charmer as he is? Am I so insecure? But she doesn't seem to notice, coyly puts her head to one side, watching me with her dark eyes, searching, appraising. I'm simultaneously attracted and afraid. Like a rabbit caught in headlights.

"I can't believe we didn't see each other," I say.

"We've eyes only for ourselves, don't we, darling?" she says playfully, turning to George and running her fingers over his hand.

I watch, feeling superfluous and glance at George. He's gazing at her, lost. Lileth breaks the spell and addresses me.

"So, you're George's best friend?" she asks. "I've been waiting to meet you."

"Well, here I am," I say stupidly and grin like a lune.

"What is it that you do?" she asks.

"Head of IT at the Council House. Very boring. Been there for years."

"I'm sure it's interesting. And necessary."

"Well, yes, without me, things wouldn't run smoothly, it's true. Only yesterday, I refigured the planning system and upgraded the operating system…"

"You are obviously an important man," she interrupts. I don't know whether she's impressed or mocking me. But it's immaterial.

"We need to go," says George, looking at his watch. "We have cinema tickets. The film's on in ten minutes."

"Perhaps we could meet again when you have more time?" I look at her hopefully. She gives me a long, lazy smile with a hint of a promise. Or am I imagining it?

"I'll see you for a drink in the week," George says, placing his hand territorially in the small of Lileth's back. They leave the café and I look for The Guardian. Someone else has picked it up. I glance out of the window and see George and Lileth walking away. He's developed a stoop, perhaps because she's so petite.

I don't hear from him for a couple of weeks, then out of the blue, he phones. We meet early doors at the Dog & Duck. George buys me a pint of Guinness.

"Sorry it was a bit stilted the other day," he says. "Wasn't expecting to see you. I was ill at ease." He smiles to himself. "I still haven't got used to being part of a couple. Feels strange."

He doesn't look good, I notice. His shoulders are folded forward. There are dark circles beneath his eyes and his skin has a greyish tinge. He should be glowing. Instead, he looks worn out.

"So, how's it going?" I ask, giving an encouraging nod.

"Yeah, good," he says, in a lacklustre way. "Still can't believe she wants to marry me."

"You don't have to rush into it," I play the sensible card. "Why not get to know each other first?"

Then he does a strange thing. He grasps my hand, squeezing it tight and gives me a look of desperation.

"You don't get it, do ya? I love her so much it hurts. I can't risk her leaving me. Marriage is the only way of keeping a girl like that."

"Yeah, I get it. I know where you're coming from. It's just… you don't look too good."

"I'm not getting much sleep," he admits. "She's very demanding."

This is not a conversation I want to have. I study my pint.

"It's like she's sucking the energy out of me," he says. "I can't think straight. If this is love, it's exhausting."

Now I'm the agony aunt.

"Well, she's younger than you, and you're from different worlds, with different expectations."

He sighs. "You can say that again."

He starts to give me details I don't want to hear. I cut him off mid-stream.

"Tell her you're not up to it."

"And risk losing her? How can I?"

I look at his face, creased with anxiety, his skin blotchy and florid. Something isn't right.

"What d'you know about this girl?" I ask.

"Not much," he admits. "She works as an au pair for a local doctor. Lives in, looks after the kids, does light domestic duties. Doctor Santos, I believe. A fellow Brazilian. Lives in a big house on Lady Barton Road."

It's the local millionaire's row, lots of big houses, performance cars and gated entrances.

"How long's she been there?"

"I don't know. I haven't asked."

"Did she come from Brazil or was she already in the UK?"

"I don't know."

"Where did she study?"

"University of Rio de Janeiro, she says."

"Does she have any family?"

"Stop asking all these questions, will you. It's making me feel worse. I don't care. I've never felt like this about anyone." He places his hand on his heart. "She makes me feel alive."

He looks more like death, I think, but I don't say anything.

He's spared further questions by the arrival of the woman herself. Lileth stands at our table, looking amazing in tight white jeans and a figure-hugging white sweater. She eyes me with suspicion and I know she doesn't trust me. Her dark eyes glitter, reminding me of a snake and I half expect a forked tongue to flick from her mouth. She acknowledges me briefly, then speaks to George.

"We need to go. I have a taxi outside. We must be at the airport in fifteen minutes."

"Airport," I repeat. "Where are you going?"

George smiles weakly. "Sorry. I didn't get round to telling you. We're going to Antigua. We're getting married there."

So, that's it. There's nothing I can do to stop it.

They're gone for three weeks.

I know they're back because he answers the phone when I call. But he's distant and vague, says he's not feeling well. He doesn't want to meet up and as good as tells me to leave him alone. That's when I decide to go round.

I ring the bell and knock, but no one answers. I'm about to leave when I remember George keeps a spare key under a stone to the left of the porch.

Amazingly, it's still there and I let myself in. The house is in darkness, the curtains drawn and the inner doors closed. A dank mustiness hangs in the air, concealing another sweet odour that lingers beneath, familiar but unidentifiable. I look into each of the downstairs rooms, finding them unoccupied, before going upstairs.

I tread softly, not wanting to announce my presence through a squeaky stair, and make my way onto the landing. I look into each of the bedrooms, one by one, until just the back room remains. The smell is stronger now.

Silently, I turn the doorknob and look inside. It's so dark, at first I can't see anything. The smell is overpowering, putrid and foul, interlaced with a heady sweetness. I cover my nose with my hand.

As my eyes grow accustomed to the gloom, I see movement. Someone's lying on the bed and a dark figure sits astride, crouched over. I blink, trying to see. It's Lileth and she's naked, dark hair hanging forward, concealing her face.

For a moment, I think it's some kind of sex ritual. But it's not. It's something much darker. I must have gasped because she turns briefly and I swear I see a long, black, forked tongue protruding from her lips, dark liquid dripping from her mouth. The figure on the bed moans and she turns back, plunging her hands suddenly into its chest cavity, ripping it apart. There's a muted scream, followed by a viscous, sucking sound and she pulls something out, holding it high. It's black and pulsating. She thrusts it into her mouth, blood spurting as she bites, and I realise it's a human heart.

My legs turn to jelly and I stagger backwards. I'm falling on to the landing and down the stairs, into the hallway, reaching the front door. I hear her behind me, but I'm too quick. I pull open the door, feeling fresh air on my face, and crawl on to the driveway, out on to the road beyond. Then oblivion takes me.

I come round lying in a hospital bed, the world stark and white around me. There's a monitor alongside, a steady bleep registering my pulse. I look down and see a drip attached to my hand. A dark-skinned, smiling nurse enters the room.

"Welcome to the land of the living. You've been out for some time."

She shines a light in my eyes and puts a thermometer under my tongue. I watch her movements, trying to remember.

"Gave us all a bit of a scare, but your vitals are fine. I'll get doctor."

She leaves the room and I lie back, looking up at the ceiling. I remember a dark house, trying to climb a stairway without making a sound, opening doors and looking into rooms. Was it a dream? Then I recall a dark figure sitting in the darkness, turning to look at me. A sensation of uncontrollable fear fills my mind and I feel a scream building.

Before I can make a sound, the door opens and a doctor in a white coat enters, followed by the nurse.

"How long's he been unconscious?" I hear him say, reading my notes.

The dark-skinned nurse answers. "A week. They think it was the shock of finding his friend."

"George," I mutter. "What's happened to George?"

I try to sit up, but the dark-skinned nurse gently pushes me back.

She shakes her head. "I'm sorry. He'd been dead for some time when you found him. It must have been dreadful for you. Try not to get too agitated."

The doctor gives me a shot and I lie back drowsy. The bad memories are obliterated.

A month later, I'm back at work. Nobody really knows what happened to George. He had some kind of chronic fatigue condition. Maybe had a heart attack. They say rats attacked and, by the time I found him, there wasn't much left.

He got married in Antigua, that much I know. He returned home, while Lileth went to Brazil to see her family. By the time she returned, it was too late. George was dead.

Naturally, she inherited his estate. There were no dependants, he'd changed his will in her favour and there was no one to contest it.

I try to find out more about her. I ask a friend who works as a postman if he's heard of a Doctor Santos on Lady Barton Road. He says there was a Doctor Santos there once. But that was over twenty years ago. He hasn't lived there for many years.

I miss George. I miss meeting up with him at The Dog & Duck, having an early doors pint and putting the world to rights. But it's not all bad. In fact, life's quite good at the moment.

Against all the odds, I'm getting married. Me, the gawky confirmed bachelor, who couldn't get a date for love nor money. Her name? It's probably too soon to announce. But I will. It's Lileth. Mutual grief brought us together and now we're inseparable.

Funny how the wheel of life turns.

I can see what George meant, though. This relationship stuff takes it out of you. I feel quite exhausted. She's very demanding.

Feeding time

I see from afar
The window's ajar
An invitation
For gratification.

Far from my home
Forever I roam
Always I thirst
Evermore cursed.

She lies on the bed
Hair glorious and red
Throat extended and white
What a perfect delight.

Her pulse in my ear
Is all I can hear
Strong and demanding
Loud and commanding.

Focused and still
I move in for the kill
My teeth pierce her skin
Let feeding begin.

The red mist descends
The agony ends
I consume in haste
Oh glorious taste.

Murder in Mind

I see what goes on
They think I don't know
Where they meet, when they kiss
What they do, where they go.

Suspicion's a drug
That's cruel and unkind
Eats away at your heart
Plays tricks with your mind.

If I can't have him
Then neither can she.
No-one has ever
Got the better of me.

I want her to suffer
The way that I do
Feel the doubt, feel the pain
Not knowing what's true.

But how best to despatch?
How shall it be done?
Send him to his Maker
With no place to run.

Poison is good
With its painful embrace
I want her to remember
His dying face.

Or a knife in the ribs
As he looks into my eyes.
I'll be the last thing
He sees as he dies.

A walk on the cliff
One quick push and it's done
As he falls to his death
He'll know that I've won.

He thinks I'm a mouse
Boring and small
I want him to know
It's not like that at all.

Revenge is the key
That makes me walk tall.
Knowing she's left alone
And he's had the fall.

So pour me another
Let drink dull my pain
And blunt the sharp thoughts
That slice through my brain.

Ply me, indulge me,
As I sit her and scheme
It's no crime to plot
It's no sin to dream.

Does an innocent gift have the power to protect from evil?
Or does it bestow the ability to curse?

The Evil Eye

I recently came back from a trip to Turkey with the usual round of souvenirs and presents. There were exotic boxes of Turkish Delight, fragrant and sweet, for my mother and aunty, beautiful gemstones fashioned into pendants and rings for my two nieces, and for my next door neighbour, an elderly lady who had kindly been feeding my cat while I was away, a wall hanger, resembling a large eye, made from brightly coloured blue, black and white glass.

Such eyes were everywhere in Turkey. Every souvenir shop was full of bracelets, pendants, necklaces, rings and wall hangings all displaying the blue eye. I asked the shop owner what it represented and he explained it was a Nazar, a talisman offering protection against the Evil Eye.

"If someone looks at your good fortune with envy or desire, even if they appear to be smiling, they will be sending you bad luck, and misfortune will befall you," he said. "That is why we wear the protective eye, to deflect the negative energy and keep us safe. An eye for an eye. And it must be blue. For maximum protection."

He showed me an eye pendant hanging in the front of his shop. There were three kinds of evil look, he told me. "The first is given unconsciously, causing harm unintentionally. The second causes harm with intent. And the third, which is the most potent, is the invisible eye, evil that cannot be seen, sinister and deadly."

I was perturbed and fascinated and, from that moment on, I saw Nazar pendants wherever I went. They were hanging in homes, offices and shops, even in cars. Everyone in Turkey, it seemed, believed in the protection of the blue eye. Personally, I wasn't sure about its protective powers. I thought it looked pretty, and when I saw the large, glass, blue eye wall hanging, I thought it would go very well in my neighbour's porch.

It was wrapped in white tissue paper and survived the journey home, arriving intact. With great excitement, I took it round to my neighbour, thinking how much more interesting she would find it than the usual fancy biscuits, chocolates or decorative mats I brought back as thank you gifts.

She opened it and gave a start, holding it up so that it caught the light.

"An Evil Eye! Why thank you. I wasn't expecting that."

"You don't like it, do you?" I asked, looking at her with disappointment. I'd been so sure she'd find it intriguing. "I thought it would go well in your porch. But it's okay. I'll have it back. You can have some Turkish Delight instead."

"Oh, no, I didn't mean to be ungrateful," she said, looking embarrassed. "I like it. You're right. It will look very nice in my porch. And it will protect the house."

"What is it then? You had a strange look when you opened it."

"No, it's nothing. Nothing at all. It's just… Oh, never mind."

But I had to know. "No, tell me. I'm intrigued."

"It just reminds me of a strange tale my old university professor told me. I've never forgotten it."

"Well, now you have to tell me," I demanded. "You can't leave it there."

She gave me a strange look and said, "Very well. I'll make coffee and I'll tell you his story."

When she'd placed the coffee cups on the table, accompanied by a plate of chocolate bourbons, she began to tell me the tale.

"It was many years ago, when I was a young undergraduate at Oxford. I was in Brasenose, one of the first men's colleges to take women. I was studying Classics, learning about the culture and languages of Ancient Greece and Rome. I spoke fluent Latin and Greek. All forgotten now." She laughed and paused to sip her coffee. "My professor was a very learned chap, a typical Oxford don, with white sideburns, a long white beard and flowing black robes. He was possibly in his late fifties, I'm not sure, but we were all in awe of him. He seemed to take a shine to me. I was very studious and earnest in those days. He'd often invite me to take tea with him after a seminar. There was nothing improper, you understand? Just a meeting of minds."

"Of course," I said, not particularly bothered whether it had been improper or not. I wanted to know where the Evil Eye came into the story.

"I went to his rooms for my weekly tutorial. We were discussing Ovid's Metamorphoses, if I'm not mistaken. Or was it Thucydides' Peloponnesian War? Never mind, it doesn't matter." She continued, "It was a bitterly cold day in January. I remember he had a roaring fire in the grate. I went in and found him to be in a state of some agitation. 'Thank you for coming, my dear,' he said, which was odd, because I was supposed to be there. His face was red, as if he'd been drinking, although I couldn't smell alcohol on his breath. His hair was on end, as if he'd been running his fingers through it. He seemed nervous and ill at ease. He looked me straight in the eye and said, 'Sit down, my dear. There's something I need to tell you.'

"I sat down on one of his comfy Chesterfields, not knowing what to make of the situation. 'You find me in a nervous state, I'm afraid,' he said, sitting opposite, then jumping up again and walking to the window. He spoke into the distance. 'There are two things I must tell you in order to put things in perspective. Firstly, I recently put forward a paper, detailing the results of some private research I undertook over the last couple of years. It doesn't matter what the subject is. Let's just say, I believed my discovery to be quite revolutionary and, if upheld, set to turn the classics world upside down. Needless to say, my paper was rejected, found wanting in certain areas.' He turned to me. 'It's a blow, a real body blow. I was so sure of my findings. I believe politics to have played a role in this decision, but I have no proof, and so my work was thrown back at me. Hence you find me in this state of agitation, coming to terms with disappointment and thwarted academic ambition. Where I go from now, I am unsure.' He looked kindly at me. 'Don't get me wrong. I value my teaching work. It's just… I'd hoped to elevate myself, you understand?'

"I nodded, not sure what to think, his outburst totally out of character from a man usually in control and sure of himself, revered for his knowledge and opinion. I could see why such a blow was causing him pain. 'And the other thing?' I prompted. 'What was the second thing you wanted to tell me?'

"He replied, 'To understand things better, I must tell you that I am also a scholar of the esoteric. I study the subjects of myth and superstition, delving into the unknown, learning about the darker sides of man's nature, studying ancient texts on taboo subjects that have no place on an undergraduate curriculum.'

"I stared at him, unprepared for such an admission. Now he had my full attention.

'The works of Alistair Crowley, for example, I have found to be of extraordinary interest, not to mention more ancient findings.'

My neighbour broke from her tale and addressed me directly. "Alistair Crowley was the famous English occultist, a scholar of magic and Western esotericism."

"Yes, I know," I replied, keen for the story not to go off at an unnecessary tangent. "Please go on. What happened next?"

She looked into the distance and sighed, before turning to me, sipping her coffee and continuing.

"As I said, my professor was extremely agitated, which in itself was a strange occurrence from a man held in such esteem, and usually so commanding. To see him as an ordinary person, subject to everyday emotions, was strange enough, but then his story took an altogether unexpected turn. He paused, as if gathering his thoughts, and then asked me, 'Tell me, have you ever heard of the Evil Eye?'

"I had heard of such a thing, but knew little about it as my studies were limited to classical texts and ancient languages. 'I believe it's some kind of amulet that people use to ward off evil,' I answered. 'Maybe a gypsy thing, I'm not sure.' 'The Evil Eye exists in many cultures,' he replied. 'It's believed to be a curse, placed on the victim by an evil or malevolent glare. To be most effective, it's placed when the victim is unaware. If you are the recipient of the Evil Eye, you are certain to undergo misfortune or injury, or in extreme cases, death.'

"Well, let me tell you," said my neighbour, taking a bourbon biscuit and glancing at me, "this was most unexpected. Perhaps not so much the content of his words, for it was factual, and knowledge of the Evil Eye is well known in folklore. What threw me most was his conviction, as though he actually believed, what I thought to be, mumbo jumbo."

She bit into her biscuit and chewed for a moment, before continuing.

"I'm sorry, Professor," I answered, 'but what has the Evil Eye to do with your paper being rejected?' Although, I must admit, I was beginning to see a possible link.

"He turned to me, with such anguish and torment in his eyes, I could barely look at him. 'What have you done, Professor?' I asked. He answered, 'A crime so heinous and so beneath me, I am ashamed to my very soul. Last night, I went to the home of the lead scholar on the board of representatives, the individual I believed to be the prime cause of my paper being rejected. To say that he and I were rivals, having crossed swords on many occasions, was an understatement. Beneath our carefully crafted veneer of respectability and mutual respect, ran a deep loathing for one another. We approached the subject of the classics from opposing camps and on this occasion, he had the upper hand because of his academic status. I knew it was he that had recommended my thinking to be ridiculed. We had a malt whiskey together and conversed in polite terms, but his manner was so superior, so patronising as to raise some kind of demon within me. He took no account of my viewpoint… the possibility that I could have uncovered some new and ground-breaking knowledge, the years of research I had committed to my subject, the long hours spent deep into the night reading ancient texts, translating near-impossible hieroglyphics…'

"I didn't dare rush him at this point," said my neighbour, pausing again in a most irritating fashion.

"And?" I asked, desperate to hear what the professor had done. "What happened?"

"He cursed the scholar," she declared with satisfaction, adding, "and I'm sure it was well deserved."

"How d'you mean cursed?"

"He put the Evil Eye on him, of course."

"Did he tell you that?"

"Oh yes. The poor man was nearly in tears with guilt. I can remember his very words. He told me, 'Margaret, as I was leaving the house, putting on my hat and coat in the hallway, the vile man made some quip about trying harder next time, as if I was some lowly undergraduate. He suggested I throw my work on the fire and start again. It was the final straw. Something inside me snapped and I could bear it no longer. As I left the house, I turned and made the sign of the Evil Eye, fixing him with such a glare of malevolence and dislike as he closed the door that I thought he would wither and die on the spot. He didn't of course, but it was done and I knew there would be consequences…'

"How do you make the sign of the Evil Eye?" I asked, transfixed by her words.

"Well, I'm not going to do it, obviously," she answered, "but you make a horizontal 'V' with your index and middle finger of one hand, pointing into the curved fingers of the other hand. As if you were making a kind of eye shape. Don't try it," she cautioned, seeing me trying to arrange my fingers.

"Did anything happen to the scholar as a result?" I asked, placing my hands in my lap.

"Oh yes. That was why my professor was in such a state. That morning, just before I arrived, he'd had a phone-call. After he'd left, there'd been a fire at the scholar's house. No one survived. He and his wife and their three children all perished."

My mouth opened in shock. "Crikey that was quick. Do you think it was the work of the Evil Eye?"

"Who knows? There could have been any number of reasons. The authorities attributed the fire to an electrical fault. But it certainly spooked the professor. And there's more…"

She looked at me darkly.

"The professor was beside himself with fear. He told me that once you put the Evil Eye on a person and something horrible happens, the evil comes back at you. Then he showed me a photograph. It had arrived in the morning post, one of a number taken by his brother on a recent trip they'd taken to the Lake District." She leaned forward and so did I. "On one photo, there was a fault with the reproduction. It was quite eerie. It showed a black line running straight through his face. He was convinced he was about to die because of the curse he'd put on the scholar, and that this photo heralded a warning."

"What happened?" I whispered.

"Two weeks later, there was a terrible storm. Trees were uprooted, roofs ripped off and walls collapsed. The professor was out in his car. No one knew why. He was driving along a country lane, when a branch came down from an overhead tree. It went straight through the windscreen and impaled him through his eye socket. He died instantly. It was in exactly the same position as the black line in the photo."

She stopped, letting the words hang in the air.

I stared at her, wide-eyed.

"That's why I'm a little nervous of the Evil Eye. Even though it does look pretty," she glanced at the blue eye, lying amidst the tissue paper on the table. "I believe it holds a hidden power we know nothing about."

"I'll throw it away," I declared, about to pick it up, when she stopped me.

"No, I'm being silly. You're giving it to me as a gift, not as a curse, aren't you?"

"Yes, of course. I just thought it would look nice on your wall."

"Then I'll hang it up," she said, picking it up and carrying it through the house to the front porch. I followed. She hung it on a spare hook on the wall and there it glinted, catching the light in a mesmerising manner.

I left and went back home, more than a little spooked by her story and determined never to put a curse, and certainly not the sign of the Evil Eye, on anyone, no matter how much they annoyed me or I disliked them.

That night there was a fire at Margaret's house. I was awoken from a deep sleep by the sound of a siren and shouting. When I looked out of the curtains, I saw smoke billowing into the air. A fire engine had drawn up outside her house and firemen were unloading hoses.

As fast as my shaking hands would allow, I put on my dressing gown and ran into the front garden. Margaret's house was ablaze, orange flames leaping against the windows, black acrid smoke pouring into the night sky. An ambulance was pulling away.

"How's Margaret?" I asked one of the firemen, who was training a hose on the house. "What happened?"

"Get back," he shouted. "It's too dangerous."

A window exploded and there was a scream from the nervous crowd of neighbours who'd gathered to watch. I thought of the eye hanging in the porch and Margaret's story the night before. Was this my doing? Had I inadvertently put a curse on her? Surely not? I bore her no ill will or envy. And surely the eye would have protected her. It must be a coincidence.

Margaret survived but she never came back to live there. She was badly burned, and when she recovered, she went to live with her daughter in London. She'd been disfigured and didn't want anyone to see her. They think a lighted candle started the blaze. Margaret had always used candles, so it was entirely possible. A couple of days after the blaze, I stood in front of the blackened bricks and charred remains. Unlike the rest of the house, the front porch had escaped relatively unscathed. I could see the blue eye hanging on the wall and, before they came to board up the house, I opened the porch door and retrieved it.

As I felt its cold blue surface beneath my fingers, a recent conversation came to mind. I'd been complimenting Margaret on her skin, how unlined she was, despite being in her mid-seventies. I remembered going back home and looking in the mirror, thinking how lined and haggard I looked in comparison, even though I was only half her age. If I'm honest, I'd been envious, wondering what her secret was. Now, her skin was burned and red, forever marred with ugly burns and scars.

I took the Evil Eye home, wrapped it up and put it in a drawer. I couldn't bear to see it, but neither could I throw it away.

That was two months ago. Now, I live in dread of the evil coming back at me. Will it be an accident or just bad luck? Either way, I know something is coming.

In Arabic, it's known as the Eye of the Envious.

Who is the mysterious girl on the train,
and why does she keep re-appearing?

Girl On The Train

I first saw her late one afternoon on the 5.33 from New Street Station. I nearly missed the train. It was waiting at Platform 4 and I had to run. I only just made it, jumping on to the train just before the doors closed. It was crowded, with no seats left, but that's nothing new. You were lucky to get a seat at this time. I saw a few people I recognised, other workers who usually caught this train. But I'd never seen her before.

I was standing close to the door, holding on to one of the upright poles when the train jerked to a halt. As the train stopped, I carried on moving, Newton's first law of motion. I held on to the pole, anchoring myself against the momentum, but was aware of someone immediately to my left and turned to apologise. It was a girl with a pretty face and long dark hair.

"Sorry. Didn't bump into you, did I?"

She smiled. "No, you're okay."

"It's a bit crowded," I commented. "Always the same at this time of night."

"Yes." She smiled again. I noticed she had brown eyes.

The train jerked forward and the lights flickered, momentarily pitching us into darkness. As the train moved forward again, the lights came on and I looked to my left, expecting to see her. She'd gone.

I looked up and down the compartment, but she wasn't there.

It was strange, but I was sure there was some explanation and didn't think much more about it.

The next time I saw her was a week later. I was waiting on the platform at New Street Station. I'd missed the 5.33 and was waiting for the 6.13. Once again, the

161

platform was crowded with commuters. It was a dreary, dark evening with a pre-winter chill in the air and I pulled my jacket around me, hoping the train wouldn't be late. All around, people huddled, looking drab and tired. Then I saw her, standing in front of me, facing the platform. She was dressed in a brown coat, just as before. She must have felt my eyes on her back, because she turned. A smile of recognition passed over her features.

At that moment, the train approached the platform, announcing its presence with a long blast of its horn. Distracted, I looked into its headlights. When I turned back, she'd gone.

I looked up and down the platform, searching for her, but she'd disappeared. I shrugged, puzzled, assuming she'd moved and was hidden by the crowds.

I didn't see her for some time after that and, if I'm honest, I forgot all about her. I didn't even think to look for her. She was just someone I'd encountered on a couple of journeys.

Life carried on. Winter came and went, crisp and cold, with sparkling frosts. I looked forward to spring and seeing swathes of yellow daffodils. I got a promotion at work, moving up to a management position, with a salary rise. Buoyed up by my extra responsibilities and income, I suggested to my boyfriend we get married and he agreed. We set a wedding date in the summer and spent long hours planning the day: church, venue, bridesmaids, wedding dress, food, flowers and so on. I hadn't realised there'd be so much to arrange nor how much it would cost. But it was a once-only event, so I threw myself into it. We got a mortgage and moved in together, our very first place.

Life was good and I had no complaints. My company was bought out by an American conglomerate and, for a while, I feared for my job. But I was competent at what I did and they chose to keep me on, with another pay rise. I was on my way up.

Summer arrived and we got married. It was everything I thought it would be. I got emotional saying my vows and shed a few tears. We honeymooned on Ibiza and came back suntanned and relaxed. Life was bowling along at a fast pace, getting better with every passing month.

And then I started seeing her again.

Only this time it was different.

Autumn arrived, wet and damp. This year, there were no crisp autumnal mornings, with a hazy mist lying over the fields as the sun warmed the land. From the start, this autumn was bleak. A bone-chilling dampness permeated the air and it was permanently dark, the sun obscured behind grey, heavy clouds.

Station platforms have their own particular dreariness when it's cold and damp. A combination of grey concrete, biting wind and resigned commuters makes them cheerless, forlorn places.

I felt utterly miserable, stamping my feet to keep warm, watching my breath steam in the cold air, willing the train to arrive early, which, of course, it never did. It was a stark reminder that not everything in life was easy. No matter how good you thought things were, something always brought you back to earth.

It was late September. Probably a year since I'd seen the girl in the brown coat. I can't be sure, but it could have been the same day and time when I last saw her.

I was on the 5.33 from New Street, once again standing up, holding on to an overhead strap, trying to keep my weight evenly balanced on both feet. I looked down the train and there she was, sitting on one of the seats facing me. Same brown coat, long brown hair and brown eyes. It was definitely her. And she saw me, because I saw the beginnings of a smile on her lips. As before, the train jerked to a halt and the lights flickered, momentarily plunging us into darkness.

When the lights came on, she'd gone. An old woman in a headscarf sat in her place, which didn't make sense. There'd been no time for the girl to move.

For the rest of the twenty five-minute journey, I looked for her, but didn't see her. It was a mystery, and I alighted from the train feeling curiously cheated. I felt now that I had to see her, if nothing else than to prove to myself she wasn't a figment of my imagination.

Next morning, on the 8.01 into work, I saw her. She was on the platform.

I was sitting on the train, looking idly out of the window. There was just one more station to go before we arrived at New Street. I was thinking about a meeting I had that morning. As the train pulled away from Adderley Park, I saw her clearly, walking along the platform, as if she'd just alighted. I pressed my face to the glass, but the train was moving and she was gone in a flash.

Now, she was beginning to bug me. Who was she? Why did I keep seeing her? Was my mind playing tricks?

Then, something happened to prove she wasn't a figment of my imagination. It should have made me feel better, but it didn't.

It was two days later and I was on the late train. Our team had gone out for a meal after work to celebrate a major new piece of business we'd won. I'd orchestrated the deal and was going to make a lot of commission. It wasn't every day you won business like that, and when they suggested a second bottle of bubbly, I was happy to join in.

By the time I reached New Street Station, I was feeling pretty mellow. Despite the chill night air, I felt warm inside and was looking forward to getting home.

The 21.33 pulled up, on time, at the nearly deserted platform, its carriages well lit and welcoming. The electric doors swished open with a faint hiss and I stepped into the nearest carriage. There were maybe half a dozen people sitting there, with plenty of free seats, so I don't know why I decided to walk through the train to the rear carriage. Perhaps it was because, subconsciously, I was looking for the girl.

The guard blew his whistle and the train set off.

As I approached the rear carriage, I saw her through the glass in the partition door. She was sitting, facing me, in a four-seater section, with a table in front of her. Now, at last, I had the opportunity to speak to her and prove she was real.

I pressed the button that opened the linking door, taking care not to let her out of my sight, and stepped into the carriage. I didn't sit next to her. That would have been over-friendly, given there was no one else in the carriage. Instead, I sat on the other side of the aisle, so she was diagonally opposite. She looked over and smiled, recognising me.

I smiled back and said, 'Hello'.

She didn't fade or disappear. She actually spoke.

"Hi. How are you?"

This was more than I was expecting.

"I'm good, thank you. Been working late?"

"Working late." She repeated my phrase as if considering it. "No."

It wasn't quite the response I'd been expecting and I wasn't sure what to say.

"I went shopping," she announced. "It's my mother's birthday tomorrow."

"That's a coincidence. It's my husband's birthday tomorrow. 23rd September. Libra," I added, showing I knew my zodiac signs.

She frowned. "No. It's 23rd October. My mother's Scorpio."

"Okay. If you say so."

I looked at her, mystified, and tried changing the subject. "I've just been having a celebratory meal with my workmates. We've won a big piece of business. It's really exciting."

"Wow. What d'you do?"

"I work for a sportswear company. I'm in sales management. How about you?"

"Second year student at Birmingham University. I'm studying psychology."

"Sounds interesting. I always fancied doing psychology. But you know how it is, life goes in a different direction."

"Sure. You can't always control life."

The train was slowing down, approaching Adderley Park and she stood up.

"This is my stop. It was nice talking to you."

"Yeah. Take care. See you again."

"Yeah. Bye."

She moved into the aisle, making her way towards the exit doors, a large, brown leather bag hanging from her shoulder. As she passed me, I saw a copy of the Birmingham Mail in the top of her bag and clearly saw the date. Monday 23rd October.

I turned and watched her walk to the door. I saw her push the button to open the door as the train stopped. I saw her step on to the platform and start walking towards the exit. The doors closed and the train started moving. I looked out of the window, expecting to see her walking, ready to give her a wave, but the platform was empty. There was no one there.

I knew the station at Adderley Park. I went past it twice a day. From the rear carriage, it was a long walk to the exit. She should have been on the platform. So, where was she?

The girl in brown was starting to get inside my head. The more I saw her, the more things didn't add up.

And then I started to see her everywhere.

I saw her waiting for the 5.33 the next evening, but lost her in the crowd. I saw her sitting in the carriage, two rows in front of me, but when I looked again, she'd vanished. She began to appear in my dreams and, every time, the sequence would repeat. I'd ask her if she'd been working late, she'd say no, she'd been shopping for her mother's birthday the next day. I'd say it was 23rd September, my husband's birthday, Libra, and she'd say no, it was 23rd October, Scorpio. I'd look away and when I looked back, she'd be gone.

It got to the point when I was seeing her half a dozen times a day and I was starting to doubt my sanity.

I mentioned it to a friend over a drink one evening. It was now 15th October and I'd begun to dread the arrival of 23rd October.

"I have a feeling something's going to happen," I said. "Every time I go to sleep, she's in my dreams. Every time I'm on the train or the platform, I see her. I don't know who she is or why I'm seeing her. The closer we get to 23rd October, the more intense it's becoming."

"You think she's a ghost?" asked my friend, looking at me as if I'd taken leave of my senses. "Or are you hallucinating?"

"I don't know."

"I think you've been working too hard. Or perhaps it's the shock of getting married."

"Yeah, very funny."

"You look tired. Perhaps you should see the doctor."

"What for? There's nothing wrong with me. There's a reason for this. I know it." I frowned and looked at my friend. "If something happens to me, if I don't survive…"

"Now you're being dramatic."

"Maybe. But something's not right."

On the morning of 23rd October, I didn't see her. She wasn't on the train. She wasn't in the crowd or on the platform. I hadn't dreamt about her the night before and I began to wonder if I'd been going through some weird psychotic episode that had played itself out. Maybe I'd seen something subliminally that had lodged in my brain. Perhaps I'd switch on the television tonight and there'd be a new series, starring the mysterious girl in brown.

At 5.33, I stood on the platform at Birmingham New Street, searching the crowd for her. She wasn't there and I felt a weight lift from my shoulders. I hadn't realised how the sightings had begun to affect me. I'd begun to get paranoid.

The train arrived and I got on. It was very crowded, but I found a seat in the rear carriage. I sat down and breathed a sigh of relief. I'd be home soon and could relax. I was looking forward to seeing my husband and enjoying a takeaway and a bottle of wine. I smiled to myself, thinking of him waiting for me at home.

My husband. My home. My life. It felt good.

The train set off and soon the dark night was flashing past.

I looked across the aisle and, suddenly, it was all too horribly familiar. The woman sitting by the window was reading the Birmingham Mail and I'd seen her before. Slowly, she lowered the paper and I stared straight into the eyes of the girl in the brown coat.

There was no time to react.

There was a screeching of metal on metal, a loud bang and the lights went out. I was aware of the carriage falling to the left and objects hitting me. I grabbed the table in front of me, holding on for dear life, not knowing what was happening and which way was up or down. I was unable to see or hear anything beyond people screaming, glass breaking and wood splintering. It was like being thrown into a massive spin dryer.

There was another huge impact and I lost my grip on the table, landing somewhere below. I must have blacked out for a while, because I don't remember anything landing on top of me, but when I came to, I was pinned down by something heavy.

Amidst the screaming, people were using torches on their mobiles, giving pinpricks of illumination throughout the carriage.

I tried to use my arms but I couldn't move. Something was wedged around me, holding me in a massive vice. Now the sound of the injured filled the air, people moaning, crying, calling for help.

Smoke was filling the carriage, seeping insidiously around me, bouncing off the torchlights. Panic hit me. I had to get out. Smoke wasn't a good sign. Smoke indicated fire, and I wasn't ready to be burnt alive. I was aware of a body lying across me and tried to kick it away with my legs. Nothing happened. I tried to wriggle my toes, but there was no sensation. Now, the true horror of my situation hit home. If I couldn't use my legs, maybe I was paralysed. Or worse.

I was trapped and at the mercy of the emergency services, if they could get to me in time.

I looked down to see how bad my situation was and came face to face with the man who'd been sitting opposite. He was lying across me, his head at a weird angle, blood dripping from his mouth, eyes staring ahead.

With superhuman effort, I pushed down the panic. I had to keep a clear head. I had to focus. There was too much going on in my life to leave it behind. There had to be a way out.

That's when I became aware of an arm reaching across me, long hair brushing my arm, and a face I recognised looking in to my eyes. It was the girl in brown.

"Okay. I'm going to get you out."

"Save yourself," I muttered. "Get out. We don't know how long we've got."

"Stop speaking and conserve your energy," she instructed. "First, I'm going to get this man off you."

She placed her arms around the dead man in a weird embrace and slowly dragged him from me. That enabled me to assess my situation. Now, I could see the table to which I'd been clinging had come away from the floor and slammed into the side of the carriage, breaking through the window and trapping my legs beneath.

"If I can lift that table just a few inches, I can pull you out," she said.

"I don't think so," I started to say, but she held a finger to her lips.

She disappeared for a moment, reappearing with a large piece of metal.

"This should do the trick."

Somehow, she managed to get the metal bar under the table, using her body as leverage to force it up the required few inches.

All the while, the smoke was getting thicker and I was having difficulty breathing. I felt drowsy and had the sensation of drifting away. I was lying on a lilo, drifting out to sea, the ocean wide and blue around me. It wasn't unpleasant but her words cut through, bringing me back to reality.

"No you don't. Keep your eyes open. Focus on me."

"Okay. Thank you. What's your name?"

"Mandy."

"Mandy. Fly me to the moon, Mandy." I was delirious, talking gibberish.

Her voice was sharp. "You have to get out. You've everything to live for. You've a baby on the way."

At least, I think that's what she said. I wasn't thinking clearly by then.

She moved behind me, placing her arms under my shoulders, pulling me away. I don't know how she did it, but somehow she got me out of the carriage and on to the embankment, pulling me through gravel and thick tufted grass until I was out of danger.

I was dimly aware of her walking back towards the wreckage, but it was hard to see. I could swear I saw her going back into the carriage, but I can't be sure. Next thing

I knew, someone was putting an oxygen mask over my mouth and I was being lifted on to a stretcher.

"Mandy." I struggled to speak, wrenching the mask off my face. "She's in there. You have to get her out."

"They'll find her. Don't worry. We need to get you to hospital."

I heard a loud explosion, followed by more screaming. Then I slid into darkness.

Later, we learned there'd been a points problem. An investigation was under way as to whether it was human error or mechanical fault. The first three carriages had buckled, crashing into each other, causing mainly crush injuries. The rear carriage had derailed, falling sideways into the embankment. Ten people lost their lives. An explosion in the rear carriage claimed most of those.

I was one of the lucky ones.

I was in hospital for two months. I'd broken some vertebrae, causing temporary paralysis, but that was all. As the nerves and bones began to heal, I regained full use of my legs. Other than that, I suffered minor cuts and bruising, and smoke damage to my lungs. But everything mended okay.

It was miracle enough that I survived, but there was cause for even greater celebration. In hospital, they told me I was pregnant and, against all the odds, that the baby had survived. I was pregnant! I cried for an hour when they told me.

"The girl on the train…" I said to my husband. "She knew. She said I had everything to live for, that I had a baby on the way. How did she know? And what happened to her?"

I went through the list of those who'd perished, looking for Mandy or Amanda. I was sure she'd gone back into the carriage just as the explosion ripped through. She wasn't on the list. I saw a list of all those who'd been travelling. She wasn't on that either. I even spoke to people who'd been in the rear carriage. No one remembered her. It was as if she hadn't existed.

My husband was desperate to find her, to thank her for saving my life and that of our unborn child, and began looking back through the records.

He found out a girl called Mandy had killed herself on the tracks five years earlier. She'd been nineteen, a second-year student at Birmingham University studying psychology. There was no reason. She'd been shopping to buy a present for her mother's birthday the next day. Apparently, she was pregnant.

She died on 23rd October, five years to the day before the train crash.

How d'you explain it?

I'd been seeing her on and off for twelve months before the accident. Was she a foreteller of doom? Or a guardian angel, sent to protect me, perhaps to atone for the innocent life she'd killed. I certainly wasn't pregnant when she first started appearing. So, why me? How did she know I'd become pregnant? Was it fixed in the stars?

I never saw her again. And for a while, I gave up work. I couldn't face travelling on the train. The memories were too raw.

None of it made sense. But one thing I know for sure. I wouldn't be here if it wasn't for the girl on the train. And neither would my child.

When our daughter was born six months later, we named her Amanda.

It seemed the right thing to do.

Camping

What's that noise outside the tent?
A guardian angel, Heaven-sent?
Or something bad that's died earth bound?
A zombie or a black hell hound?

Is there a killer on the loose?
A maniac with a hangman's noose?
Will they find us in the morning dead?
Our bodies severed from our head?

Fear runs amok in the dead of night
In a lonely field far from the light
How can I sleep so filled with dread?
I wish I'd stayed at home in bed.

Pat Spence

Halloween

Cobwebs, spiders and creatures that creep
Crawl up your bedclothes while you're asleep
Blood and guts and all things gory
It's all part of the Halloween story

Nasty scares in the dead of night
Horrible things that give you a fright,
Ghoulies, ghosties, vampires that bite,
Banshees, mummies, second sight.

Zombies walk, the living dead
Led by a horseman without a head
Skeletons smile with evil grins
At last, the witching hour begins.

Werewolves howl and pumpkins flicker
 The dead awake on this night of Wicca.
Evil flows and knows no bounds
Fanned by ghouls and Baskerville hounds.

Spectres rise from centuries old graves
Dance round churchyards in moonlit raves
Underground crypts dark and dank
Full of cadavers decomposing and rank.

Witches fly with pointed hats
Astride their broomsticks, and vampire bats
Drink human blood with fangs sunk deep
In unwitting victims while they sleep.

A big black dog with eyes of red
Carries the curse, you'll soon be dead.
A bloodcurdling scream hangs in the night,
Straight from the lips of the woman in white.

The unholy walk on this night of dread
When the veil is lifted 'tween living and dead
If you value your life you'll stay unseen
Safely locked indoors on Hallowe'en.

A dog owner is rushed to hospital with a mystery illness, but who will walk her dog in her absence?

The Dog Walker

I first met Bill and Buster outside the supermarket in our local town.

I'd popped in to get a few essentials, a bottle of Sherry and some cheese sticks, and decided, while my car was parked in the car park, I might as well go to the nearby shops. I was walking up the concrete ramp that led from the supermarket into the back of British Home Stores, since re-opened as Dunelm, when I noticed a man sitting on a ragged old blanket by the wall.

"Can you spare any change?"

I've always been one to find spare change for someone begging on the street. After all, they're not there by choice. How quickly loss of job, income or relationship can turn into loss of everything. Sadly, there are too many casualties bearing witness to the situation. It shouldn't happen, but it does, all too often.

When I heard the words, I reached for my purse to see if I had a couple of pound coins. As I passed them to the man, I noticed there was a dog sitting beside him, nestled inside the blanket.

"Oh, you have a dog." I reached down to pat him.

Two bright brown eyes looked up at me. It was a grizzled, scruffy old mutt, but seemed bright enough.

"Yeah, this is Buster."

"Hi, Buster. Pleased to meet you." Buster's tail thumped beneath the blanket.

"He looks old."

"He's fourteen."

"D'you have food for him?"

The man opened a carrier bag, lying alongside him, revealing half a dozen cans of dog food and a couple of packets of dog biscuits.

"He never goes without," he said, scratching Buster's head. "I feed him first. If there's enough left, I feed myself."

"He's obviously very precious."

The man looked at me with sad, tired eyes that had seen too much. "He's kept me going over the years. I got him as a puppy. He's been with me ever since."

I thought of my own pampered, pedigree pooch, a Cockerpoo called Brodie. He only knew the good life. He wouldn't last two minutes on the street.

"What's your name?"

"Bill."

"Pleased to meet you, Bill. I'm Sarah. I'll see you again. Take care."

I gave Buster one last pat and went on my way.

I didn't think too much about Bill and Buster over the coming week. I had other things on my mind. What was I going to do for my fiftieth birthday? Where were we going to go for our holidays next summer, a Greek island or a Mediterranean cruise? Was it worth buying now, in late November, to get a cheaper price? Should I buy that red coat I'd seen in John Lewis? Or should I settle for the cheaper version in Marks and Spencers?

I'm ashamed to say, middle-class living held greater sway in my thoughts than one homeless man and his dog.

A week later and I passed by Bill and Buster again. They were in the same place, outside the supermarket.

"Hi, Bill? How are you?"

I don't know if he recognised me.

"Hi. Not so good. I've got a cold. I ache all over."

"Have you taken anything for it? You need to go to the doctor's."

"I've taken some paracetemol. I'll go to the walk-in centre later. See if they'll give me antibiotics."

Of course. He didn't have an address. He couldn't go to the doctor's.

"Why don't you go, now? You need to start taking something soon."

"I'm waiting for my friend to come and mind Buster. He should be here soon."

"Okay. Well, here's a couple of pounds to get a cup of tea."

"That's great. Thanks."

With that, I went on my way.

That night, a freeze set in, all the way from Siberia. I looked out of my warm, cosy house into the cold, dark night and thought of Bill and Buster. Where were they? Were they outside? Were they freezing somewhere? I hoped they had somewhere to go, a homeless hostel or a friend's floor, maybe.

Next morning, my car windscreen was frozen and I thought of them again as I chipped off the ice. It was bitterly cold, everywhere twinkling and white as the weak sun shone on the hoar frost. The wind was biting and cold, and although I was wearing a goosedown jacket, mohair scarf and leather gloves, I could feel it in my bones.

Did Bill have a coat, I wondered? What was it like at two in the morning when you were living rough, when the temperatures plummeted and the cold was at its worst?

On impulse I drove to the supermarket, on the pretext of buying some milk. I looked for Bill but he wasn't there. Good. That meant he was somewhere else, possibly inside. Or something worse, God forbid.

Then I was on a mission. I went back to the supermarket in the afternoon and there he was.

"How are you? Did you get some medication?"

"Yeah, thanks. I'm taking it now. Hopefully, should be feeling better in a few days."

He didn't look good. His face was pitted and lined, his eyes bloodshot, and deep grooves cut into his jowls on either side of his face. He wore a dirty woollen bobble hat and fingerless black woollen gloves. I wondered how old he was. It was impossible to tell. Living rough added years to a person's age, no doubt about that.

"Where did you stay last night?" I asked.

"We got a place in a hostel. There's only a few hostels that take animals, so having Buster makes it difficult, but we got lucky last night."

"Good. It was freezing outside. If you can't get a place, where do you sleep?"

"There's an alcove round the back of the supermarket. We sleep there."

"I hope you find a place tonight."

"Yeah, so do I. A woman gave Buster a dog coat, but it doesn't fit him. Meant for a smaller dog. He's my priority."

He showed me the fancy tartan dog coat lying under the blanket. A nice gesture, but that was all. No practical use. I bent down and patted Buster.

"I'll bring you a blanket and a dog coat that fits. If you're not here, I'll leave them round the back of the supermarket."

"Thanks."

I opened my purse and took out some notes. I passed them to him.

"There's fifty quid there. Call it an early Christmas present. Get yourself some decent food."

He looked at me with tears in his eyes and, leaning forward, gave me a hug. He was thin as a rake, all skin and bone.

"Thank you, Sarah. You're a friend."

He'd remembered my name. I wasn't just another faceless, nameless, middle-class woman who'd given him a few coins. I stood up to go.

"I hope you'll be alright, Bill. Take care."

The next day, he wasn't there. I walked around the back of the supermarket and found the alcove. It wouldn't give much shelter against the rain and wind. On the ground nearby, concealed beneath some shrubs and bushes were some damp cardboard boxes, flattened out, and a cheap nylon sleeping bag. This was where he slept. I felt tears stinging in my eyes.

Under my arm was a plastic bag containing a thick woollen blanket, a larger size dog coat, fleece-lined, straight from the pet shop, a spare pair of my husband's leather gloves and a new woolly hat. Carefully, I placed the package inside the sleeping bag. I hoped he would find it. I hoped someone wouldn't steal it.

A week later and I was struck down by a mystery illness. I went home from work feel tired and hot, every bone in my body aching with a dull throb. I took some paracetamol and went to bed, thinking I was going down with flu. My husband looked after me as best he could, although with his condition, it was difficult. Did I mention he was in a wheelchair? He'd been disabled for years, ever since he'd contracted a virus in his spine on a trip abroad. We'd designed our house to be wheelchair friendly, with grab rails and ramps, even a lift to get him to the upper floor, but life could be challenging. This was one of those times.

Overnight, my condition worsened. I was burning up, feverish and delirious. He brought me hot drinks, took my temperature and tried to help, but I got worse. Later, he told me I was saying the Lord's Prayer over and over, thrashing out wildly at invisible things in the air, before lapsing in to a period of unconsciousness.

Eventually, not knowing what else to do and unable to care for me, he called for an ambulance.

I don't remember any of it, certainly not the paramedics coming into our house or being wheeled out, on a stretcher, into a waiting ambulance. I vaguely remember being in a white room and a doctor in a white coat looking into my eyes with a flashlight, but nothing else. Apparently, they were baffled as to my condition and, for a while, put me in an isolation ward. There was talk of sepsis and poison, my husband told me later, of some kind of nerve agent, although I think maybe he was joking.

It was the aftermath of the Skripal poisoning in Salisbury, so maybe the authorities were a little paranoid. I mean, I was hardly a Russian spy.

Eventually, they decided it was a virus, allied with a bacterial infection. I was pumped full of antibiotics.

I knew nothing of this. I remained stuck in some kind of weird limbo, unresponsive and unconscious, imprisoned in my own private nightmare. I ambled through a strange white mist, desperate to keep walking, but finding it difficult to pick up my feet. Strange fronds brushed my face and branches laced with snow whipped my body. It seemed to go on and on, a continual walking with no end in sight.

Occasionally, people would appear through the mist, faces I recognised, looking pale and drawn. Other faces I didn't recognise peered into my face, pulling away branches, trying to make me more comfortable.

Sometimes, I heard familiar voices, talking about everyday things. I heard my husband's voice telling me he loved me, talking about my friends, my family and dog. I specifically heard him talk about Brodie, how he was pining for me, missing his walks with me.

"Brodie's lost without you," he said. "I'm going to get someone else to walk him. I can't do it myself, not with the wheelchair and spending so much time at the hospital."

I don't know why those particular words stuck in my mind, but they did. I suppose I was missing my dog. After all, he was my baby, dependent on me. I missed his soft brown eyes, his small furry body and his look of excitement every time I walked into the room. I'd bonded with Brodie closer than any other living thing, even my husband, if I'm honest. Not being with Brodie was a cruel separation, the one thing I'd always dreaded.

Strangely, Brodie never appeared in my ethereal, misty world. I remained trapped in a cold, sterile environment that had me locked in its grasp.

Slowly, I recovered.

My husband tells the story of one day seeing my eyes flicker, about three weeks after I'd been admitted. I was in the High Dependency Unit, all kinds of tubes and monitors attached. Doctors and nurses appeared, checked my vitals, and said it was a good sign. I was coming back.

My initial recovery is faint in my memory. Perhaps I've erased it because it was so difficult. My first recollection is of sitting up in my hospital bed, drinking a weak kind of soup. High nutrition food, I think they called it. I also remember looking outside through the small window in my room and seeing snowflakes swirl in the air, soft and feather-like. I asked my husband what time of year it was and he said late December.

I'd missed Christmas.

He said the country had been going through a terrible cold spell, with freezing conditions and heavy snow.

"It's like the arctic out there," he said. "People have been stuck in their cars for days, sheep are dying in snowdrifts as big as a house and everything has come to a halt. It's been going on the whole time you've been in hospital. If you had to choose a time to be stuck here, this was it. It's grim out there and they think it might go on for another week."

As I recovered and became more aware, they allowed me to watch the small television in my room. They said it would be a good stimulus. I turned on the news and saw for myself how the UK had been going through some of the most difficult conditions in living memory. Roads were impassable, councils had run out of grit, and people in remote, country locations were being rescued by the armed forces. It seemed a world away from my warm hospital room, with its light green walls, green flowered curtains and clean white sheets. My world had shrunk to the four walls I knew so well and I wasn't in a hurry to leave.

My husband informed me I'd lost three weeks of my life. It seemed my body had gone into a voluntary coma to help me heal and recover.

"You've been pretty poorly," he told me. "I came every day. They said it would be good for you to hear my voice."

"I heard you," I said, "in my weird alternative universe. I heard you talk about Brodie. How is he? I've missed him."

"Brodie's good. Missing you, as well."

"Did you manage to take him for walks?"

My husband grinned. "Much as I like to think of myself as superman, I know my limitations. There was no way I could take him for walks every day, so I called a charity called GingerButtons. It's a dog walking service for anyone who is unable to walk their dog, whether because of age, illness or some other factor."

"Oh. Okay." I was unsure how I felt about someone else walking Brodie, somebody unknown getting close to my baby, doing what I should have been doing. There again, Brodie needed exercise, and my husband couldn't have done it, especially not in the wintery conditions.

"Who's been walking him? Is he safe?"

"Yes. It's a nice bloke called Bob. He said he has a dog of his own. Seems to have a real affinity with Brodie. And Brodie absolutely loves him. His tail starts wagging even before Bob's pressed the doorbell. He's been taking him out once a day, even in the snow. He comes around 2 in the afternoon, which is when I've been popping home from the hospital. I can't tell you how grateful I was to find GingerButtons, despite the silly name."

I was in hospital for a further week, building myself up and having physio sessions to strengthen my muscles. It's amazing how quickly your muscles weaken when you're not using them. When I first swung my legs over the edge of the bed and attempted to walk, I could barely stand.

"You've had a tough time," the doctor advised. "Take your time getting back to normal. Gentle exercise, good food and fresh air, if this freeze ever goes, should do the trick."

The day I left hospital felt very strange. I was still weak, and institutionalised by hospital routine. It's easy to become passive when some else takes control, telling you what to do, when to eat, when to sleep. Outside seemed loud, bright and frightening. I was vulnerable and out of control, glad I had my husband at my side to guide me.

The big freeze was over, thankfully. Everywhere was grey, wet and soggy. The remnants of dirty snow lingered at the sides of the road and there was a constant drip-dripping from trees, shrubs and gutters. It was a wet, dirty world I emerged into and I was happy to get home, lock the door and sink into the sofa in our lounge. Brodie came bounding towards me, eyes bright, ears high, tail wagging furiously.

"Brodie boy. I've missed you." I buried my face in his fur, luxuriating in its softness, inhaling his familiar doggy smell. He seemed clean and he looked healthy, black button nose wet and brown coat gleaming. He wriggled out of my grasp, running manically around the lounge in excitement, barking like crazy.

"Brodie, come here, you daft mutt." He bounded on to the sofa and squashed in beside me, looking up expectantly. I stroked his head. "Bet you wonder where I've been, boy. Well, I'm back now and I'm here to stay. Starting tonight, I'll take you for a walk. It won't be far, but at least it will be me. I'll ring GingerButtons and tell them we don't need them anymore."

"Sure you're up to it?" asked my husband, bringing in a cup of tea.

"Oh yes. I've missed our walks. This will be the best tonic for me."

That night, I took Brodie out for a brief walk. Just round the block, but enough for me to get some fresh air.

When you've been ill, nothing prepares you for your return to normality. Everything is different and new, the colours more vibrant, the smells more acute and the sounds sharper. It's as if everything you saw before was under wraps and now it's raw and unfiltered, and you have to get the most from every moment.

As I walked down the street, drinking in the damp and the cold, I remembered Bill and Buster with a flash of guilt. I wondered how they'd fared through the terrible freeze, whether Bill had found the package I'd left. I hoped they'd found refuge. It all seemed a lifetime ago.

Earlier that afternoon, I'd called GingerButtons to tell them we didn't need any more dog walking.

"What was the name and address again?" asked the woman who answered the phone. "Sorry, I've got no record of anyone coming to that address for dog-walking."

"Someone definitely came," I said. "I was in hospital, but my husband said somebody came every day for three weeks. His name was Bob."

"We were very short staffed over the cold spell," she replied. "We certainly wouldn't have sent someone out every day. And we don't have a dog-walker on our books called Bob. Everyone is vetted before they're allowed to dog walk. D'you have his surname?"

"No, I don't, sorry."

"Well, as long as your dog is okay, no harm done."

"I suppose so. Whoever it was did a good job and we're immensely grateful."

I hung up baffled and would have remained in ignorance, were it not for the fact I broke a glass a couple of days later.

I was reaching up to get a glass from a top shelf. My fingers failed to get a proper grasp of the glass and it came tumbling down onto the ceramic kitchen floor, shattering into silver shards.

Sighing deeply, and still of the mind-set where small setbacks were major incidents, I swept up the pieces of glass and took an old newspaper from the rack to wrap them in. It was the local free sheet from a few weeks back, I noticed. My husband obviously hadn't got round to throwing out the old newspapers.

With a sudden lurch of the heart, I read the story on the page I'd opened.

'Homeless man and dog found frozen to death.'

Beneath the headline was a picture of Bill and Buster, obviously taken during the summer months. Bill was sitting on the pavement, smiling at the camera, and Buster was standing alongside him, looking very alive and alert. I started to read.

'Homeless man, William Robert Thomson, better known as 'Bill' and his dog, Buster, were found frozen to death on Tuesday morning in grounds behind the supermarket on Grange Road. A well-known figure in the town centre, 45-year-old Thomson, had been given special permission by the supermarket to beg outside and shoppers frequently stopped to chat and pet his dog, Buster, who was believed to be 15 years old.'

I felt dizzy and cold, my breath coming in short, shallow pants. I left the paper with the broken glass on the floor and sat on a kitchen stool, hardly believing what I'd read. No. It was impossible. Surely, they would have gone to a hostel?

I remembered Bill's words, "It's difficult to find a place with a dog. There's only a couple of hostels that take dogs and they fill up quickly."

While I'd been fighting for my life in hospital, Bill and Buster had been fighting for survival out on the streets. I'd come through. But they hadn't. What a cruel twist of fate.

I looked at the date on the paper. It was three weeks old. That meant they'd barely survived the first night of the big freeze. Years of malnutrition, ill health and abuse had taken their toll. They'd had no chance against the severity of the weather.

"You all right?" asked my husband, coming into the kitchen. "What's happened?"

"Oh, nothing. I broke a glass. Just had a bit of a shock. You know that homeless man and his dog I used to see outside the supermarket, the one I took the blanket and the dog coat for? Well, they were found dead three weeks ago."

My husband picked up the paper and looked at the picture.

"He can't be dead. They've got this wrong."

"What d'you mean?"

"That's the guy who came to do the dog-walking. He came every afternoon. He didn't have a dog with him. He was alone. But it's definitely him. He said his name was Bob, not Bill."

I stared at him, the blood draining from my face. "Are you sure?"

He read the article. "His second name was Robert. I suppose he could have shortened it to Bob. He said he was from GingerButtons."

"Think back. Did he actually say he was from GingerButtons? They say they never sent anybody. They were too short staffed."

"I don't know. Maybe he didn't. Maybe I assumed that's where he was from. I can't remember, sorry. I had bigger things on my mind. Like whether you were going to pull through or not."

He placed the paper on the kitchen table. "Anyway, it's immaterial. Going by the date on the newspaper, this guy was long dead by the time the dog-walker came to our door."

We never did get to the bottom of it. Whatever the identity of the phantom dog walker, he obviously had an affinity for dogs, as Brodie clearly loved him.

Was there a rational explanation? Or was it Bill, repaying a kindness from beyond the grave? I'd like to think so.

And I'd certainly like to think that Bill and Buster are in a better place now.

*A couple create a 'haunted hotel'
in an effort to boost business…*

Cats' Home

Midge Morgan spread the local newspaper out on the breakfast table and started to read as he ate his bacon and eggs.

"No! I don't believe it."

"What?" asked his wife, Hattie, sitting opposite at the breakfast table.

She looked up from the gossip magazine she was reading, cigarette between fingers with long, red, manicured nails, peroxide blonde hair curling around her bony, over made-up face.

It was Saturday morning and they were having a leisurely start to the day.

"That hotel they want to build at the end of the road's got planning permission."

"No!"

"A big fat yes."

"What about the objections?"

"Thrown aside."

He read from the article, "'Permission granted to convert an existing, red-brick, three-storey Victorian mansion into a luxury 20-bedroom hotel'."

He looked up. "That's us done for. Who'll want to come here when that's down the road?"

His wife stared at him, taking in the implication of his words.

They'd lived in Lilac Avenue for a year. It was a middle-class street, typical of the area, wide and tree-lined, with picturesque detached Victorian houses set in large gardens on either side of the road. Theirs was one of the smaller establishments, a compact redbrick, with a balustrade veranda wrapped around its ground floor, and pretty wooden shutters framing the sash windows.

They'd inherited the house from Midge's Aunty Mabel, who'd died suddenly. Midge had been surprised to find he was the only beneficiary, as he'd never got on with her. She'd regarded him as an upstart and a layabout, which, in truth, he was. She'd positively hated Hattie on sight, refusing to come to their wedding, calling her a trollop and a tart.

They'd had no contact over the years and he fully expected her estate to go to the local cats' home.

The inheritance came with two conditions: firstly, that they lived in the house for a period of not less than ten years and, secondly, that they took care of Mabel's ten cats.

A Victorian house in an affluent suburb was a considerable improvement on a two-bedroom flat in an inner city tower block and they'd moved in straight away. Hattie couldn't bear cats, said she was allergic to them. Midge hated all animals.

In the first week, the unfortunate creatures went to the local cats' home. Or that was the story. Mounds of earth in a secluded patch at the bottom of the garden told a different tale, as did the bloody spade in the shed.

After a few months, Midge and Hattie decided to turn the house into a boutique hotel, offering luxury accommodation at a premium price. The location, close to a major exhibition centre and events venue, would guarantee a steady supply of guests.

Showing a level of enterprise he'd never before exhibited, Midge drew up a business plan and secured a bank loan to finance the renovations. Hattie supervised the interior design, transforming the house with expensive but hideous designer furnishings. Zebra and leopard-print wallpaper, ornate gold coving, faux Doric columns and colour-changing crystal chandeliers displayed her inherent lack of taste. They installed an industrial size kitchen; equipped every bedroom with state-of-the-art waterbeds and fitted magnificent en-suite bathrooms dripping with gold, Carrara marble and steel.

They had a website designed, subscribed to booking sites and tourist organisations, and placed advertisements in glossy magazines. They hired a chef, employed local girls as waitresses and chambermaids, and appointed themselves as 'front of house ambassadors'.

For the first few months, all went well. Bookings flooded in and the hotel was busy.

Then things started to spiral downwards as they failed to secure repeat bookings. Conferences and events were taking place locally, but the attendees weren't staying with them. It seemed a case of once bitten twice shy as far as guests were concerned.

The day-to-day running of the business was also proving a challenge. Managing a hotel, even a small one, was more difficult than Midge and Hattie had realised. There was constant maintenance required on the house, they couldn't hold on to staff and the hours were arduous and long.

"I just want some time off," complained Hattie, after another chambermaid walked out and she'd spent the day making beds and cleaning rooms. "I wasn't made for this kind of work."

She angrily pulled off a broken nail and threw it in the bin. "I wish we'd never inherited this horrible house."

They made the decision to close the restaurant for evening meals and downgraded their status to 'luxury bed and breakfast'. That made life easier, but they still found it hard to attract customers.

"Why don't people come back?" asked Midge. "Business people visit the area on a regular basis, yet when I offer them a long-term discount, they're not interested."

They considered lowering the prices, but they had a considerable loan to pay back and needed to recoup their investment.

They looked at Trip Advisor to find some answers. It seemed people weren't impressed by Hattie's décor.

'Lacking in atmosphere. Bereft of taste….'

'Sumptuous décor, if you like that sort of thing. I don't…'

'Yuk. Tacky doesn't do it justice.'

'It is what it is. We won't be back…'

Now, with a new luxury hotel about to open up the road, things weren't looking good.

"We need to do something to make our place stand out," said Hattie, "something that makes it different, makes people want to come and stay. But what?"

"I've got an idea," said Midge, reading another article in the paper. "Listen to this, Hat."

He read from the paper, "'Haunting Increases Visitor Numbers at Local Restaurant… Ever since staff at The Vinery reported seeing a grey lady, who mysteriously fades and disappears at one of the tables in the restaurant, business has boomed. Customers have reported feeling a strange presence sitting beside them, while experiencing an unexplained cold spot'."

He looked up excitedly. "It's called 'paranormal tourism' and it's really popular. People love ghosts. Why don't we create our own haunting?"

Hattie smiled and stubbed out her cigarette.

"I like it. Let's become a haunted venue. If we can get paranormal groups in to investigate, we'll be mentioned on paranormal websites and people will want to come and stay. The press will love it."

They spent the next few days googling 'haunted hotels' and found a rich source of information. They read reports of strange sounds, bumps in the night and objects moving unaided. They found stories about unexplained atmospheric changes, footsteps in empty rooms and a haunted chamber where an old-fashioned woman wrung her hands in sorrow. They read about a ghostly baby crying at night, a lady in a white gown drifting down a corridor and one hotel where a Walter Scott novel fell to the floor every night, opening at the same page each time, where there was a reference to the place being cursed.

After that, their imagination went into overdrive. They made up a story about a young maid who'd lived in the house during the 1870s. She'd been pushed down the stairs at the top of the house by a jealous lover, managing to crawl back up to the servants' quarters before dying in an upper room.

They created cold spots in the said room by programming the radiator to go off at certain times; Midge punched himself in the nose to make it bleed, creating a 'blood stain' at the bottom of the upper stairs; and they made a recording of footsteps walking across the room and strange knocking sounds, hiding the recording device behind the wooden panelling and turning it on via a remote control in Midge's pocket.

They came up with stories of objects moving by themselves in the breakfast room, of voices heard in the kitchen when it was empty and beds shaking mysteriously at night.

"We don't want to overdo it," said Midge, "just make it believable enough to be possibly true."

Then it was simply a case of feeding the story to the press. They invited journalists from local newspapers and radio stations to visit, telling them their story and even providing a photograph, created by Midge using Photoshop, of Hattie sitting in the upper room, with the faint outline of a white lady behind her.

"I'd no idea she was there," Hattie told the journalists. "I thought I was alone. It was quite a shock to see her in the photo."

Midge had even included a few 'orbs' for good measure.

"I have it on good authority from a local medium that these faint white orbs in the photo reveal the presence of spirits in the room," Hattie told the journalists.

They showed the journalists the 'blood stain' at the bottom of the upper stairs, before taking them into the 'haunted room', where the heating had been off all day to make it feel cold and the lights turned low to give it a creepy feel.

"Here's a picture of the lady in question," said Midge, showing them an old sepia print of a woman in a maid's uniform he'd picked up at an antiques sale. "We found it hidden in the eaves when we renovated the place."

The journalists commented on the cold spots and the ghostly atmosphere, joking that they wouldn't like to spend the night there. As they left the room, Midge turned on the recording device and they heard footsteps walking across the wooden floor and a strange knocking coming from behind the wooden panelling.

It was a compelling performance and it had the journalists fooled. They reported it as a genuine haunting and challenged paranormal investigators and mediums to stay at the hotel.

Groups of paranormal investigators arrived with their thermal cameras, night vision lights, full spectrum recorders, motion detectors, EMF Meters and all manner of electronic wizardry.

One group declared it a real haunting and had evidence to prove it, another was unconvinced and couldn't find anything, while yet another found evidence of hauntings in other rooms of the house.

A local medium visited the house and said she detected an angry female presence in the drawing room, accompanied by a ghostly cat.

"It's Aunt Mabel come back to haunt me," laughed Midge. "The more the merrier. You can't have too many ghosts in a haunted house."

The real breakthrough came when a local TV reporter did a piece to camera. She was very nervous, which added to the atmosphere, concluding there were definitely unexplained phenomena in the hotel.

That led to a visit from Horrible Hauntings, the paranormal investigative TV series, who filmed an overnight stay in the house. Midge and Hattie didn't have to do anything. The Horrible Hauntings team were so keen for the story to be real, they provided their own special effects. The result was a spooky, compelling TV show, with scenes filmed in infra-red, adding to the scary atmosphere, and a dramatic re-enactment of the servant girl arguing with her lover, falling down the stairs and crawling back to the upper room to her death bed.

After the programme was aired, the hotel was well and truly on the paranormal tourism map. The phone rang continuously. It seemed people were desperate to stay and find proof of the afterlife.

Midge and Hattie obliged with gusto. They made recordings of hideous screams and a woman crying, which they played in the early hours, and Hattie would occasionally appear with horrible scratches on her arms, made by her own fearsome talons, but attributed to the venom of a resident demon.

They played the Horrible Hauntings programme on constant loop in the reception area and hung framed photos of ghostly apparitions, produced by Midge on Photoshop, throughout the hotel.

Their plan worked beautifully. Within six months, they'd made so much money, they were able to pay off their bank loan. They employed a top chef and reopened the restaurant, they hired a manager, who took care of the staff.

It was true that some members of staff were too scared to work in the hotel and left within days, but others relished its notoriety. They were encouraged to report further sightings and evidence of hauntings to the local press, whether true or not.

Midge and Hattie were able to put up their feet and take off as much time as they wanted. They bought a villa in Spain, where they spent weeks at a time.

"Who'd have thought it?" declared Midge, lying on a sunbed in the Spanish heat. He shifted his rapidly expanding girth with difficulty and swigged from his bottle of beer. "People are idiots. They'll believe anything. Ghosts, honestly! What a load of old tosh."

Things started to go wrong when they returned from Spain and Midge got drunk in the local pub. His brother had come to stay and they'd gone to the pub for lunch. One beer led to another and before long, they were inebriated.

"Go on, tell me the truth," demanded his brother. "The hotel's not really haunted, is it? You made it up."

"Yeah," laughed Midge, slurring his words. "We fooled 'em all." He laughed loudly again. "We made up the story about the woman throwing herself down the stairs, got the idea from the Internet. I made the photo of the white lady using Photoshop. Those suckers bought it all. Hook, line and sinker."

He regaled his brother with further details of the deception and the two fell about laughing at the stupidity of the media, the naivety of investigators and the gullibility of the general public.

In the booth immediately behind them, a local journalist listened with interest. Earlier on, she'd interviewed a man who'd written a book about combustion engines. He was an opinionated bore and she'd rapidly lost interest, sighing with relief when the interview ended and the man left. She'd ordered herself a large glass of wine and sat back, rubbing her temples, trying to relax.

Hearing Midge, her ears pricked up and she began to record him on her phone. Forget the combustion engine story, this was much bigger. She had proof of a major deception.

The story appeared that weekend in the local paper and was immediately picked up by regional TV. Midge turned on his television to see his hotel on screen accompanied by a recording of his own voice, declaring the haunting to be a hoax.

Next day, the daily tabloids featured it, attacking Midge and Hattie for playing on people's superstitions and making money dishonestly. After that, the national news ran the story, playing a clip from Horrible Hauntings, followed by Midge's drunken admission and a reporter speaking to camera at the front of the hotel.

The phone rang and a guest cancelled. Then another. And another. Over the next few days, all future bookings were cancelled. Midge and Hattie's boom time was over. Rubbing salt into the wound, the new hotel down the road was doing extremely well.

"Perhaps it's time for us to shut up shop," declared Midge, standing in reception and looking around.

The hotel seemed quiet and empty after being so full of guests.

"I think we should sell up."

"What about the terms of the will?" asked Hattie. "We're supposed to stay here for ten years."

"Forget that. Who's gonna know? We've made enough cash. Time to retire to Spain."

Hattie took a drag on her cigarette, exhaling a large plume of smoke into the air.

"Whatever. I've never liked it here. Too much like hard work."

That night, Midge was awoken by a sound from the top of the house. It was a loud knocking, as if someone was hammering on a door. Leaving Hattie sleeping, he went to investigate, mumbling grumpily to himself.

"Probably a window left open. Wait till I see the chambermaids tomorrow."

He climbed the stairs to the upper level. The knocking continued. It seemed to be coming from the so-called 'haunted' bedroom.

He stood outside, listening. He wasn't scared. He knew only too well any ghosts in the house were his own creation. The knocking stopped as he opened the door. He flicked on the switch and looked around. The windows were shut and the door to the en suite closed. All seemed well. He frowned and stomped around the room.

"Could have been a branch knocking against the window, I suppose. I'll take a look in the morning."

He left the room and closed the door behind him, turning to go back down the stairs. He didn't see an object on the top step until it was too late. It was black and furry and mewed loudly as he stepped on it. Midge pitched forward, arms splayed out to break his fall, fingers clutching the air.

Down he tumbled, unable to stop until he reached the bottom, where he lay in a crumpled heap, a pool of blood gathering on the floor.

Some time later, he looked up, shaking his head to clear his vision. That had been a close call. Since when had there been a cat in the house? Not since he and Hattie had moved in. He'd made sure of that.

A movement down the corridor caught his eye and he struggled to focus, gasping in surprise at the figure that materialised before him. It was Aunty Mabel, faint and insubstantial, surrounded by a number of shadowy cats, weaving around her ankles.

She smiled at him, her teeth black and her face disfigured by decay.

"Hello, nephew. I was wondering when we'd meet again. All that haunting business. So unnecessary when you had the real thing all along."

For the first time in his life, Midge felt real fear, and a scream left his lips.

Later that night, Hattie awoke and, seeing an empty space next to her in bed, went looking for Midge.

She found him, looking like a broken marionette at the foot of the upper stairs. It seemed he'd lost his footing and fallen, breaking his neck in the process. Strangely, the pool of blood around his head covered the exact spot where they'd created the fake bloodstain.

Gently, she nudged his side with her toe to make sure he was dead, then shuddered involuntarily as something touched her leg. If she didn't know better, she'd have sworn a cat had just brushed past her.

She took out a packet of cigarettes and lit up, considering her options. Inhaling deeply on her cigarette, she reached for her mobile and dialled 999.

"My husband's dead, looks like he's broken his neck. Can you send an ambulance?"

She imagined life as a rich widow. She could sell up, find a younger man, live the dream. No doubt about it, Midge was old, fat and boring. Now, events had played into her hands.

She looked down at her dead husband and smiled broadly.

"It was good while it lasted, Midge, but it's time to move on."

She was about to go downstairs to wait for the ambulance when she heard a knocking sound. It seemed to be coming from the room at the top of the stairs.

"Idiot, he must have left that recording device on," she muttered, climbing up and going into the room to investigate.

All was silent. The window was shut and the en suite bathroom empty.

Now she heard a sound outside the room, a scrabbling kind of noise, like an animal would make. She left the room and peered across the landing, straining to see in the dim light.

Moving cautiously to the top of the stairs, she looked down at Midge's prostrate body, gasping in horror at the dark, moving shadows that swarmed all over him. They mewed as they pawed, flexing claws in and out.

One large black shadow with enormous yellow eyes glanced up and with one swift, fluid movement, bounded up the stairs towards her.

"Get away," she screamed, kicking out at the ghostly figure.

Just like her husband, she lost her balance and pitched forward, fingers grasping the air, tumbling down and landing by his side, crumpled and broken.

When the ambulance arrived, they found husband and wife, lying side by side in a grotesque embrace. Both were quite dead.

Six months later and the hotel had a new identity.

A codicil in Aunt Mabel's will decreed that should Midge and Hattie die intestate, the local cats' home would inherit. The trustees immediately submitted plans to make it their new headquarters.

Now, cats of every shape and form filled the house. Some were in pens awaiting adoption. Others roamed free.

There were gingers, tabbies, pure white and tortoiseshell, black cats, grey cats, short coated and long, moggies and pedigree, old and young, all claiming the house as their own.

Aunty Mabel drifted into the reception area, holding her favourite Persian cat asleep in her arms. There she found her fat nephew and his unattractive wife, their heads at odd angles, walking towards the front door, kicking at the cats weaving around their legs.

"Get away," shouted Midge, as a cat leapt onto his shoulder.

"Leave me alone," shrieked Hattie, as another tried to climb her leg. "We're leaving."

Aunty Mabel smiled, revealing a row of blackened, stumpy teeth.

"I don't think so. Don't you understand? You can check out any time you like, but you can never leave."

She drifted up the stairs, leaving Midge and Hattie surrounded by caterwauling cats.

Turning back to them, she called over her shoulder, "You had your chance, nephew. Now it's payback time. Welcome to my world."

Midge and Hattie put their hands over their ears, but nothing could dim the sounds of the cats.

Magic to Tragic

From magic to tragic
An easy transposition
He thought he could do it
A simple supposition.

Sleight of hand was his forte
Making coins disappear
Then bringing them back
From your mouth or your ear.

The card that you signed
And placed in the pack
Would appear in a bottle
Oh, he'd got the knack.

How they wondered and marvelled
And watched him with awe
With eyes like saucers
And wide-open jaw.

He took to the stage
Pulling rabbit from hat
Making doves reappear
How does he do that?

He became more adventurous
That's when it went wrong
Over-reached himself
It didn't take long.

Throwing knives at a girl
It all went awry
A slip of the hand
And she lost her eye.

Sawing a woman in half
Took a turn for the worse
It's as if he invoked
A terrible curse.

She cried and she screamed
As blood flowed galore
Making the stage
A theatre of gore.

From magic to tragic
His fall was complete
He hung up his wand
Admitted defeat.

Reviled by the public
Career down the pan
He retired to the coast
A sad, broken man.

The moral is simple
Only do what you're able
If you saw someone in half
Always use a trick table.

*Midsummer night is a time of magic, when fairy folk
seek to entice mortals into their world…*

A Midsummer Night's Madness

23rd June 1968

Maya Jefferson stood in front of the mirror and looked at her reflection. She was dressed in a flowing white wedding gown, its silk folds clinging to her body, a mock gardenia garland adorning her long golden hair.

Her sister, Saska, stood by her side.

"You look perfect. I'm so envious. I wish it was me."

"Your turn will come," laughed Maya, a combination of apprehension and excitement making her voice higher than normal.

Just one more night, then it was her eighteenth birthday and her wedding day, a double celebration. What better coming-of-age present than marriage to her childhood sweetheart? Tomorrow would be their two-year anniversary. Sam Winterborne had first asked her out on her sixteenth birthday and they'd been inseparable ever since.

"D'you think I'll meet someone like Sam?" asked Saska wistfully. "He's so lovely. And he adores you. I can't imagine anyone feeling that way about me."

"It's all about timing," laughed Maya. "Finding the right person at the right time. It hasn't happened yet. You're only fifteen."

"But what if it doesn't happen until I'm old?" What if it doesn't happen at all? I don't want to be left on the shelf."

"That's something you'll never be," said Maya. "You're far too pretty. Another year and the boys will be queuing up to ask you out."

People were always commenting how alike they looked. Saska had her sister's same slender, willowy figure, the same long golden hair that fell in soft curls around her face and the same bell-like voice, with an infectious laugh that drew people in. They turned heads wherever they went.

"Oh my God, take the dress off," shrieked Saska, glancing in the mirror and seeing a sudden movement in the reflection.

"Why? What's wrong?"

"Sam's coming. He's crossing the field. He can't see you wearing the dress."

Maya ran to the window. Sure enough, there was Sam, walking across the field that ran behind their cottage. Seeing a figure at the window, he looked up and waved. Maya jumped back. But it was too late.

"Oh no! He saw me. D'you think that means bad luck?"

"No, said Saska, decisively. "What could go wrong? The church is booked, the wedding feast's arranged and the vicar's given his blessing. Best of all, Sam's besotted with you. We'll probably be going to the christening this time next year."

"Not if I can help it," laughed Maya, unzipping her dress and letting it drop over her hips onto the floor. "I want to live. See the world."

"Does Sam know?" asked Saska, hanging up the wedding dress while her sister slipped into skinny blue jeans and T-shirt.

"Oh yes. Sam and I have plans. We don't intend to stick around."

"You don't?" Her sister sounded shocked. "I thought it was all settled. You're moving into that little cottage on the High Street. It's so pretty with those pink roses growing up the front. I know it needs work, but it's nothing Sam can't handle."

Maya wrinkled her nose.

"I'll be eighteen tomorrow, Saska. I'm not ready to live in a tiny rented cottage, down the road from mum and dad. I don't want get a job in the village shop and go home every night to find Sam doing DIY. There's time enough for that later." She dropped her voice. "Don't tell anyone. We're leaving."

"Leaving? Going where? And when?" A look of anxiety crossed Saska's pretty features. "You can't."

"Tomorrow night. It's all sorted. Sam's got a friend in London. We'll stay with him for a few weeks. After that, we're going travelling. We'll be eighteen and married. No one can stop us. We want to see the world while we're still young."

"What about me?" asked Saska. "You can't leave me behind."

"You can visit. When we're settled in our apartment in Paris, I'll send for you. You can stay with us."

"Promise?"

"I promise. And you must promise not to tell anyone about our plans. Deal?"

"Okay. Deal."

They went downstairs to find Sam sitting at the old pine kitchen table, a steaming mug of tea in front of him.

"Hi, sweetheart," he said, standing up and giving Maya a peck on the cheek. "How are you? All set for tomorrow?"

"Absolutely," she beamed, pulling a kitchen chair alongside him. "Can't wait. I hope you didn't see my dress when I was at the window. We don't want any bad luck."

"Just a glimpse," he admitted. "Don't worry. It's just an old wives' tale.

Saska sat opposite, taking secret looks at Sam. In her eyes, he was perfect, with wild, unruly dark hair, soulful brown eyes and a mouth that was made for kissing. He wore an old white linen shirt, creased and frayed, rolled-up sleeves revealing muscular sunburnt arms, the result of long hours working in the fields.

"How's my favourite maid of honour?" he asked, catching her staring. "Ready for the big day?" He winked at her.

"Yes, I'm ready," she said, feeling the colour go to her cheeks and wondering whether to tell him she knew about their plans. She was spared making the decision by the entrance of her grandmother.

"Is there a cup of tea going?" asked the old lady, letting herself in through the kitchen door and sitting at the table.

"Hello, Mrs Jefferson. Everything okay with you?" asked Sam.

"All the better for seeing you, Sam," she laughed. Sitting down alongside him, she placed a wrinkled old hand over his. "You take care of my Maya, won't you? She's very precious."

"Of course he will, Gran," said Maya, embarrassed. "You don't have to ask."

"Oh, don't mind me, darling," answered her Gran. "I'm just envious. Takes me back to my wedding day. Best day of my life. Your Granddad and I were happy for nearly sixty years." She glanced at Sam. "You remind me of Stan. He used to work on the farm. We had so many happy times, especially at harvest time."

She looked into the distance, remembering the past. "The whole village would come out to help. The harvest supper was magical. Singing and dancing till the early hours. It was a harvest supper night when Maya and Saska's father was conceived."

"Too much information, Gran," said Saska, putting her hands over her ears.

Sam grinned. "Guess your family's been in this village for a long time, Mrs J?"

"At least five generations. This cottage has been in the family for over a hundred years. It's where I grew up, before Stan and I moved down the road. But enough of that. Is everything ready for tomorrow?"

"Yes, it's all sorted. Mum and her friends have done a fabulous job decorating the village hall," said Maya.

"And dad's hired an old fashioned Rolls Royce to drive her the huge distance to church," said Saska. "All one hundred and fifty yards."

"You can't blame him for wanting to give her the best," said Mrs Jefferson, sipping her tea. "Even if the car's more for him than Maya."

They all laughed, a sense of excitement building. The evening sun shone through the kitchen window, bathing the room in golden light, and the sweet smell of freshly cut grass wafted in through the open door.

"It's a glorious evening," said Mrs Jefferson, breathing in the aromatic air. "Midsummer night, longest of the year. There's nothing better than walking through the meadows in moonlight."

"Even better than harvest supper?" asked Saska, grinning.

"Midsummer night has its own magic," said the old lady, mysteriously. "They say the veil between the mortal and fairy world is lifted."

"Oh yes," said Sam, laughing. "Which fairy story have you been reading?"

"You may mock," said Mrs Jefferson, raising an eyebrow, "but we country folk have grown up with the old ways. Midsummer night is a time for magic. The fairy folk are out in force, looking to entice any unwitting young person into their world."

"What d'you mean?" asked Saska, nervously.

"Rumour has it," said the old lady, lowering her voice and leaning forward, "if you find a fairy ring on midsummer night, it's a door into their world. Whatever you do, don't step inside."

"Or what?" asked Maya.

"You'll be enchanted by their magic. If the fairy king takes a fancy to you, he'll make you queen for the night. They say once you've loved the fairy king, no mortal man will measure up."

"Better stay away from the fairy king, Maya," joked Sam. "Don't want you measuring me up against him."

"And there's a terrible price to pay," continued Mrs Jefferson.

"What's that?" asked Maya, fascinated.

"Time moves differently in the fairy realm," replied her grandmother. "Spend a night with the fairies and they'll take away your youth."

"It's all make believe, isn't it, Gran?" asked Saska nervously.

"Of course, dear," she answered, patting her youngest granddaughter's hand. "Just stay away from fairy rings, that's all."

An hour later, Sam was walking home towards the house he shared with his mother and brothers. Maya had accompanied him across the field and they'd shared a long, lingering kiss in the balmy night before she'd returned home. Now, he took the pathway that led alongside the dark wood and across the meadow. He couldn't have been happier. The following day he was to marry the love of his life. He thought of her slender body and long golden hair, her welcoming smile and easy manner. What a future stretched before them. In another day, they'd be in London, looking forward to a new life together, exploring the world, creating their own magic.

He was so lost in thought, he nearly kicked over a line of mushrooms growing in the middle of the meadow. He stopped just in time, amazed at their size. As he bent to pick one, he realised it wasn't so much a row as a circle of white-topped mushrooms and long white stalks.

"A fairy circle," he murmured. "Well I never. Better make sure I don't step inside. I don't want the fairy king taking a fancy to me."

He walked around the circle, laughing at his superstition, but feeling a flash of apprehension. Strange he hadn't noticed it earlier, on his way to Maya's house.

He was soon at home, falling into bed and enjoying a deep, dreamless sleep, peaceful and happy at the prospect of his forthcoming nuptials.

Eleven o'clock at night and Maya tossed and turned in bed, unable to sleep. It was a warm night and the bed sheets were stifling and heavy. However hard she tried, she was unable to still her mind, thoughts of the coming day rushing through her head like an express train.

Kicking off the bedclothes, she got up and walked to the window, opening it wide, revelling in the cool air that entered the room. She looked out over the fields, lit by the full moon, thinking how she loved this place, but how she needed to leave. She had to spread her wings. So did Sam. They'd been here too long and everything was too familiar, too predictable. It would be a wrench, but together they would forge a new future, have new experiences far away.

She breathed in the sweet night air, letting it calm her thoughts, but feeling even less like sleeping. Hardly realising what she was doing, she pulled a wrap around her shoulders, slipped on a pair of sandals and opened the bedroom door. Her parents were sleeping in the room next door. She could hear her father's gentle snore. Just across the landing was Saska's room, the door closed.

Quickly, Maya went down the stairs, treading carefully to avoid the creaking floorboards, and into the kitchen. The old Aga made the room feel unnaturally hot and she opened the back door, stepping out into the garden.

Now she was outside, the air smelled unbelievably sweet and aromatic, night-scented stock and honeysuckle emitting a heavenly fragrance. She walked down the garden path and through the gate, into the field beyond. The long grass was wet, cooling her legs and feet, and the moon was high in the sky, illuminating the way ahead. It was a perfect midsummer night, calm, clear and warm.

In no time, she'd followed the path across the field, round the edge of the dark wood and into the meadow. Gran had been right. There was magic in the air. She could feel it in every nerve of her body. There was a tingling vibrancy in the rustling trees and a sense of expectation in the moonlit meadow.

She stopped. In front of her was the fairy circle that Sam had found earlier, the white tops of the mushrooms gleaming in the moonlight. As she looked, the ring appeared to shine brighter, contrasting with the dark grass beneath. Her grandmother's words sounded in her head, but curiosity got the better of her.

"Just an old wives' tale," she said softly to herself. "What can possibly happen?"

She kicked off her sandals and placed a foot in the circle. Nothing. She looked around. Everything was exactly the same. With a laugh, she placed her other foot in the circle, then stared in amazement as the woodland scene around her began to change.

It was as if she'd stepped into a kaleidoscope and she gasped with delight at the scene that met her eyes. The dark night sky faded away, no more than a backdrop to a myriad of colours flashing around her, shining and sparkling. As her eyes grew accustomed to the strange moving colours, she began to make out shapes and realised each was a tiny creature, no bigger than a butterfly.

"Fairies," she gasped, as they flew around, hovering by her face to get a closer look, their delicate wings shimmering with incandescent light.

She held out her hand and one of the tiny creatures landed on her palm, looking up at her curiously, a perfect person, no bigger than her finger, with big eyes and huge wings. Others followed and soon she was holding half a dozen of the creatures on her outstretched palms.

Looking around, she saw the dark wood behind her had transformed into a vivid green glade, vibrant and lush, illuminated with silver light from the enormous moon. Animals ran here and there: snuffling rabbits with white bobtails, timid deer with black glittering eyes, a vixen with her cubs, a badger with black and white striped head. Beautiful blue birds flew among the trees, darting around the moonbeams that shone through the foliage. Delicate butterflies and shimmering dragonflies hovered over brightly coloured flowers and a sweet singing filled the air.

"It's beautiful," gasped Maya. "This must be a dream. I never realised there could be so many beautiful colours or creatures."

No sooner had she spoken than she saw a figure emerging from the woods, walking towards her. It was a man with long blond hair, dressed in flowing cloak with an open green tunic, revealing a tanned body beneath. Maya watched breathlessly as he approached, mesmerised by his beauty. He was tall and slender, with even features and cornflower blue eyes. Small fairies flew around him, spinning and glittering in the moonlight, sprinkling fairy dust as they twisted and turned. On his head was a golden crown.

"Now I'm definitely dreaming," whispered Maya. "It's the Fairy King."

Then he was stepping into the fairy ring, smiling and extending a hand towards her. Nervously, she placed her hand in his and as their fingers touched, a tingling sensation travelled down her arm and through her body, filling her with the warmth and wellbeing of a summer's day. Instantly, she felt relaxed and energised, at one with the strange world around her. She looked into his eyes and was smitten, diving into ever-changing pools of brilliant blue, immersing herself in their shining intensity.

"Come Maya," he said softly, and she was lost.

She wanted this man like never before, every nerve ending on edge, every fibre of her being yearning for his touch. Somewhere deep in her memory, she heard a distant voice saying 'Beware', but she closed her mind and it disappeared. There was only one possible outcome from this otherworldly meeting. Never had she felt such desire coursing through her veins.

"There's a glade in the woods where the velvet moss is deep and soft, and the honeysuckle forms a fragrant curtain. There shall we lie together," he said softly.

His voice was like a silver shadow skimming over her skin, electrifying and enticing, filling her with sensations she'd never before experienced. A powerful, all-consuming desire filled her. She was transfixed, helpless as a fly in a web.

Gently, he leaned forward and kissed her lips. It was the touch of an angel, soft and caressing, yet so intense it took her breath away. She pulled back and stared at him, not comprehending the feeling that rose within her.

"Don't fight it, Maya," he said softly, looking into her eyes. "Do you want me?"

"Yes," she whispered, surrendering to the magic and the moment.

"So be it," he said, leading her by the hand out of the fairy ring and across the meadow.

A glow appeared in the lush green foliage and a magical pathway appeared before them, shimmering and silver, guiding them forward. Silently, he led her into the wood, fairy dust glittering, tiny fairies placing sweet-smelling flowers in her hair.

A curtain of honeysuckle hung before them, and he parted it, guiding her in.

"Lie down," he commanded, indicating the lush green bed of moss.

Silently she obeyed, lying before him, feeling the wrap fall from her shoulders.

"You are beautiful, Maya," he said, leaning over her and gently running his fingers over her skin, "and you are mine."

His touch was soft but she felt a bolt of electricity shooting through her and gasped in pleasure. Her skin felt alive, responding to his touch in an unimaginable way. Slowly, he leaned over her, kissing her gently. Then he was alongside her, over her, engulfing her in a blur of passion and desire, creating sensations she had never known. It was exquisite and primal, an ancient dance from days gone past, and she lost all sense of self and identity, giving herself to his potent magic. Past, present and future ceased to exist, all leading to this one point, this magical union. She was captivated, entranced and ensnared, lost in the moment, belonging to him now and forever.

* * *

The early morning sun was bright and unyielding, and she awoke with a start, blinking against its intensity. Feeling the early morning dew on her skin, she sat up abruptly, unsure where she was. Then her eyes opened wide as she remembered. She looked around for the fairy ring but it had vanished. There was nothing except the verdant green meadow grass, spiders' threads heavy with dew, daisies opening to the sun.

Memories of her midnight lover filled her mind. She could still feel his hands on her body, his fingers light as a butterfly's wing. She shook her head, trying to clear the thoughts that crowded in.

"A dream," she murmured, "just a dream. And now I have a wedding to prepare for, with a real-life, flesh and blood man, who can give me far more than a fairy king ever could."

Smiling at the whimsical thought and gathering her wrap about her shoulders, she looked around for her sandals. They were gone. She frowned. She definitely remembered taking them off as she'd stepped into the fairy ring. There again, if the fairy ring was nothing more than a figment of her imagination, perhaps her sandals were too.

She glanced at the sun. It was still early.

"Hopefully, I can slip back and no will know," she said to herself, standing up and stretching. "I don't want anyone to know I slept out here."

After a night in the meadow, she felt spent. Typical. Just when she needed to be fresh and glowing, she was tired and washed-out.

"A cup of coffee will do the trick," she declared and started walking across the meadow.

It looked different somehow, but she couldn't say exactly why, attributing the sensation to tiredness. In a few minutes, she was walking alongside the dark wood, memories of a very different woodland setting, green and inviting, filling her head. Then she was walking over the field towards her parents' cottage.

"I hope nobody else is up," she said under her breath, "otherwise I'll have some explaining to do."

She approached the gate leading to the garden and stopped, a puzzled expression on her face. Strange, she didn't remember the garden gate being this colour. It had always been natural wood. And looking into the cottage garden, things were different. What had been a wildflower patch was now a vegetable bed, with triangular canes planted in rows, ready for runner beans.

She shook her head, trying to clear her thoughts but feeling befuddled and unclear. An anxiety took hold of her that she couldn't explain.

A little girl, blond and pretty, wearing a red-checked gingham dress, ran into the garden. She stopped and stared at the woman standing by the gate.

"Hello," said Maya, smiling. "Who are you? What's your name?"

"I'm Maya," answered the little girl.

"Oh, how strange. That's my name too. Where are you from?"

"I live here," said the little girl indignantly. "Who are you?"

There was a noise from inside the cottage and a young blond woman stepped into the garden.

"May-bells, breakfast. Come on. It's ready."

She stopped when she saw the figure at the gate and her voice grew tense.

"Maya, come here. What have I told you about talking to strangers?"

The little girl ran to her and stood behind her, peeping round.

"Can I help you?" asked the young blond woman.

"I don't understand," faltered the figure at the gate. "I'm Maya. I live here. Today is my wedding day. Today I'm eighteen."

Putting her hand to her mouth, the young blond woman stepped back, a look of horror passing over her face.

"Oh my God, it can't be. Mother! Mother, come quick," she called out.

"What's the matter?" asked a voice inside the cottage.

The young woman's face drained white and further words refused to come. She stared open-mouthed.

"What is it?" repeated the voice and an older woman, with long white hair, stepped into the garden. She stood rigid when she saw the figure at the gate.

"Maya, is it you?" she gasped. "After all this time?"

Maya stared, uncomprehending. The woman looked familiar, but she couldn't place her. "What d'you mean after all this time? Who are you?"

The older woman walked up the garden pathway and opened the gate. She gently took Maya by the arm.

"I'm Saska. You'd better come in."

They sat at the kitchen table and Saska poured her a cup of coffee.

"What date do you think it is, Maya?" she asked quietly.

"24th June 1968. My wedding day."

"And how old do you think you are?

"I'm eighteen today."

"It's not 1968 and you're not eighteen," said Saska slowly. "If you don't believe me, take a look in the mirror." She indicated a small ornate mirror on the wall by the dresser.

Frowning, Maya stood and walked towards it. She looked at her reflection and gasped. Instead of a young face with firm skin and long blond curls, an old woman looked back, with lines around the eyes, crows' feet and thin greying hair.

"What's happened? I don't understand?" she cried out in alarm, stepping back.

"It's 24th June 2018," said Saska, standing by her. She took her sister's hand. "You're not eighteen. You're sixty-eight. And I'm sixty-five."

"No," faltered Maya. "That can't be."

"You went missing on your wedding day in 1968," said Saska. "No one knew what happened to you. They found your sandals in the meadow by a ring of toadstools, but there was no sign of you. You simply disappeared."

Maya looked at her, eyes wide open as comprehension dawned.

"The fairy king," she said faintly. "Gran warned us." Her voice became urgent. "D'you remember the day before, Saska? We sat in the kitchen and Gran said don't step into the fairy ring."

"Vaguely," laughed Saska, nervously.

"She said if you stepped in the fairy ring, you'd enter the fairy world."

"Yes, but she was joking."

"She said that time moves differently in the fairy realm. That the fairies would take your youth."

"And did you…?"

"I did. I stepped inside and met the fairy king."

Her words hung in the air. For a moment, neither spoke.

Then Saska laughed. "It's an old wives' tale, Maya. It can't possibly be true. Where've you really been?"

Maya grabbed her sister's hand.

"What was I wearing when I went missing?" she demanded.

Saska swallowed. "Your pale blue nightgown and a white wrap."

"Just like these."

"Yes." Saska's voice was no more than a whisper.

"Where's Gran? I need to speak to her."

"I'm sorry, Maya. She's gone. She died over forty years ago. Mum and dad, too. They never got over your disappearance.

"And Sam. What happened to Sam?"

Saska looked down.

"It was difficult for him. He was the last person to see you alive. He was arrested on suspected murder. The way you'd been talking about leaving the village and going travelling, they thought you'd changed your mind about marrying him."

"But we were going together," said Maya. "We had it all planned."

Saska shrugged. "They assumed you'd told him it was over and, in a fit of anger, he'd killed you."

"But you know that wasn't true. And where was the body?" pointed out Maya.

"Exactly. They couldn't prove anything and the case was dismissed."

"So what happened to him? Where is he?"

Saska looked her sister in the eye for a moment before answering.

"When all the fuss had died down, he married me. On my seventeenth birthday."

Maya stared.

"That's not possible. He loved me."

"He never stopped loving you, Maya. But you weren't here. And I was. I was the next best thing." She paused. "He always said you'd been taken, that you'd never have left him."

The young blond woman who'd been listening to their exchange without uttering a word spoke now.

"So, this is my long lost aunt?" she asked. "This is Maya come back from the dead fifty years later?"

"Meet your niece," said Saska, glancing at her sister. "Sam and I had a daughter. This is Tia."

"And Sam? Where's Sam?"

"He died a couple of years ago. He had a massive heart attack while he was helping with the harvest. That's him there." She indicated a photograph.

Maya picked up the framed photo and there was Sam. Older, lined, with greying hair, but still Sam. Her Sam. She threw the picture on the table.

"No," she screamed. "No. Tell me this is a nightmare and I'll wake up. It was only yesterday I was kissing Sam. Only yesterday we were looking forward to our wedding day."

"No, it wasn't. It was fifty years ago."

The small blond girl started to whimper.

"Mummy, I don't like this lady. Tell her to go."

Maya looked at the child through the tears forming in her eyes.

"And this is…?"

"Maya. My granddaughter. Named after you, so we'd never forget you."

The older Maya stared at her younger namesake and spoke in a choking voice, "You lived my life, Saska. You always wanted Sam. Thanks to a moment of midsummer madness, you got what you wanted. And what about me? That one night cost my youth, my dreams and my future."

"I'm sorry. I never intended it."

Maya placed her hands on the child's shoulders and looked deep into her big blue eyes. She spoke sharply.

"Listen to me Maya. Never step in a fairy ring. D'you hear? Stay away from fairy rings or you'll end up like me. Out of place, out of time and out of options."

The little girl began to cry all over again.

"Mummy, make her go away. She's the wicked witch from the wood, isn't she?"

Never pay for a witch ball. As soon as money changes hands, the evil comes right back at ya'…

The Witch Ball

Fenella Fotheringay-Smythe had wanted a witch ball for a long time.

She'd seen a number of witch balls hanging in The Museum of Witchcraft and Magic in Boscastle, a place she'd visited with her husband, Rupert, one summer while on holiday in Cornwall. Fenella asked if they could buy one, but her request met with a resounding 'no'.

The next time they saw a witch ball was in an antique shop in Whitby. Actually, there were a number of beautiful witch balls, in various colours, hanging in the shop's window. Fenella stared in awe at the shiny green, blue, red and silver baubles, looking like large Christmas tree decorations, catching the light, glinting and winking at her temptingly.

In great excitement, she marched inside and demanded to buy one.

"They're not for sale," said the owner, a dour Yorkshire-man with a big beard.

"What d'you mean? They're in the window."

"They're in't window cos' they're protectin' the premises," he informed her, bluffly.

"I'll pay double," she persisted. "I don't want them all. Just one."

The man stared at her with a steely gaze. "They're not for sale," he repeated.

"Call yourself a shop," she said, in disgust. "You'll never make any money if you refuse to sell items in your window."

"Even if they were for sale, I wouldn't sell you one," answered the man.

"Now, see here, my good fellow…" Rupert leaped to his wife's defence. "There's no need to take that tone."

The man ignored him and continued. "You should never sell a witch ball for money. They're meant to keep evil at bay. As soon as money exchanges 'ands, the evil comes right back at ya."

"What poppycock," exclaimed Fenella. "They're antiques, like everything else in this shop. What would you do? Give them away?"

"Aye, I would," said the man. "I'd sell you another small item for the amount the witch ball's worth, and then I'd give it you for free. That way, the evil wouldn't come back at ya'. Or me." He looked at her closely. "People don't understand these things. They think a witch ball is a nice decoration. They forget its purpose."

His face moved closer to hers and, instinctively, she backed away.

"Some of 'em are filled with hair or nails or skin, to ward off or contain the evil. Some of 'em are very powerful. And you wouldn't want that power workin' agin ya."

Fenella bristled, looking at his beard distastefully and trying not inhale the man's odour of old tobacco and beer.

"Come on, Rupert," she said, in exasperation. "There's no point staying here. We're not going to get what we want."

She grabbed his arm and pulled him from the shop, the man's words ringing in her ears.

"Mark what I say. Don't underestimate the power of a witch ball."

With one last, longing look at the brightly coloured metallic balls hanging in his window, catching the sunshine, Fenella strode down the street, Rupert in her wake.

Nobody denied her what she wanted! Now, she was more determined than ever to acquire a witch ball. It would look simply delicious hanging in the upper window of their Chelsea mews. She imagined the comments it would draw from her friends. Regarded as something of an interior design guru, she would start a new trend within her circle. People would find the idea of an object that repelled evil to be fascinating. There was nothing like a bit of witchcraft or magic for gaining people's attention. It would be quite the talking point at her next dinner party.

And then, it seemed, she saw witch balls everywhere.

They visited a museum in Oxford and saw an exhibition about witchcraft. What was hanging there in a display, bright and tempting? Witch balls. She visited an ageing pensioner as part of her 'Help the Aged' work. What was hanging in the woman's front window, bright green and luscious? A witch ball. She asked the woman if she'd sell, but was met with another abject refusal.

"Ooh, no dear. It's been there for years. Keeps me safe. I'd never part with it. Not for all the tea in China."

"I'm not offering you tea. I'm offering a lot of money," pointed out Fenella, but to no avail. The woman wouldn't be parted from her witch ball.

It seemed every old cottage she walked past, whether in the city or country, had a brightly coloured witch ball hanging in the window, resplendently blue, green, red, gold or silver.

"I'd no idea they were so prevalent," she said, in exasperation, after yet another of their jaunts. "How come everyone's got one except me?"

She became obsessed.

"I must have one," she hissed at Rupert. "It's the one thing I want, the perfect finishing touch for the upper lounge. And no," she cut him off before the words were out of his mouth, "I'm not buying one from the Internet. How would I know if it's an original? I don't want a modern replica. I want a genuine, old witch ball. I simply couldn't trust to buy one online."

At which point, fate played into her hands.

She and Rupert were visiting the stunning Lydford Gorge, located near Dartmoor, an area known for its proliferation of local superstitions and supernatural sightings.

They discovered The White Lady Inn and checked in for a couple of nights. The old coaching inn lay in the shadow of a ruined castle, a place with an allegedly heinous history, reputedly haunted by the infamous Judge Jeffreys. He'd been a cruel and heartless man, who had carried out a savage retribution in the aftermath of the Monmouth rebellion of 1685. It was said he sent his prisoners to the gallows in the morning and tried them in the afternoon. The ancient castle was reputed to sigh with the suffering and desperation of events long past, ingrained in its dour stonework.

"A bit creepy," shuddered Fenella, reading from a leaflet. "But this is lovely." She gazed around their spacious room, beautifully decorated in pastel shades, pieces of art deco adding taste and colour.

"And it looks out over the old castle," said Rupert, gazing at the view from their window.

"Yes, well, we don't want to be reminded of that," said Fenella, pulling the curtains, with a sharp tug. "I'd rather not think about people being executed. It's very unpleasant."

Later that evening, they walked down the old wooden stairway into the restaurant. It was very olde worlde, with lots of dark wooden beams, old pews and low lighting. A wonderful aroma assailed their nostrils. The place had a reputation amongst foodies for the quality and originality of its dishes, and it didn't disappoint.

Fenella chose the deconstructed oyster with pickled daikon and pepper coulis. Rupert selected the Lobster Roulade with a parsley smear and petite herbs. They shared a plate of bone marrow Pommes Dauphines.

"Oh my God, I don't believe it," said Fenella, raising a glass of Chateauneuf Du Pape to her shiny, glossed lips."

"What is it?" asked Rupert.

"Look over there," she said in a whisper, gazing over his right shoulder.

He turned around. There, twinkling in the candlelight, was a large green witch ball.

"That is magnificent," she whispered. "It's huge. And I'll bet it's original, knowing the local folklore. There was plenty of witchy stuff going on around here a few hundred years ago."

She finished her food, hardly daring to take her eyes from the magnificent orb that dangled before her.

Afterwards, they took brandy in the bar and there, lo and behold, she found a further three witch balls.

"Oh my! I have never seen such beautiful specimens."

They began chatting to the barmaid, a middle-aged woman with scrubby black hair, a ruddy complexion and strong local accent.

"Have you always lived round here?" asked Rupert.

"Oh, yes. Born and bred round these parts. Never been away."

"I see. We're from London," he informed her. "Pretty well travelled. We go all over the place."

"Oh, I wouldn't wanna leave here. It's where I know, see?"

"Not a particularly cheerful place, having that castle next door," ventured Fenella. "A bit depressing, if you ask me."

"Oh, that place doesn't bother me. It's been cleansed by dowsers. The residue of evil's long gone. They did all the ley lines around here."

"Really. How fascinating," said Fenella, stifling a yawn.

"The place that's really strange is that area over there." She pointed behind her and they both turned to look.

"What, you mean the optics?" asked Rupert.

"No. I mean down the road, where Dartmoor begins. Forms a triangle. It's dark there."

"Couldn't they install street lighting?" asked Fenella.

"Not that kind of dark. I mean dark dark. Where dark forces dwell. They reckon," she leaned forward conspiratorially, "there've been more suicides in that triangle than anywhere else in the country."

"Oh dear," said Rupert. "Sounds horrible."

"It's a powerful place," she informed them. "I fell pregnant to a warlock after convening with him up by the big stones. After years of trying."

"Good for you," said Rupert, unsure how to respond. "Can you top up my glass, please?"

"All sorts has gone on round 'ere," she continued, filling his glass with Courvoisier. "Down in the Gorge, there's the White Lady Waterfall and the Devil's Cauldron. And up on Dartmoor there's hauntings and highwaymen… beasties and battle sounds…will o' the wisps and witchcraft."

This was a topic with which Fenella felt much more comfortable.

"Ah yes. That's why there are so many witch balls here."

"You've noticed, then." The barmaid eyed her suspiciously. "You a witch? There's still a coven meets up."

"Oh, no. I don't go in for that sort of thing. Not in Chelsea. But I would rather like to acquire a witch ball." She looked hopefully at the barmaid.

The woman shrugged her shoulders. "Not up to me, is it? They don't belong to me."

"Who would I speak to, then?"

"The owners, I guess. You wanna be careful meddling with things like that, though. They're not ornaments, you know?"

"Oh yes, I know all about that. Some old grizzly in Yorkshire warned me off his balls. Where are the owners? Are they around?"

"No, they don't live here. They're city folk. Bought it as an investment. Did it up then buggered off. We don't see much of 'em."

"I see. So, how do I get in touch with them?"

"Leave it with me. I'll let you know."

It was frustrating, but as good as she was going to get. Fenella had no option but to wait and see if the barmaid was as good as her word. She didn't feel too hopeful. The woman was clearly not the full shilling.

The next morning at breakfast, the barmaid sought her out.

"I've 'ad a word with the owner. She says you can 'ave a witch ball if you want. The cost is five hundred quid. Cash."

"Really? You mean I can buy one?"

The woman shrugged disinterestedly. "S'what she said. Pick the one you want. Leave the money on reception."

"Oh my." Fenella was overcome, not quite believing she'd reached the end of her quest after searching for so long. To find one now, and for it to fall into her lap so easily, seemed almost beyond belief.

She turned to the barmaid. "I want that big green one there." She pointed to the magnificent green witch ball hanging in the restaurant. "I'll get the money today. In fact, I'll get it now. Where's the closest cashpoint?"

The barmaid eyed her disagreeably. "S'not for me to say anything, but it's not right."

"What do you mean?" asked Fenella, distastefully.

"This pub, see, 'as been 'ere for 'undreds of years and, over time, a lot of old things 'ave been accumulated.

It's not right for some city folk to march in 'ere and start selling 'em off. They belong 'ere. This is where they should stay."

"Yes, well, that's your opinion," said Fenella. "If the owner is happy to sell, then I'm happy to buy. It's got nothing to do with you."

"Maybe not, but someone 'as to look after the interests of the place. You can't let the crows in to start pecking off the flesh. It ain't right."

"Look here," said Rupert, stepping into the affray. "You're the hired hand. You should know your place."

"Oh, I know my place all right." The woman raised her large bushy eyebrows. "And I say, you shouldn't take what don't belong to you."

"Absolute poppycock," said Fenella, wiping her mouth with her linen napkin and rising from the table. "Come on, Rupert, let's go and find a cashpoint."

She pushed past the barmaid, Rupert following. As they reached the doorway, the woman called after them.

"You should never buy a witch ball. Soon as the money leaves your 'and, the evil comes right back at ya. That ball's been collecting evil for a long time. Best not disturb what you don't understand."

With a flick of her hand, Fenella dismissed the woman.

"Honestly, these local people, who do they think they are? If everything was left in situ, we'd never discover anything. What about the Egyptian pieces in the British Museum? Or the Elgin Marbles?"

"To be fair, the chap in Whitby said the same," pointed out Rupert.

"Another local idiot!" said Fenella, decisively.

Within a couple of hours, they had found a cashpoint, withdrawn five hundred pounds and deposited the money at reception. Fenella ceremoniously led the way in to the restaurant and supervised the taking down of the witch ball.

Now, it sat, packed with newspaper, in a large cardboard box on the back seat of Rupert's Range Rover.

Things started to go wrong almost immediately.

Rupert, not realising how much rainfall had fallen recently, got the car stuck while attempting to drive through a ford.

"It's a bloody off-road vehicle," complained Fenella, about to open the door, as Rupert tried to turn over the engine. "It should have taken this in its stride."

"Don't open the door," shouted Rupert. "You'll let the water in."

They sat, stranded, in the middle of the ford, waiting for over an hour for the rescue vehicle to come. Eventually, they were towed out and, miraculously, once on the other side, the engine started at once.

They carried on their journey, but not for long. The engine began to make a strange rattling noise and a number of lights appeared on the dashboard.

"What the devil's going on?" asked Rupert, frowning. "It's a bloody new car. Only had it a few weeks."

A smell of burning and the appearance of small flames from beneath the bonnet gave him no choice.

"Time to bail out," he announced. "I don't fancy being fried alive in here."

"Get the witch ball," shrieked Fenella, opening her door in panic, thick acrid smoke already filling the cabin.

They stood by the roadside and watched while flames devoured Rupert's beautiful new Range Rover. By the time the fire engine arrived, it was too late. The car had been consumed.

They returned to London by taxi. Back at home, Fenella lost no time in hanging the witch ball in the first floor lounge of their Chelsea mews. She placed it in the front window, where it hung, majestic and bright, its metallic green surface reflecting the lounge behind it.

"Perfect," exclaimed Fenella, the drama of the burning Range Rover forgotten. She had achieved what she set out to do, as she always did. People didn't say 'no' to her. And if they did, it simply raised the bar and she rose to the challenge.

The next morning, at the breakfast table, Rupert received a shock.

"I don't believe it," he gasped, looking up from his tablet. "That property company I invested in, the one that was guaranteed to make a killing… It's gone bust. Overstretched itself. A glut of properties it couldn't sell."

"Is it a big hit?" asked Fenella.

"As big as they come. That was meant to provide our pension." His face was white as he took in the implications of the disastrous news. And it didn't stop there.

Two days later, he received a call from his Financial Adviser. The new build project in Cape Verde, in which he had a considerable investment, had fallen apart.

"Apparently, there is no project," he told Fenella. "Never was. We've all been taken in."

Fenella glanced at the witch ball, hanging magnificently in the lounge window. She had a dinner party planned that weekend and couldn't wait to show her friends the new acquisition.

"Don't worry, Rupie," she said. "Daddy will never see us starve. Just be more careful with future investments. Now, leave me alone while I plan the dinner party."

The dinner party was a great success. She brought in caterers and put on a lavish spread.

After dinner, the guests retired to the lounge, where they were treated to their first view of the witch ball. Their effusive comments were all she had dreamed of and more.

"Wow, how splendid."

"I love it. So original."

"Oh, Fenella, you were always ahead of the crowd. Where can I get one?"

"It's magical. I so want one for my country house."

Fenella sat back, luxuriating in the adulation. She'd known her set would love it.

Unfortunately, the evening was spoiled by a conflagration in the kitchen. No one knew exactly how it started. A tea towel too close to the gas ring? It seemed improbable, given that she'd had the food delivered by caterers. But there was no other probable explanation. The fire brigade was called and, as with the Range Rover, dowsed the flames with foam.

Next morning, she surveyed the blackened, smoke-damaged scene.

"No problem," she said to Rupert. "The insurance will cover it. I was tired of it anyway."

She set about placing an insurance claim and organising a new kitchen. She didn't cook, so it was hardly a great mishap, just an inconvenience. She wondered idly whether their run of bad luck had anything to do with the arrival of the witch ball, but dismissed the thought as superstitious nonsense. These things only meant something if you let them. That's how they worked.

But the bad luck continued. The next day, she had her handbag stolen while out shopping, and had to spend an unpleasant morning cancelling her credit, debit and store cards.

In the afternoon, the heel came off her stilettoes while walking down Sloane Street. An x-ray revealed nothing more than a sprained ankle but, out of necessity, it was strapped up and she was issued with crutches. The embarrassment of it! Not to mention the inconvenience. Later at home, rushing to answer the telephone and rendered clumsy by her injury, she knocked over her favourite vase. It was a Susie Cooper original, valuable and irreplaceable. Stooping to pick up the pieces, she stood up too quickly, going dizzy in the process and banging her head on the shelf.

By the time Rupert returned home, she was in a sorry state, sitting on the sofa with her bandaged ankle propped up and an alarming black bruise appearing around her eye. She was already on her third gin and tonic.

"My God, old girl. What happened? You look like you've gone ten rounds."

"Ver' funny, Rupie. I've had a run of bad luck today and I'm not in a good mood. Pour me another, will you?"

Handing him her glass, she momentarily saw her reflection, curved and distorted, in the surface of the witch ball. She looked more closely, forcing her eyes to focus. For a second, she could have sworn she saw a figure standing behind her. She looked over her shoulder, but no one was there.

After the day she'd had and the amount of alcohol she'd consumed, it was no surprise she was seeing things. She settled back on the sofa, glass in hand.

"So, what kind of day have you had?" she asked Rupert. "Can't have been any worse than mine."

Although Rupert didn't like to admit it, his day had been worse.

First, he'd had a letter advising him of abnormal prostate test result and asking him to make an appointment as soon as possible. Rupert didn't do illness, certainly not his own. He scrunched up the letter and threw it in the bin. Distracted and out of sorts, he crashed his car on the way to the office, not realising the vehicle in front had stopped. Both cars incurred minor damage, but it involved insurance companies and was extremely tiresome.

At the office, he found his secretary had phoned in sick and the agency was unable to find a replacement at such short notice. That meant he had to take his own phone-calls and make his own coffee. Then a major client dropped a bombshell. They were leaving him and going with a competitor.

Just when it seemed the day couldn't get any worse, it nose-dived again. His mistress, or as he preferred to call her, his occasional woman, telephoned and announced she was pregnant. She had the temerity to suggest he divorce Fenella and set up with her. The very thought! Why would he want to cut off his wealth at source? Out for lunch with a colleague, he ate bad prawns and spent the afternoon running to the bathroom.

By the time he arrived home, he had no stomach to hear Fenella's woes. He went upstairs to run a bath, returning to the lounge for a large whisky while he waited for the bathtub to fill. Sitting on the sofa, he promptly fell asleep and was awoken some time later by water dripping on his head.

"Where's that coming from?" asked Fenella, looking up.

"Oh, Christ! It's the bath."

Rupert leapt from the sofa and ran upstairs, where he found water seeping under the bathroom door. He turned off the taps, but it was too late. The damage was done. Downstairs, water dripped down the central chandelier, causing the lights to pop and fizz alarmingly. There was a sudden loud bang, the lights fused and the house was plunged into darkness.

"Bloody hell!" shouted Rupert, midway on the stairs. "Is the torch still in the bureau, Fenella?"

"I think so," answered Fenella, from the sofa.

Feeling his way down the stairs and around the lounge furniture, Rupert edged across the room, recoiling as he felt something brush past him.

"Was that you, Fenella?" he called through the darkness.

"Don't be ridiculous, Rupert. I'm on the sofa. I've got to keep my leg up."

Something brushed past Rupert again and he felt his skin crawl. An earthy, acrid smell filled his nostrils. Then, mercifully, he reached the bureau and located the torch. Cautiously, he flashed the beam around the room, seeing Fenella on the sofa, but no one else.

"I'll light some candles," he announced. "Then I'll phone the electrician."

Downstairs, in the kitchen, he found a box of candles and some old candlesticks. He brought them upstairs, placing them at strategic points around the lounge, and lit them. A low, flickering light filled the room.

"Looks almost romantic," said Fenella, slurring her words.

Something inside Rupert snapped.

"It's not romantic. It's bloody disastrous. I've had the day from hell. In fact, I've had the week from hell and I've had enough." He turned on Fenella. "This bad luck started when you bought that bloody witch ball." He glared at it, pinpoints of candlelight reflected in its shiny surface. "Why did you even want one? It's a bloody eyesore. Looks like an over-sized Christmas tree bauble. I want it out of here."

In a sudden fit of rage, he picked up the nearest object, a cat ornament cast in bronze, and threw it at the witch ball. His aim was true. It hit the ball right in the centre, shattering it into hundreds of tiny green shards, leaving the jagged remains hanging in the window.

"No!" screamed Fenella. "What have you done?"

Rupert looked aghast. He was not a violent man. He had no idea what had made him do that.

"And what is that?" asked Fenella, looking at the lounge floor.

What looked like a long skein of hair, matted and knotted, lay amongst the tiny pieces of green-mirrored glass.

"Ugh! Is it alive?"

Rupert fetched the decorative poker from the hearth and tweaked it.

"No. I'd say it's pretty well dead. Like its owner, no doubt."

"What d'you mean?" asked Fenella.

"That chap in Whitby told us they put things inside witch balls. Pieces of hair and skin and what not. To contain the evil."

"Oh gross! You mean that's the hair of someone who's dead?"

"Could be. The ball was pretty old."

"And if it's broken…?"

Rupert shrugged. "I don't know. The evil is released, I guess."

Fenella stared at him, horrified. "The evil is released!" Her voice rose to a shriek. "Why, in God's name, did you throw something at it?"

"I don't know. I've had a very bad day. I thought it was responsible for all the bad luck we've been having." His voice dropped. "I didn't mean to smash it."

"Great! As well as bad luck, we've now got to contend with the very evil it's supposed to be protecting us against!"

"If you believe all that claptrap. I didn't think you did."

"I didn't. I don't," she declared forcefully. "What's the matter with you?"

She stared through the flickering candlelight at Rupert, who was gazing horrified at a point just over her left shoulder, the whites of his eyes showing clearly. He swallowed loudly.

"Just get up slowly, Fenella," he whispered "and walk towards me. Whatever you do, don't turn round."

As soon as he said the words, he regretted them. Of course, she turned to look.

Her scream filled the air, as she came face to face with a dark figure materialising behind her. It appeared to be an old woman, stooped and bent, with matted hair and a hooked nose. Small yellow flames licked at her flesh and the acrid, earthy smell grew stronger.

Fenella, attempting to rise from the sofa in panic, tripped over the coffee table, knocking over a candlestick. The lit candles fell into the curtains nearby, the fabric catching light immediately. At the same time, the water-damaged ceiling finally succumbed and collapsed, the large ornate ceiling Rose crashing down and catching Rupert on the brow. He fell forward, unconscious, landing on the Persian rug and taking with him another candlestick. The flames flickered around his suit sleeve, teasing and tasting, before taking a hold.

A gusting wind, ungodly and foul, swept through the lounge, fanning the flames, causing them to flare. Forced back by the heat, Fenella attempted to reach the stairs leading down, but acrid smoke filled her lungs and she fell, coughing and choking, landing alongside Rupert.

The last thing she heard, before unconsciousness claimed her, was the cracked, wizened voice of the long-dead creature in their lounge.

> *"Tried by water, found guilty as hell.*
> *Crackling flames my final death-knell.*
> *Released at last, after years lying dead*
> *I rise again, my evil to spread."*

* * *

Twenty-four hours later, the scene was declared safe for accident investigators and they entered the building. Searching through the smoking remains of the once desirable Chelsea mews, they found a puzzling scenario. Two charred bodies were identified from dental records as being those of Fenella and Rupert Fotheringay-Smythe.

A third set of remains proved more problematic. They appeared to be those of a woman in her late seventies, severely deformed by arthritis. No dental records were found and her identity remained a mystery.

DNA testing proved inconclusive, although did throw up something of an anomaly, suggesting that the bones came from the eighteenth century.

At the same time as the fire in Chelsea, two hundred miles away, on the edge of the Dartmoor National Park, a fire broke out in the kitchen of a recently refurbished, old coaching inn. Despite the fire brigade's best efforts, the building was totally destroyed.

The two events were never linked. Why would they be?

In a small cottage in a little backwater, not too far from the Chelsea mews, an old-aged pensioner glanced at the witch ball hanging in her window. She'd seen a black reflection flit momentarily across its mirrored surface, and quickly crossed herself, thankful she hadn't given in to temptation and sold it to that woman from Help The Aged.

God knows she needed the money, but some things shouldn't be sold. The price was just too high.

Evil

I've been around since ancient times
Insidious, creeping, sly and cold
Just as pow'rful now as then
Nothing's changed since days of old.

I prey upon the weak and lost
The godless ones so easily led.
One small chink is all it takes
For me to get inside your head.

Moral weakness I adore
Nothing has a sweeter sound
Avarice and vanity
Place me on familiar ground.

Selfishness and gluttony
Envy, jealousy and pride.
All are music to my ears
I'm ready waiting by your side.

Destruction, desolation, death
Mayhem, madness, that's my aim
Confusion, crying, I don't care
Pain and suff'ring. It's a game.

I'm the voice upon your shoulder
I'm the one who makes you act
I'm the one who feeds your ego
Join with me, let's make a pact.

Earthly riches, power and fame.
They're the empty promises I make.
Too late you learn they're made of dust
I never, ever give. Just take.

So, let me have your empty soul
Join with me where you belong
I'll raise you to new earthly heights
Every lost soul makes me strong.

Killing, maiming, cheating, lying
Stealing, hurting, cursing, crying.
Join my ever-growing throng
I revel in a world gone wrong.

And the insects shall inherit the earth...

Puffball Spiders

The male spider approached cautiously, detecting the presence of the female by the scent on her dragline. He had to be careful. He didn't want to be mistaken for prey.

Gently, he plucked the strands of her untidy web, sending her a vibrational message. On high alert for her next feed, the female responded quickly, darting forward with a view to kill. She was somewhat larger than the male, so timing was crucial if he was to achieve his aim. As soon as he detected her movement, he exuded sperm on to his extended palps. He was just quick enough. She paused, detecting his purpose, and now, the courtship could begin. He rose up in front of her, waving his legs in an exotic dance, drumming his extended palps together, making further vibrations. She was entranced, all thoughts of feeding forgotten, reproduction now top of the agenda. Not that she was easily wooed. On the contrary. She made him wait, playing hard to get, while he wearied himself with his excessive courtship.

Mating, when it happened, was swift and successful. She had what she needed and now he was extraneous to requirements. Exhausted from his extended dance, he failed to move quickly enough and rapidly became prey.

She ate him voraciously, hungry after the mating game. His demise or survival was of little consequence. He would have died soon after anyway. Now, at least, he provided much needed nourishment.

Her eggs were laid soon after, deposited in a silken sac, hidden within the messy strands of her web. Now, it was a waiting game. Mating had taken place late autumn and, as winter arrived, the temperature plummeted, making survival of the spiderlings unlikely. They would not emerge until spring.

Gerald Mahoney woke bright and early. The red gold rays of the sunrise filled his bedroom. Wood pigeons cooed on the chimneystack, starlings chattered on the telephone wires and, through the open window, the fresh aromas of early spring assailed his nostrils. This was what he'd been waiting for. It had been a long, arduous winter, with frozen earth and biting winds. His old bones weren't what they used to be and he'd been forced to stay inside, huddled by the fireside, keeping the cold and the arthritic pain at bay.

Today, the tide had turned. This was the day he'd get back to the allotment and start planning future endeavours. Finding out if the fennel, rosemary and thyme had survived; planting sage, oregano and basil; sowing seeds for carrots, runner beans, peas, courgettes, lettuces and tomatoes. Perhaps trying pumpkins this year, definitely giant sunflowers. And rhubarb was a must.

When you got to this age, you never knew when your time was up, so you went the distance, outsmarting death with a full harvest.

He breakfasted quickly and made a flask of coffee, packing his pipe and a pouch of tobacco, along with a bar of dark chocolate, into his canvas kitbag. He stood outside the back gate for a moment, savouring the sun's brightness, drinking in the chill air, and feeling the call of spring in every cell of his body. He might be old and rickety, but it still felt good to be alive.

It took him twenty minutes to walk to the allotments on the far side of the village, behind the manor grounds. It was deserted when he arrived, the hour too early for others to show, dewdrops creating delicate patterns on spiders' webs, the sun not yet hot enough to burn away the early morning moisture.

He walked through his plot, making mental notes as to what needed clearing, which shoots were appearing and how he would organise his new crop. The old lean-to had survived the wind and snow, still standing at the top of his patch. He wouldn't have been surprised to find it in pieces, given its age and general decrepitude. Like me, he thought. Keeps going against all the odds, like the proverbial creaking gate. He turned the key in the rusty lock and the padlock sprang open.

Pushing open the door, its hinges stiff with disuse, he peered into the dark interior. It took his eyes a moment to adjust. His tools were still there, lined up on hooks, just as he'd left them; two spades for light and heavy digging, a fork, hoe, edger and strimmer. On the workbench lay his shears, trowels and secateurs, clean and ready for use.

He inhaled deeply, relishing the musty, earthy smell. He'd had so many happy times sitting in this shed, smoking his pipe, whisky flask alongside, listening to the racing on his small transistor. Now, God willing, he was about to enjoy another season.

The rising sun threw more light through the open door, illuminating corners and crevices that had been dark throughout the winter months. Now his eyes saw something unusual.

"Hello. What's that?" he murmured, stepping forward to investigate.

Suspended on an unseen thread that lead from the handle of a spade to the far corner of the lean-to was a curious, teasel-like object, maybe two inches across.

"Some kind of seed lodged on a spider thread? Rosebay willowherb, maybe?" he wondered.

The object looked almost fluffy, covered in soft creamy-coloured down like the top of one of his cacti. As the light grew stronger, it began to vibrate and Gerard moved closer, trying to see more. Was it alive or had a sudden draft of wind given it movement?

Amidst the fluffy bristles, he could just make out legs and two eyes. Whatever it was, the thing was alive.

"You're a spider," he declared. "I've never seen one like you before. What a beauty!"

He could swear, as he spoke, that the fluffy creature opened its eyes and looked right at him. Slowly, it began to move on the horizontal thread that held it in place. Gerard looked on bemused.

"It's all right," he said, gently. "I'm not going to hurt you. You're safe."

Initially, he thought the movement was defensive and the spider was afraid. He could not have been more wrong. The spider was on the offensive. It had woken from a deep winter slumber and was very hungry.

The vibrations increased, turning into a spinning motion that grew faster and faster, until the creature was nothing more than a cream-coloured blur, its soft furry down expanding outwards with the momentum. Gerard was now inches away, his head craning forward, his rheumy old eyes open wide in amazement.

As the creature reached the peak of its spinning, the fluffy bristles detached from its body, flying out in all directions.

Some went into Gerard's eyes, causing instant irritation. He backed away, rubbing his eyes and breathing deeply, inhaling some of the flying missiles into his nostrils. Tiny barbs on the end of each fluffy bristle hooked into the soft nasal membranes, releasing their poison and causing instant swelling. The wetness of the membranes caused hairs on the bristle to expand, interweaving with others to produce a mesh.

Unable to breathe through his nose, Gerard inhaled through his mouth, drawing further venomous fluffy strands into his windpipe and ultimately his lungs. Wherever they landed, the barbed ends lodged, causing Gerard to cough and choke, as he tried to breathe.

Death was swift: a combination of septic shock, as the poison flooded his system, and lack of oxygen, as the mesh and swelling cut off his air supply. The last thing he saw, before the bleeding in his eyes prevented vision, was the eyes of the creature looking into his, as its spinning subsided and it became still.

Once life was extinguished, the hungry spider set to work, eating its fill, new bristles already starting to grow.

Somewhere deep within the web, the spider sac wriggled, the sudden light and warmth creating the stimulus its occupants craved.

Gerard Mahoney was found the next day.

Ralph Rogers had the next plot along, and many a time the two men had chased the breeze, sitting on an old wooden bench, sharing a tot from Gerard's flask.

Visiting the allotments early the next morning, he was alarmed to see the door of the lean-to wide open. There was no sign of Gerard and it was unusual for the door to be unlocked. He was most particular about closing up the night before.

Ralph frowned, wondering if there had been a robbery, then experiencing a stab of fear at the thought the inevitable may have happened. Neither of them was getting any younger. The end had to come sooner or later. If you had to go, this was surely the best place. Only he didn't want to be the one to discover his friend.

Laughing off his fears, he approached the lean-to. The sun's rays were just beginning to infiltrate its dark interior, and the exterior brightness made it all the more difficult to see inside. He paused in the doorway, wondering what he'd find.

Nothing could have prepared him.

Something was lying trussed up at the back of the lean-to. It was hard to tell whether it was an object or a person because it was tightly bound by a dense array of silvery threads, shimmering in the emerging rays. As the light grew brighter, a myriad of spider's threads was revealed, criss-crossing the interior.

Ralph felt bile rising in his throat. He didn't want to take a further look, but out of loyalty to his friend, he knew he must.

Parting a way through the cobwebs, he grasped a small hand fork from the workbench and clearing it of sticky thread, cautiously approached the bound-up thing on the floor. He chose the end that could possibly have been a head, slipping the tines of the fork into the web mass and lifting it up, then pulling it away with his other hand.

The sight that met his eyes may once have been Gerard, but it no longer resembled a living thing. The face had been eaten away, clumps of purple flesh left clinging to the skull beneath. Ralph felt nausea rising and turned to the door of the lean-to, desperate for fresh air and normality. He was denied both.

A motion in the corner of the lean-to caught his attention. It appeared to be a teasel, caught in a spider's web, circling round and round. He frowned, wondering what was causing the sudden movement, given the lack of wind. He peered closer, seeing legs and eyes that quickly disappeared as the spinning intensified, lost amidst a puffball of creamy fur. Without warning, the thing exploded, creamy-white shards flying in all directions.

Like his friend's before him, his end was quick, as the flying bristles entered his nose and mouth. Clutching his chest, Ralph fell to the floor, his skin already turning a poisonous purple.

Now, something else was happening inside the lean-to. The egg sac finally burst, scattering its inhabitants far and wide. Hundreds of tiny, fluffy puffball spiders shot into the air, some anchoring to the wooden interior, others floating outside, where a gentle breeze picked them up, carrying them away, across the village and further afield.

A day later, on the other side of the village, Verity Parker, president of the Women's Institute and Chair of the Planning Committee, opened her bedroom curtains and looked out over the front garden. It was a beautiful day. Bright green daffodil shoots had appeared in the dark earth, pushing through the last of the snowdrops and crocuses.

Alfie, her border collie, bounded into the room, looking hopeful.

"All right, I'll take you for a walk," she promised.

She paused, as something caught her attention in the corner of the window. It looked like a small puffball, covered in soft, yellow fur, spinning around like a Catherine Wheel.

"Wow! What is that?" she exclaimed. "It's so pretty."

She looked more closely, a smile of delight on her face, as she watched the small creature spin around. As the spinning reached its peak, the baby puffball spider shot its load of venomous barbs into the air, its motion giving them momentum.

Verity staggered back, clutching her throat and trying to breathe as the tiny yellow threads embedded inside her, releasing their poison and thickening to a mesh as they encountered the wet membranes of her mouth and nose. Others went into her eyes, causing instant bleeding and excruciating pain. Alfie, rushing to his mistress's side, met the same fate, the tiny mesh of yellow threads quickly blocking his airways, the poisonous barbs spreading their venom throughout his body.

More spiders entered through the open bedroom window.

Half an hour later, when her husband, Thomas, walked into the bedroom, he found his wife and dog lying on the floor, tiny spiders already starting to feed. By then, at least twenty or thirty more tiny puffball spiders were spinning on their threads, ready to explode. He didn't stand a chance.

All over the village, in homes, shops and gardens, local people were meeting a similar fate.

A strong south-westerly didn't help. Soon, tiny spiderlings were being blown all over southern England, maturing quickly with the ready availability of food.

Mating followed and, given the warm weather, gestation was fast.

Within weeks, the puffball spider army was growing at an alarming and uncontrollable rate. It was an invasion of epidemic proportions, spreading quickly across the country and causing thousands of fatalities.

"Stay inside. Close all windows and doors," advised the World Health Organisation's public service announcement. "Under no circumstances attempt to remove a puffball spider. If you find one, vacate the room immediately. Do not re-enter. Alert the authorities immediately. These spiders are lethal. If you approach a spider that is spinning, you will die within seconds. As yet, there is no antidote."

At Euston Station in London, a clutch of newly-hatched puffball spiders caused mayhem and mass extinction. Travellers waiting in the main concourse became aware of hundreds of tiny puffball spiders flying through the air on fine threads. As each of the spiders landed, it began twisting and turning before spinning at high speed, emitting hundreds of fine, highly poisonous, soft bristles into the air.

Panicking travellers had nowhere to escape. As people ran from one spinning spider, they encountered another and, within seconds, the air was thick with bristles. People placed handkerchiefs and scarves around their faces to prevent inhalation, but only a few were lucky enough to escape.

The invasion progressed, and public places became no-go areas and a state of national emergency was declared. Supply chains broke down as the crisis deepened, resulting in food and drug scarcities. Hospitals were deserted as doctors and nurses fell victim to the spider attacks. Westminster was silent, politicians either dead or hiding within their homes. Looters, looking to profit, were killed instantly, either by spiders or army personnel policing the streets in airtight radiation suits. Soon, they became the only visible sign of human life.

Airborne spiders reached the Continent and attacks began abroad, spreading throughout Europe, the Middle East, China and beyond, eventually reaching America and Australia.

Within six months, the spinning puffball spiders had become the biggest threat to human life on planet earth, eclipsing global warming, warfare and asteroids.

As for the spiders themselves, they appeared to be indestructible. The authorities tried to kill them with insecticide, but the spiders were as resilient as cockroaches. When sprayed, they simply folded their bristles into their bodies, locking them together to form a protective shield, and waited until the chemicals ceased to pose a threat.

In laboratories deep within isolated decontamination units, scientists studied the spiders, using carbon dioxide as anaesthetic and examining them under electron microscopes. The creatures were found to possess a highly advanced sensory system, comprising a series of soft cuticular bristles covered in fine chemoreceptive hairs.

Each of the soft bristles contained no less than 3,500 minuscule sensory slits, continually opening and closing, making them highly sensitive to the slightest flow of air. As soon as the frictional force of prey was detected, the sensory slits triggered the spinning motion and ultimately, the release mechanism.

The tip of each bristle ended in a tiny hook, making it easy to 'anchor' to a host. When connected to a damp surface, such as a nasal or mouth membrane, the highly sensitive hairs expanded and locked with the hairs from other bristles to produce an impenetrable mesh, quite sufficient to cause asphyxiation.

Once embedded in the membrane, the bristles released poison of a similar chemical make-up to that of digitalis, the toxin produced by foxglove plants, and in such strength as to be fatal within seconds.

Unmatched as predators, the puffball spiders were an evolutionary phenomenon. As 'wandering' spiders, they had abandoned web building in favour of free-roaming hunting, catching their prey by tactile sense rather than web, which was utilised only for purposes of reproduction and to protect the resulting egg sac.

Sheer numbers rendered them unstoppable and deadly to the human race.

Until one day.

Annabel Philips, aged 21, sat at her dressing table, brushing her hair in front of the mirror. As advised by the public health notices, she had remained indoors, keeping all windows and doors firmly closed, retreating to an upstairs room that was uncluttered and airtight.

Staring into the mirror, she froze as she saw the reflection of a tiny puffball spider suspended in the window behind her.

She reacted instinctively, doing the only thing she could think of. Grabbing a can of hairspray from the dressing table, she rushed to the window and, just as it began to spin, gave the creature a hefty spray, fixing its tresses in a tight hold. Unable to form its usual protective shield, the spider was suddenly vulnerable.

Then, it was simply a matter of knocking the spider into a glass tumbler and dropping in a lighted match. The highly flammable hairspray caught light immediately and the creature was incinerated.

With a sense of elation, Annabel donned the protective suit with which they'd all been issued and went searching for more spiders. Half a dozen puffballs met with a similar fate.

After which, she picked up her mobile and dialled the number on the public service leaflet that had come through her letterbox a few weeks earlier.

Maybe, just maybe, she had found the solution...

Good

I cannot give you riches
Power or position
I cannot raise you to new heights
With instant recognition.

I do not aim to make you great
Make others seek you out
Set you up above the rest
That's not what I'm about.

It's not about the money
It's not about the fame
It's not about competing
Winning every game.

Rather, live a simple life
Show respect for others
Treat them as you would yourself
Look on them as brothers.

See wonder in a sunset
Feel the magic of the moon.
Find beauty in a smile
Hear the robin's tune.

Where evil walks, good will prevail
It's always been the same.
Replacing wrong with what is right
Has always been my game.

Rest assured, I'm watching
Totalling loss and gain
Balancing and restoring
Bringing hope instead of pain.

I've been around a long, long time
And still I fight the fight
Battle-scarred and weary
Defending what is right.

The devil lies in waiting
Don't join his empty throng
Together we are growing
Together we are strong.

The inspiration behind the stories

Rejuvenate

Since writing 'The Blue Crystal Trilogy', a paranormal romance that takes its inspiration from the Victorian novel 'She' by H. Rider Haggard, I have been fascinated by the quest for eternal youth. Our celebrity-driven society is obsessed with the need to stay young and hold back old age. This story looks at what happens when a rejuvenation trial goes horribly wrong.

Miss Hissy

My good friend, the late Liz Armour, was convinced the new sat nav in her husband's car became aggressive whenever she was in the vehicle, and called her Miss Hissy. At the time, Liz suggested I write a story about this. I'd like to think she would have been happy with the result.

Road Boys

Driving back from an Eagles concert some years ago, my husband was convinced a man, dressed in white, stepped out in front of the car. He didn't have time to stop and when he looked in the rear view mirror, the man simply wasn't there. We heard later that a man had been killed on that particular stretch of road. I've heard of other people encountering something similar on the site of a fatality.

A road near my village has seen more than its fair share of fatal accidents and, whenever I drive down it, I recall my husband's experience, often wondering if the road is haunted and whether the ghosts are lying in wait for further victims. It's true that the council levelled the road camber to make it safer, and also that someone cut down the row of trees causing so many deaths. The rest is from my imagination.

People reading the story have told me it makes them drive slower when travelling on this particular road, so hopefully I'm doing my bit for road safety. I'd like to think so, given that my own brother was killed on the roads.

Corky

When writing this tale, I was thinking of Marianne Dreams by Catherine Storr, in which a young girl, bed-bound through illness, draws a picture and, as she dreams, it comes to life. I remember reading this story and looking out over the back field from my bedroom window, wondering whether stationary objects, such as large standing stones - or scarecrows - could actually move. This story also indulges my fascination with possession and displacement, always very creepy subjects.

The Tulpa

When I was in my teens, I was fascinated with the occult and the unknown. My early reminiscences are recorded here, along with my fascination for a book called Mysterious Worlds by Denis Bardens. One story, in particular, captured my imagination, telling how the Belgian-French explorer and spiritualist, Alexandra David-Neél used an ancient Tibetan technique to bring a creature from her imagination into the physical plane. It was a small step to turn this into a contemporary horror story, using the name of my daughter's imaginary friend, Triff-Traff, created when she was young.

Can't Let Go

Can love transcend death? Especially if an accident tears a family apart? I'd like to think so. There again, is the haunting real? In cases of intense grief, does the mind play tricks? This is a sad story, with a bittersweet ending…

Magnet Fishing

I've never had a go at magnet fishing, but saw a story about it on the local TV news and became fascinated. Then I found lots of stories about unusual finds on YouTube. Around this time, another story also made the news. In Sweden, a young girl found an ancient sword in a lake. It was dated to pre-Viking times. I put the two stories together and created a classic horror story, complete with treasure hunting, ancient artefacts, museums, curses and a disused millrace.

Room 408

Last year, we stayed in an old country house in Yorkshire and, yes, number 408 was a haunted room. My daughter was with me and yes, she did experience someone breathing above her in the night. It was spooky stuff, crying out to be made into a story. It also made me think of the abandoned hotel in Stephen King's The Shining. The result is a Gothic horror story, complete with a storm, Yorkshire moors, an old hotel, ghosts and the undead…

The Green Man

The Green Man is an ancient fertility symbol, representing pagan beliefs and often found carved in old churches and chapels. In my story, the Green Man is something more primal and evil. I imagined him as a malevolent Teletubby, preying on innocent youth. Is he really a murderous monster that lives in the woods? Or is this simply a study of insanity?

Lileth

The Aztecs have always held a grisly fascination for me, especially their macabre practice of plucking a heart from the breast of a living sacrifice. The members of the tribe who carried out this practice were known as Eagle Warriors and, actually, although barbaric and cruel, the practice was used as a means of quelling insurrection with minimal loss of life. Rather than put prisoners to death en masse, a few were selected for sacrifice, sending a clear message to the others. In this story, a woman, possibly a modern-day Aztec, carries on the practice. Although, in ancient folklore, Lileth or Lilith was a female demon, so maybe she is not quite as modern as she seems.

The Evil Eye

'Evil eye' bracelets, necklaces and ornaments can be seen everywhere when travelling in Turkey and Greece. They are said to provide protection against evil forces, a belief that goes back nearly three thousand years. This story tells how the evil eye is given and the danger of dabbling in such matters. It's written in tribute to the early nineteenth century ghost-story writer M.R. James, which means it includes, of course, an Oxford Professor of antiquarian studies, a respectable elderly lady and the ever-present threat of evil.

Girl on the Train

Remember the 10CC song 'I'm Mandy Fly Me'? That's what gave me the inspiration for this ghostly story. Of course, there are numerous tales about ghosts appearing to warn of impending doom, and railway stations, in particular, can be emotive places. I put the two together to create a tale of tragedy and redemption.

The Dog Walker

My friend, the late Liz Armour, suggested this story. During a bout of illness, she and her husband were unable to walk their dog and used a local dog-walking service. The person who arrived on their doorstep was odd and inarticulate, but appeared to have an affinity with animals. Around this time, I became friendly with a homeless man, who used to beg in our local town, his dog alongside him. One day, he simply vanished. I never knew what happened, but a harsh winter that year got me thinking. I put the two events together to create this story.

Cats' Home

A hideous couple get their come-uppance. That's the premise of this ghostly morality tale, based on the rise of paranormal tourism and the idea of creating a 'hoax' haunting. Of course, there are real ghosts, too. And animal cruelty can never go unpunished...

A Midsummer Night's Madness

When I was little, I read a story about a girl who ventured into the woods on midsummer's night, spent the night with the fairies and returned the next morning as an old woman. The tale stayed with me and I wanted to write my own version. It's well catalogued in folklore that spending a night with the fairies carries a terrible price. Imagine the nightmare of losing fifty years overnight and discovering your sister has stepped into your shoes and lived your life...

The Witch Ball

My husband and I had been looking for a witch ball for a long time, but couldn't find one that was for sale. Eventually, the owner of an old coaching inn near Lydford offered to sell us one. We wrestled with our conscience, ultimately refusing, as we knew money should never change hands and we didn't want the evil to come back on us. Some time later, we acquired a witch ball in an antique shop in Whitby. In keeping with tradition, the owner gave it to us, and we paid the money for another small object. Our blue witch ball now hangs in an upstairs window, protecting our house. I often wondered what would have happened if money had exchanged hands. This story gives one potential outcome… (Incidentally, the White Lady Inn is fictitious, but I would recommend staying at the Castle Inn, Lydford. It's a wonderful old place!)

Puffball Spiders

One evening, I saw a 1975 TV adaptation of M. R. James' ghost story The Ash Tree, in which a family of demonic spiders attacks the aristocratic owners of a stately home. It was a story I had read some time before and it obviously played on my mind because, that night, I dreamed my own version, in which an invasion of puffball spiders attacks a community. The puffballs are evil creatures, like something out of a sci fi film, and, I have to say, my dream was a full-length adventure, in glorious Technicolor. It became this story.

Thank you for reading Truly, Madly, Creepy

If you have enjoyed reading this book,
please leave a review on Amazon/Goodreads.
Thank you. Pat Spence.

Contacts

Follow Pat Spence

On facebook:
https://wwwfacebook.com/patspenceauthor

On Twitter:
https://twitter.com/pat_spence

Visit the website
www.patspence.co.uk

Acknowledgements

Thanks go to:
Danusia Hutson for editing, Amelia-Anne, Steve and
Judith Weir for reading, and Andrew Aske for cover
design (www.aske-associates.com)
All those, including members of New Street Authors and
Solihull Writers groups, who have listened to my stories at
regular events over the years, usually at The Gunmakers
Arms, Birmingham and The Happy Heart Café, Olton.
Your support is much appreciated.

Other titles by Pat Spence

The Blue Crystal Trilogy:
Blue Moon (Book One)
True Blue (Book Two)
Into The Blue (Book Three)

Abigail's Affair
(A quirky love story set in the UK and Australia)

Find Your Sparkle
(A 30 day self-help plan to look good and feel great)

All titles available on Amazon.co.uk and Amazon.com

Follow The Blue Crystal Trilogy on Facebook:
https://www.facebook.com/bluecrystaltrilogy

See the Blue Moon trailer at:
https://www.youtube.com/watch?v=SFvsXiPem4Q

Coming soon…

Two supernatural novels:

The Step-Daughter
Extended families can be difficult, especially step-daughters, and especially one who dislikes you from beyond the grave. When a lonely 40 something librarian meets an eligble local man, it turns her life around, resulting in an unexpected marriage and baby. But all is not what it seems in the big house on the edge of the village…

Lepers' Lane
Somebody is watching. But is the watcher supernatural or in the physical realm? Or is it all in the mind? A family relocates to a stunning location on the North York Moors, but their house lies on an ancient pathway that is still used. Add a husband's misplaced affair and a wife's paranoia into the mix, and the family is soon under threat from present day and long dead horrors.

Due for publication 2019/2020.

About the author

Pat Spence is a freelance copywriter. She has a degree in English, lives at home with her husband and daughter and, over the years, has worked as an advertising copywriter, magazine editor, trainer, massage therapist and aromatherapist.
She also performs stand up comedy.

Printed in Poland
by Amazon Fulfillment
Poland Sp. z o.o., Wrocław